Hand of Titan

A Priest of Titan, Volume 2

Paul Mouchet

Published by Paul Mouchet, 2020.

HAND OF TITAN

First edition. December 31, 2020.

Written by Paul Mouchet.

To my copy editor and big sister Louise, thank you for helping me bring my stories to life.

To Brian Mullen, my good friend and content contributor on this novel, thank you for your words and inspiration.

To my wife, who believes in me, even when I struggle to believe in myself.

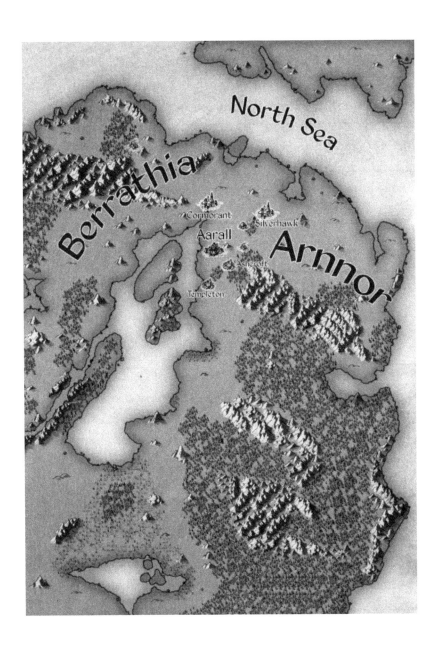

North Sea

Berrathia

Cormorant

Silverhawk

Aarall

Arnnor

Ashcroft

Templeton

Chapter 1

KIT AND INDIE COULDN'T help but laugh while watching the antics of Runt, as the dire wolf chased anything and everything that caught his attention. He seemed to particularly enjoy chasing butterflies. Perhaps it was their bright colours, perhaps it was the haphazard way they flitted about, or perhaps it was because chasing them simply brought him joy.

As the trio approached the outskirts of Aarall, the territorial capital of Luna Nord, and the second largest city in the kingdom of Arnnor, Kit couldn't help but feel concern for how the citizens were going to react to a dire wolf approaching.

"I'm really worried that Runt is going to cause quite a stir when the people see him," Kit shares with Indie, just as Runt comes back to walk beside her.

Runt looks over at her, his eyes seem to indicate that he, too, is worried about how people might perceive him. Kit gives him a reassuring scratch behind his ear. His head is practically level with Kit's shoulders, causing her to laugh to herself. After all, even though Runt is a larger than average dire wolf, he's only a puppy, a puppy that was magically enhanced by the old woman in the hut. Kit had considered that the old woman may have been the lesser deity, Fenrir, in Berrat form, but she never thought to ask her. Well, truth be told, she had thought about it, but she didn't have the courage to go through with it.

"Don't worry, Runt, I've got this covered," Kit says to him as she continues to scratch his head. "Just stay close and leave it to me to deal with the people."

From a distance, one can really see just how massive Aarall is. Its outer walls are so large that it would take the better part of a day to walk around the city. Mount Toka, the tallest and most dangerous mountain in all Arnnor, rears up to the east. The giant ice statue of

Titan, reaching thousands of feet into the sky, seemingly carved from the side of the great mountain, stares down at Aarall and the Temple of the Fist.

As they get closer, the riot of colours from the merchants' tents, spreading out on either side of the city's main gates comes into view. It's late afternoon and the marketplace outside the city walls is still doing brisk business. Kit was hoping that the crowds would have died down, allowing them to slip through the gates unnoticed, but that is not to be.

"Look at the big puppy!" The shrill cry of a young girl startles Kit out of her thoughts. She's racing toward them as fast as her little feet will carry her. Runt's ears perk up at the sound of her voice. He's practically begging to go see the little girl, but Kit sternly tells him to stay. He gives a small whimper before sitting beside her.

Both Kit and Indie do their best to head off the little girl, but she slips past them with ease. A moment later, she's got her face buried in Runt's chest. "Runt, I'm so happy to see you," she whispers into his think black fur. She pulls herself away so that she can look at him more closely. "I think you're going to cause a panic if Kit brings you into the city."

"What?" Kit is completely taken off guard by the child. "How do you know my wolf's name? How do you know *my* name?"

"I may be old," the child replies, "but I don't easily forget the names of people I love." And with that, the small girl wraps her arms around Kit's waist, giving her a big hug. When she pulls away, she starts to giggle, seeing the completely baffled look on Kit's face.

The little girl gives her a wink. "We've met before, in my house to the north." She walks over to Runt and begins scratching his head and ears. Runt quickly returns the favour, giving the small girl's face an enthusiastic tongue-bath.

Still seeing that Kit does not know who she is, the child giggles wildly. The sound of her laughter is sweet and melodic. "I made the armour you're wearing. I changed Runt here so that he would be big enough to protect you."

"You? You're the old woman in the hut?" Kit blinks at her in disbelief, as nobody else knew how Kit procured her armor or the fact that Runt is just a puppy.

"You know, people don't like to be called *old woman*," she says with a grin. "But I suppose I never did properly introduce myself. You may call me *Fenrir*."

Indie immediately falls to his knees and bows his head. Kit, unsure how to react, follows suit. "Again, you grace me with your presence. How can I be of service to you?"

"I am here to help you," Fenrir offers. "After you left, I was afraid of what might happen if you brought Runt into a city. I came to give you this." Fenrir holds out a thick collar, made of black leather and a bright green metal of some sort. As Kit takes the collar from her, Fenrir turns to Runt. "This collar is for you to wear. While you have it on, you will appear to be a popular domestic dog."

Runt quietly growls at the prospect of wearing the collar.

"Don't worry," Fenrir assures him. "Kit will always see you as you. So will any friends, as long as she permits it." Fenrir giggles wildly again. "Anybody who is Kit's enemy, will also see you in your true form. That way, they'll know better than to mess with her, or you."

This seemed to satisfy Runt. He moves closer to Kit, motioning to put the collar on him. As Kit ties up the buckle, Runt shimmers for a moment, but otherwise Kit sees no change in him. "So, what does he look like to anybody who doesn't know he's a dire wolf?"

"He'll appear to be a very large golden retriever," Fenrir giggles as she says it. "I'm pretty sure everybody loves goldens, so he'll be welcome almost anywhere." No sooner does she finish, Runt begins to prance around, holding his head and tail high in the air.

Kit can't help but smile. "If you look like a golden retriever, then Lump is going to love you."

"Who's Lump?" Indie asks.

"*Lump on a Log* is the Temple's mascot. He's also a golden retriever, but I think he's also part wolf. He showed up at the Temple a couple of years ago, and after tasting some of Sister Miyuki's braised lamb shanks, he's never left." Kit grabs Runt by the face, looking closely at him. "I wish I could see what you look like as a golden. I'll bet you look a lot like Lump."

No sooner do the words leave Kit's mouth, Runt shimmers again, his wolf form shifting to that of a golden retriever. "Sweet Titan!" Kit blurts out. "You could be Lump's twin brother!"

Fenrir again begins to giggle, and she starts dancing around the three of them, singing a little song.

"Lump and Runt, two peas in a pod. One acts like a wolf. One acts like a dog. They could pass as twins, they could, because I made them both, like a good girl should."

"You made Lump?" Kit's eyes are wide in wonder.

Fenrir gives a coy look. "No, I suppose I didn't *make* him. But I did send him to the Temple to keep an eye on you. He was an orphan, wandering around Old Town. If I hadn't rescued him, he'd likely have not made it through the winter. I knew the Temple would care for him." Fenrir continues to dance around. "Now everybody's happy!"

"Why did you send him to keep an eye on me?" Kit asks, wondering why the wolf goddess would have any interest in her. "Fenrir?" Kit spins around, not seeing her anywhere.

"I guess she finished what she needed to do," Indie offers. "I can't believe she was here! I can't believe that she knows you. I mean, she *knows* you."

"Let's get moving." Kit's face is beginning to flush, and she really doesn't want Indie to see that. "We need to report back to the Captain."

As they approach the market district, merchants can see them approaching. They begin calling out, hawking their wares. Kit smiles politely, waving them off so they can pass by. Nobody seems to be reacting to Runt's presence, so the collar must be working.

Closer to the city gate is the food area of the marketplace. The smells of breads, and sweets, and cooking meats fill Kit's nose, making her mouth water. Runt starts whining at the smells, and Indie's stomach makes an audible rumble.

"We can get some food at the Temple." Kit's saying the words, but her stomach is getting the better of her, too.

"Hail, Kit! Are you buying food for Sister Miyuki?" Kit looks over at the merchant with surprise. She often buys from this merchant when Sister Miyuki needs something special for a meal that she's making.

"No, Comden, not today. I'm on my way to see Captain Harding. We just took care of the wolf problem that's been plaguing the outlying villages." Kit was going to mention the wolf poachers whom she thwarted as well, but that was information that didn't need to be shared.

"You took care of the wolves? Titan preserve us! My sister's family lost so many of their sheep and goats to those beasts that she thought she'd have to shut down her farm and move in with me. Ooh, my wife would not have been happy with that. My sister's children, my nephews, act like they were born directly in Helja. Little monsters they are! I remember a time ..."

Kit gives Comden a smile and holds up her hand to cut him off. If she lets him continue talking, they won't make it into the city before the sun sets.

"Here!" Comden continues. "I know you've got business to attend to, but you have to try my new recipe. I call it prickle-berry loaf." He hands Kit and Indie two small loaves of bread. The smell is absolutely heavenly. As Kit goes to take a bite, Runt begins to whine.

"Oh, my apologies Lump. I didn't notice you there." Comden grabs a pile of crumbs and other scraps that were piled up on one of the merchant's counters. He tosses a large hunk of bread to Runt, which he promptly gobbles down.

Kit has barely taken a bite of her own loaf when Indie starts smacking his lips. She looks over as he licks his fingers. "What?" he says as he manages to swallow the last of his loaf.

"Titan's snowballs, Indie. Did you even take time to taste it?"

"I tasted it," he protests. "It was so delicious I couldn't stop myself from *wolfing* it down." He laughs lightly, watching Runt gently taking the food Comden was offering him.

When Kit finally gets to try her own loaf, the flavours fill her mouth, causing her to moan lightly. "It tastes just like Miyuki's prickle-berry honey," she manages to say between bites.

Comden begins to laugh. "Where do you think she got the recipe, and the prickle-berry blossoms to make that honey?" He gives Runt the last of the food in his hand and points his thumbs at himself. "This guy!"

Just like Indie, Kit is also licking her fingers, not wanting to waste a single morsel. "Does she have this recipe? I know the brothers and sisters at the Temple would all enjoy having this on a regular basis."

Comden gives her a small smile. "No way, this one is for me and my customers. Besides, the supply of prickle-berries is coming to an end. We'll need to wait until fall for the next harvest." When he sees the disappointed look on Kit's face, he pulls out three more loaves. "Two of these are for you and your friend here but save the third one for Miyuki. If she likes it, maybe the Temple can buy them up for the Feast of Titan's Bounty?" He waggles his eyebrows at Kit. Comden does good business from his stall, but he knows that if the Temple is buying his goods for the Feast, it will make him even more popular among the city's population.

Kit and Indie thank the merchant for the food he's shared, and they head off toward the city gate. They had barely gone a dozen paces or so when Kit hears Indie smacking his lips again.

Chapter 2

THEY MAKE THEIR WAY to the City Watch barracks, where they would expect to find Captain Harding. Kit gets a quick greeting from a few of the guards as they cross through the gates into the Watch's compound. Most of the guards are aware that she's doing work for the Captain, so they're quick to let them through without incident.

"The guards almost look like they're afraid of you," Indie mentions as he keeps a careful eye on the men and women of the Watch. "That's got to feel good, eh?"

"They don't fear me," she can't help but laugh. "But they do fear the Captain. The last time I was treated badly, it didn't go well for those involved."

"We don't *fear* the Captain, street rat. We *respect* him."

Kit turns to see Lieutenant Karr standing behind them. He has the same cheerful demeanor he seems to always have. She can practically hear him snarling at her as he speaks.

"Judging by the look on Harding's face right now, I'm going to guess that perhaps you should be fearing him." Kit motions with her head for Karr to look behind him. His face blanches just before he spins on his heel to face the Captain, who isn't actually there.

"You worthless piece of gutter trash. I'm going to skin you alive!" The lieutenant begins to bear down on Kit, his meaty hands clenched in tight fists by his side. His face is so red that it's practically turning purple. Just as he's about to lay his hand on her, Runt steps in between. He offers the lieutenant a low menacing growl while peeling back his lips, exposing his formidable set of canines.

"Move out of my way, Lump, or I'll gut you like a summer hog." Karr has completely lost his composure at this point. This escalated much faster than Kit would have ever expected.

9

"Lieutenant!" the shout was loud enough that everybody in the compound turns towards it, including Runt. Standing just outside the gate is an enormous man, dressed in full ceremonial armour, carrying a bastard-sword that is nearly as long, as Kit is tall. "Are you looking to spend the rest of the entire cycle on latrine duty? Is one moon not enough for you?" It seems that every time Kit runs into Karr, it goes badly, and he ends up on the *dirty* end of the stick.

Karr immediately snaps to attention, saluting his commanding officer. "No, sir, definitely not, sir. I was only ..." The words fall off, like he really isn't sure what to say. He turns back to Kit, lowering his eyes slightly, "My apologies, Sister Kit, I don't know what came over me."

The Captain continues heading their way, his strides getting longer and faster with each step. It looks like he's ready to use his massive sword. Kit quickly pulls out one of the loaves that Comden gave her, holding it out to the lieutenant. "No hard feelings," she says with a small smile. "It's Comden's new recipe." As she holds it out, Karr's face is a picture of pure confusion. Kit furrows her brow and whispers, "Just take it. Make nice."

The lieutenant takes the loaf from her, but he clearly has no idea what Kit is up to.

"Lieutenant, to my office. NOW!" Even though the Captain is only a few feet away, he continues to scream like he's trying to get the attention of somebody on the other side of the kingdom.

"Captain! Wait!" Kit interrupts. "It's not what it looks like."

"What is it then, if it's not what it looks like!" Unfortunately, Kit is now catching the full brunt of the Captain's ire. She stammers slightly while trying to come up with a plausible explanation.

"Yes Kit? Do you have something to say?"

She needs to crane her neck to look up at the Captain. He's easily two feet taller than she is, possibly more.

"Well sir," she continues to stammer trying to buy herself some time. "It's my fault that Lieutenant Karr was upset with me. I made a comment, well, about you really, and he took offense to it."

"What comment could you possibly make to warrant my officer to threaten to *skin you alive*?"

"Well, nothing that bad, I don't think, but I've got a bit of a history with Karr. You know, needling him, just to get a reaction. I might have overdone it." Kit holds her hands, palms up, hoping to look adorable. It's a technique that had often smoothed over the edges with Father Hoarfrost. "It's kind of what I do." She bats her eyes a few times, as if that would help.

"Sweet Titan, girl. If you're going to work up my guards just for the sport of it, I'm going to have to find somebody else to ... do what you're doing." Apparently, Kit's child-like demeanor was enough to diffuse the situation. The Captain starts shaking his head. "What's Lump doing here? This is no place to be bringing the Temple mascot."

Runt is still watching Karr like he's ready to rip open his throat. "Oh no, this isn't Lump," Kit says with a big smile. "This is Runt. I picked him up while I was looking after the wolf problem you sent me on." She's just about to tell them that Runt is a dire wolf, but Indie is slowly shaking his head, suggesting that perhaps it was a bad idea. Taking his cue, she continues. "And this is Indie. He lives in one of the villages I visited. He's offered to help as well. You did say you were short of able bodies, so I thought you'd appreciate the extra hands. He's also pretty good in a fight."

"Pleasure to meet you, Captain," Indie offers his hand to the Captain.

"Do you know how to use that short sword you're carrying?" The Captain seems to be sizing up Kit's new friend. "If so, defend yourself!"

No sooner had the Captain said the words, than he brings his bastard-sword around in an arcing overhand strike. Indie smoothly steps to the side and draws his short sword, smashing it down on the Captain's blade. The Captain shifts his weight in towards Indie, bringing him inside his guard. He then quickly spins around, trying to catch Indie in the face with his elbow. Again, Indie deftly moves, sinking below the attack. With the Captain's back now exposed, Indie kicks him in the back of the knee, knocking the big man off balance. With cat-like reflexes, the Captain spins around again, this time sweeping the legs out from Indie, causing him to land hard onto his back.

Runt is just about to step in, but Kit's able to tell him to be still before he does.

The Captain nods his approval. "He'll do, Kit," the Captain says as he reaches out to take Indie by the arm, offering to hoist him up to his feet. "You should join the Watch, son. You'd be a welcome addition to my ranks."

Indie's look is somewhere between confusion and outrage, but Kit gives him a knowing smile. "Don't sweat it, Indie. He did the same thing to me when we first met. It's his way of making sure you're up to the task, whatever that task might be."

Indie is rubbing his backside, still looking confused. Shortly afterwards, his confusion turns to anger. "It was a test? What is wrong with you people? You could have killed me!"

The Captain begins to twirl his enormous sword like it's an extension of his arm. "I could shave you with this if I wanted. You were in no danger, other than perhaps dying of embarrassment." He then reaches out and takes the bruised young man's hand in his own. "I'm Captain Harding. I run this post. If you're a friend of Sister Standing Bear, then you're welcome here anytime. If you'd like to join the Watch, I'd take you in a heartbeat."

"Captain," Kit interrupts. "I'm not technically a *sister* yet. Even though I completed the *Rite of Abandonment* ritual, I haven't yet been awarded the title."

Captain Harding dismisses her comment with a wave of his hand. He then turns his attention back to Karr. "Is there some reason you're standing around, Lieutenant? If you don't have anything to do, I'm sure I can find you something to clean out."

"No sir, Captain, sir. Plenty to do." Just as he is about to leave, Karr inclines his head slightly to Kit. Even though she knows he hates her, she's hopeful this small show of mercy will help mend things between them.

"Enjoy the loaf!" she calls out, as Karr walks away.

"Follow me to my office, Kit. I want to hear about the wolf situation."

Chapter 3

THE GROUP FOLLOWS THE Captain into his office. Kit and Indie take a seat across from the Captain's massive rough-hewn desk. Runt moves into a corner where he can see the entire office and the door. He promptly curls up into a small ball, tucking his nose under his tail. Before the Captain takes his seat, he methodically removes his pauldrons and breast plate.

"You're all dressed up today, Ray. Hot date?" Indie looks at Kit in shock. "What?" she asks, in mock surprise.

The Captain presses his lips together, trying his best not to let her get under his skin. "Kit, if you weren't of use to me, I'd drag you by your ear back to the High Priest and let him deal with your insolence."

"But I am of use," Kit says with a wide grin, batting her eyes. "And you like having me around."

The Captain puts his elbows on his desk and his face into his massive hands. "Indie, why are you hanging out with this ... person. I require her services, so I'm forced to deal with her, but you're doing so of your own free will." He looks up from his hands, his face looking more weary than usual. "Like I said, there is a place for you in the Watch. It seems like a win, win. I get a good man, and you get away from ... her." Indie laughs at the Captain's joke, but he tries to control it so that he doesn't offend Kit.

Kit feigns shock and outrage, but when she sees she's not getting the intended reaction, she shrugs her shoulders. "Do you want to hear about the wolves we dealt with?"

The Captain sighs heavily and leans back in his chair. "Yes, Kit, that's what we're here for. Please, tell me all about the wolves."

"Do you want to hear about the poachers as well?"

The Captain sits up in his chair, his face becoming much more serious. "Poachers?"

"Yes, poachers!" Kit scooches up to the front of her chair for dramatic effect. "But first, the wolves." Kit recounts the story of the wolves, how they were poisoned by mushrooms, likely causing them to behave erratically and aggressively. She tells him how they were forced to put them down when they found them. She also tells him about the dire wolves they encountered, suffering from the same affliction.

"What about the poachers?" the Captain asks. He's clearly more interested in that part of Kit's story.

"Just be patient," she replies, holding up her hand to stop him from talking. "I'm getting to that. The story about the wolves is important."

"Then get on with it," Harding says through clenched teeth. His face is getting a bit red at this point.

"Well, I can't say for certain, but I think it was the poachers who were poisoning the wolves." Kit pushes back into the large wooden chair. It's then that she notices her feet are no longer touching the floor. She swings them back and forth a few times before continuing. Apparently, these chairs were designed with tall people in mind, and at well under five feet, Kit did not meet that criteria.

"I think they were poisoning the wolves to make them aggressive. If the cities and the outlying villages are being attacked by the wolves, then nobody is going to complain about the poachers killing off the wolves in the area." Kit gives the Captain a satisfied smirk, letting him know she's finished.

The Captain starts speaking slowly to her, like she's too dim to understand his words. "And, what. About. The. Poachers?"

"Oh, right!" she rolls her eyes at him, like she was planning on getting to it. "Well, I needed to do something, so I sent Indie back to his village to let them know the wolves had been taken care of. After he left, I started heading north, and that's when I ran into them. They were killing a dire wolf so that they could take her puppies from her."

Runt starts to whine as Kit recounts the story of his mother's death. He gets up from his place in the corner and sits beside her. "After I took care of the poachers, I found the dire wolf puppies and made sure they had a good meal."

"You *fed* them? Why didn't you just kill the pups?" the Captain's face is grim. He looked like he didn't really want to hear the answer to his question. Runt was giving a low growl when Harding asked about killing the puppies.

"Kill them? No way!" She gives Runt a scratch on his head. "I kept Runt with me, and I used the other pups as bait to catch the poachers. I knew Runt would have no trouble following his litter-mates." Runt gives Kit a smile at the comment.

"Runt was one of the puppies?" the Captain starts to chuckle to himself. "I hate to break it to you Kit, but he's not a wolf, and he's definitely not a *dire wolf*." His chuckle is now a full-on laugh. He is clearly having fun at Kit's expense. "I hope the wolves you were killing weren't golden retrievers as well."

She begins to laugh along with the Captain, with Indie staring at the two of them like they had both lost their minds. Suddenly, Kit cuts her laughter off. "We'll see who's laughing now," she says with a wide grin. "Runt *is* a dire wolf."

As the words leave her mouth, Runt begins to shimmer, and for the first time the Captain sees him in his natural form. The spell Fenrir placed on the collar is working perfectly. When Kit permitted the Captain to see Runt in his true form, the illusion was broken.

"Titan's snowballs!" he screams, scrambling from his chair to grab his sword.

Runt gives the Captain a satisfied looking smile.

"You won't need your weapon, Captain. He's on our side."

Runt moves away from Kit, around the desk, towards the Captain. When he gets within a few feet, he sits down and begins panting, his immense tongue dangling from his mouth. The Captain puts his sword away and holds his hand out to the wolf. Runt immediately starts licking his hand and rubbing his body against the Captain. As big as the Captain is, Runt's back is nearly even with his waist.

"I thought you said they were puppies," the Captain says casually as he gives Runt's thick neck fur a good rub.

"He *is* a puppy. Fenrir turned him into a full-sized wolf so that he could protect me."

The Captain's hands immediately stop petting the wolf. "Fenrir?" he asks, one eyebrow cocked up in disbelief.

"Well, that's a bit of a long story," Kit says as she calls Runt back to her side. She recounts how the wolf spirit was talking to her, helping her hunt down the poachers. Kit also goes on to tell Harding of the old woman, and the hut in the woods. "And after I took care of the poachers, the old woman, Fenrir, gave me this fine suit of armor." She stands up and twirls for the Captain, giving him a full view of the magnificent creation that she was given.

"How do you know the old woman was Fenrir? She isn't known for visiting us mortals, but when she does, she usually appears to people as a great white wolf." The Captain has that skeptical look in his eyes again.

"Well, I know because she told me so. She brought a wolf back from the dead. She helped me communicate with the wild wolves." She points to Runt with her hands. "And she made a puppy into a full-sized wolf." Kit pauses for a moment, thinking of other things Fenrir did. "I suppose she might have just been an old mage, or a necromancer of some sort, but I know in my heart that it was the real Fenrir."

"She's telling the truth," Indie offers. "I saw her myself just before we came into the city. She was just a small girl, but she gave Runt the collar he's wearing. It's what makes him look like a dog instead of a wolf." Runt yips and nods in agreement. "See? Even Runt knows it was Fenrir."

The Captain rolls his eyes. "So, in addition to everything else, now you're suggesting that Runt understands what you're saying?"

Kit smiles at the Captain. "Well, let's see how well he understands." She thinks for a moment before coming up with an adequate display. "Runt, close the door and keep the Captain from leaving."

Runt immediately closes the door with his muzzle, before moving himself between the Captain and the door. He gets into a crouch and begins to growl. The growl grows into a full snarl, the big wolf's tongue licking through his razor-sharp teeth.

"Okay, Kit, you've made your point. Runt clearly understands what you're saying."

Runt's snarl turns into a smile, just before he pounces onto the Captain, knocking him off his feet, flat onto his back and promptly starts giving his face a thorough tongue-bath.

"Okay, Runt, let him be." Kit's laughing so hard, she can barely get the words out. Apparently, even though Runt does understand, at this moment, he is choosing not to listen. He continues to give his new friend all the kisses he can manage.

The Captain reaches around his 'attacker,' grabbing him in a bearhug and rolling him over onto his back. Runt struggles for a moment to get free, but as soon as the Captain starts scratching his belly, he stops fighting.

"Okay, Runt," he says with a broad smile. "I need Kit to finish her story so that I can get back to work."

"That's really all there is to the story, Captain. Well, except for the fact that the poachers seemed to have been working for somebody." Kit shrugs her shoulders with the last comment. "I don't know who, though. I mean, why would somebody hire poachers to kill off the wolves in Arnnor?"

The Captain retakes his chair. Runt moves in beside him, trying to get him to continue scratching him. "Off the top of my head, I have no idea. But I'll ask around."

The Captain heads for the door and opens it up. "So Indie, if you do decide to join up, don't hesitate to drop by."

"One more thing, Captain." Kit's not quite ready to end the conversation, even though the Captain seems to have heard enough and is ready for them to leave. "What happened to On'nak?"

The Captain's face goes dark. "He's still in the dungeon. He'll be seeing the magistrate in a few days. His parents are hoping to plead his case, but he tried to murder you, as well as several children. I expect he'll be executed for his crimes. Truth is, I'm surprised you didn't cast judgement on him yourself."

"He's just a boy!" her voice pleading. "He believes he's fighting for a good cause, for the freedom of his people." Kit remembers back to the events at the Cheeserie with Karim's mother. "There is a man, a Berrat man, named Pental who has been getting the Berrat citizens all fired up. He's the one who brainwashed On'nak into doing what he did."

"The reason for his crime is irrelevant," Harding states. The matter-of-fact tone in his voice tells Kit that she is not going to convince him. "He's guilty of murder and attempted murder. Regardless of why, we can't have our citizens killing each other just because somebody gets into their head."

"Oh ya?" Kit challenges him. "What if somebody, a powerful mage for example, cast a spell on you, or made you drink a potion that forced you to kill somebody. Should you be executed for that?"

"That's completely different, Kit. The person would no longer be in control of themselves, so they couldn't be held responsible."

"Words, potions, spells? What's the difference?" she counters. "If somebody can convince you that what you're doing is right and just, then how can you be held accountable?"

Captain Harding's expression doesn't change. It is still hard, like it was carved from a block of granite. "Thankfully, it's not my decision to make. If you feel this strongly, you can speak on On'nak's behalf before the magistrate." He opens the door a bit more, as if to make a point. "We're done here for now, Kit. I have things to do, and you need to go see the High Priest. Father Hoarfrost has been looking for you for two days now. We both know he is not a man that likes to be kept waiting."

"Yes, sir." Kit heads for the door with Indie right behind her. A moment later, Runt comes bursting through the door, practically knocking Kit over in the process.

The massive wooden door closes. From behind the door, she hears the Captain. "Sweet Titan! What am I going to do with her?" causing Kit to chuckle to herself as they make their way to the barracks' exit.

Chapter 4

KIT, INDIE AND RUNT stop at the base of the stairs leading up to the Temple. Indie's mouth is agape as he looks at the ominous task before him.

"First time to the Temple?" Kit asks with a small laugh. "Climbing up is much harder than it looks."

"What? Seriously?" Indie's eyes are practically bugging out of his head. "It looks pretty hard, and you're saying it's harder than it looks?"

"Race you to the top!" Kit shouts out as she starts bolting up the stairs. Runt is already halfway up to the top before she's even climbed three of the stairs. A moment later, Indie catches up and threatens to pass by.

Kit digs deep, not willing to let Indie beat her to the top. "Titan, don't let me lose this challenge. Give me strength," she whispers with ragged breaths. Suddenly, Kit feels a burst of energy coursing through her. She begins to bound up the stairs with ease. By the time she's halfway up, Runt is already at the top. She continues pushing herself, even though her heart is beating so hard that she can feel it in her throat.

When Kit gets to the top, she turns around to see how close Indie is behind her. Shockingly, he still has a long way to go. "Hurry up, you big poke!" Kit's enjoying this far more than she should.

"How did you do that?" Indie asks when he makes it to the top. His face is bright red and he's sweating profusely. "I was passing you, and then you suddenly started climbing the stairs as fast as Runt."

"I didn't speed up," Kit chides. "You slowed down. You need more training."

"I'm telling you, I never slowed down. If anything, I climbed faster than I thought possible, just trying to keep up with you." Indie is still gasping for air, but his skin colour is returning to normal. He uses the sleeve of his shirt to wipe the sweat from his brow.

"Sure, whatever you want to believe," Kit says with a dismissive wave of her hands. "C'mon, let's take Comden's loaf to Miyuki."

"Aren't you supposed to report to the High Priest? The Captain made it sound like you were to waste no time."

"My duties will still be there when I get to him. We don't want the bread to go stale, do we? Besides, I want to show you around the Temple."

Indie shakes his head and lets Kit lead the way.

They head through the main hall of the Temple. There are several priests, acolytes and visitors going about their business. Nobody seems to be paying any attention to their arrival, or to the fact that Runt is a dire wolf, so they continue through to the staircase at the back. They travel down several flights of stone stairs until they get to the floor where the kitchens are. Kit has been up and down these stairs so many times that she no longer notices the quality of the workmanship; how every stone fits so neatly with the ones adjacent, that there is barely a visible seam between them.

"Why did they put the kitchens in the basement?" Indie asks as they head through a set of large double doors. Like the stonework of the stairs, the quality of the workmanship of the kitchen doors, all the doors for that matter, is beyond reproach.

"Heat rises!" Kit replies simply, like it should be obvious. Indie's look says that he needs more of an explanation than that. "Well, the kitchen fires and the clay ovens churn out a lot of heat. Like I said, heat rises, so, that heat travels up through the Temple, warming the dining halls above, as well as the main hall, the private chapels, and the classrooms."

Kit gets a bit of a sour look on her face. "About the only things the kitchen doesn't heat are the dormitories, which are perpetually cold. I complained once about how cold our rooms were and I was told, "You should offer your discomfort as a sacrifice to Titan. Consider what he must endure. Surely you can survive a bit of a chill."

Indie laughs at her comment. "It sounds more like they just don't want to bother having fireplaces built to keep you warm."

Kit gives him a shrug. "The rooms all have them, but it's considered weak to ever light a fire in them; unless the temperature drops so low that not to do so would likely mean death." She's about to continue when she sees her friend. "Hey, there's Miyuki!"

They make their way through the rows of long tables and benches to where Miyuki is delivering a basket of fresh muffins to a table of priests. Kit's mouth begins to water at the sight. "Miyuki is the best baker in all of Arnnor, but I can't wait to see her face when she tries Comden's prickle-berry loaf."

"I thought you said the dining hall is upstairs. This kitchen looks like it could seat forty or fifty people."

Kit laughs at Indie's comment. "These tables are typically used by kitchen staff for their meals, but we all come down every now and again if we're looking to grab a quick snack. The dining hall upstairs can seat hundreds of people!" She no sooner finishes speaking when Miyuki calls out a greeting.

"Oh, hello, Kit. Nice to see you." Sister Miyuki waddles over, giving Kit a warm embrace that is so full of love that it makes her homesick. "Have you been to see Father Hoarfrost yet? He's been searching for you for the past two days."

Kit can't help but roll your eyes at the question. "No, not yet. I just got back from a mission that Captain Harding sent me on." She then pulls out the loaf Comden gave her and presents it to Miyuki. "I wanted to deliver this to you first. It's Comden's new recipe."

Miyuki gives the loaf a gentle squeeze before putting it to her nose. She draws in a deep breath, savouring the aroma of the bread. She is just about to comment when she seemingly notices Indie and Runt for the first time.

"Well, hello there," she says to Indie. "And hello to you, too," she says to Runt. "You look just like Lump!" Suddenly, the chubby priest's face turns bright red. "I meant the dog, not you, good sir." Everybody has a good laugh at her jest.

When they finally stop laughing, Kit begins her introductions. "Sorry Miyuki, this is Indie and my furry friend's name is Runt."

"Pleased to meet you, sister. Kit speaks very highly of you." Indie gives her a small bow as he extends his greeting.

"She does now, does she? Well, I'm glad to hear it." Miyuki gives a chuckle before returning her attention to the loaf handed to her. "Prickle-berry bread," she states. "It seems like such a waste of a fine fruit, but Comden knows what he's doing." She pulls a piece of the bread off from the loaf. She squishes it between her fingers and gives it another sniff. "Nice texture," she muses before popping it into her mouth. Her eyes go wide as she does.

"Oh my," she says with a bit of a gasp. "This is wonderful, truly wonderful." She pulls off another piece, again enjoying its aroma before popping it into her mouth. "Oh, what a masterpiece this is. I take back my earlier comment. This is a marvelous use of the fruit."

"I think he's hoping you're going to buy up what supply he has left for the Festival," Kit whispers. It's not like anybody's listening, but it's typically bad form for members of the Temple to be advocating on behalf of vendors.

"Oh my, yes. This bread would make a wonderful addition to the Feast." Kit could see the wheels spinning in her head as Miyuki ponders the treat. "It's too sweet to be served with dinner, and I've already planned dessert." She begins to laugh. "Who cares when it gets served, as long as the guests get a chance to try it out."

Miyuki finishes off the last of the loaf and begins to lick her fingers clean. Again, her face turns red with embarrassment. "Oh, I'm so sorry. I should have shared this with you." The priest looks mortified with herself.

"We brought it for you," Indie interrupts. "We've already eaten our fill of them." Runt growls lightly. He clearly disagrees with Indie's statement.

"Oh, poor puppy. I'll bet you're starving, aren't you?" Runt begins to spin in a circle, clearing indicating that he'd enjoy some food. "Kit, why don't your new friends stay here for a proper meal while you go see the High Priest." She is giving Kit *that look* that tells her this is not a request. Sister Miyuki may be a Temple baker, but she is also one of the highest-ranking priests here.

"Yes, sister," Kit replies, bowing slightly, acknowledging her rank. "I'll head there right now."

"Good!" she says, bobbing her head as though to punctuate the statement. "On your way then. I'll make sure your friends are well looked after."

And with that, Kit turns on her heel and heads off to the High Priest's office.

Chapter 5

KIT MAKES HER WAY UP the stairs to the High Priest's office. She's feeling more nervous than she might have expected, which only goes to tell her that inside, deep inside, she knows her actions would not be appreciated by Father Hoarfrost, her mentor, and somebody she considered a friend. The fact that he even entertained audiences with her says a lot. Most acolytes would never have private meetings with him, nor would he be *personally* giving them duties.

She cringes at how she's been treating him, all things considered.

When Kit gets to the door of his office, it's slightly open, and she can hear people talking inside. Judging by the tone, Father Hoarfrost isn't happy. As Kit's just about to head off, brother Powder comes out of the room. His face is bright red. When he sees Kit, he quickly averts his eyes and rushes past.

"Come in, Kit!" the High Priest shouts. "I know you're out there!"

Kit blinks in confusion, wondering to herself. *How could he possibly have known that?*

"Titan's blessings upon you, Father," Kit offers as she walks into the room. "I can come back later if now is not a good time."

"Sit!" the old priest says. His voice is firm, but completely in control.

"I'm here to report on my assignment." Kit tries to sound formal, in an attempt to appear respectful, but the dubious look on the High Priest's face says that he's not buying it.

He holds up his hand, telling her to stop talking. He then quietly moves behind his desk and takes a seat. Each second that he spends milling about feels like an eternity. Kit just knows he's going to rip a strip off her, and the waiting is killing her. *Just get it over with,* she thinks to herself.

The priest's face goes hard. "I'll get to it in my own time, young lady."

Titan's snowballs! Is he reading my mind? No sooner does the thought pop into her head, she regrets thinking it, especially if the old priest can read her mind.

Just when it looks like Hoarfrost is about to speak, he stands from his chair and walks over to one of the office windows. He looks out at the statue of Titan. He takes a deep breath and slowly lets it out. Kit can't help but think that whatever he's going to say, it will be bad, very bad.

Still staring out the window, he begins to speak. "Are you not a member of this Temple?" Before Kit has a chance to answer, he again holds up his hand cutting her off. "Am I not the High Priest in this Temple? Did you not address me as *Father* when you came into my office?"

Slowly, he turns from the window to face her. When Kit looks past him, she can see the statue of Titan in the background. As High Priest, he *is* Titan's representative here on Orth. When he speaks, he speaks for Titan. Her studies have always stressed this.

Again, with the same methodical pace, the priest moves from the window back to his chair. He then slowly, deliberately, lowers himself into it before casting his full gaze upon Kit.

"*I* sent you on a mission. An important mission. And you, a not-yet-anointed priest, think that you can go running off on an errand for Harding?"

"But I did complete your mission," Kit squeaks out, desperately hoping to quell his anger.

"Silence!" he shouts in reply, waves of cold emanating from him. Frost begins to form on the edges of his desk and around the window frames.

"I shouldn't have to learn of your *exploits* from other members of the Temple, let alone from *prisoners*!"

"You spoke with On'nak? Was he okay? He doesn't deserve to die!" The words are tumbling out of Kit's mouth before she has a chance to check herself.

The High Priest's eyes harden even more, narrowing to something barely more than a slit. "I will tell you when you can speak. Until then ..." he just lets that hang. The room feels like it dropped several more degrees.

"The mission I sent you on was simple, but it was important. The *problem* you encountered at the fishing village is not an isolated incident. People are dying, Kit! Do you understand? They're *dying*!" Suddenly the old priest's face softens, and the room's temperature begins to return to normal.

"The boy you brought back; he tried to kill children, just because they're human; children, without fault, but he tried to kill them anyway. Then, when you saved that child's life, he tried to take yours for doing so. Is that a correct account of the mission?"

The old priest pauses for a moment, leaving Kit unsure if it's a question meant to be answered, or if he is simply pausing to make his point. Kit nods slightly, hoping that a non-verbal response won't make the situation any worse.

"The young Berrat tried to kill two people that we know of. Very likely, he was also responsible for the other illnesses in the village. Did you think to ask him that? No. No, you didn't. Instead, you let him spin you a tale of woe and hardship, and suddenly you feel that he should be freed, because somehow, this isn't his fault."

Kit keeps her head down, staring at her feet like they might somehow save her. "He was brainwashed." The words fall from her lips, again coming out before she has a chance to stop them. "His mind was not his own. The words of somebody else had poisoned him; poisoned his mind, turning it into something horrible; something ..."

Kit suddenly realizes that she's crying. Tears are falling down her cheeks, puddling on the floor beneath her. "Surely Titan can understand forgiveness! Justice doesn't always have to mean death." When she looks up, the old man's face is a mixture of pity and pride.

"Good." He says with a small smile. "Very good."

"But?" This is not the reaction Kit expected.

"But nothing. It's true, we stand for justice, and as priests of Titan we deliver justice with swift and decisive action. Often our brand of justice can be seen as harsh, possibly even cruel. But, when the lives of innocents are on the line, we need to temper that justice with compassion. That's what you did. You're barely a full priest, but you are wise beyond your years."

"I thought you were angry with me."

"Oh, I am. I'm furious with you. But I'm also proud of you." Hoarfrost offers up a thin-lipped smile with his last comment.

"How? How can you be both angry and proud?"

"I'm proud of you for looking beyond the obvious. I'm proud of you for seeing the good in people, when all they're showing you is the bad." Hoarfrost leans back into his chair, knitting his fingers together, letting his hands rest on his lap in front of him. "But even though you handled the mission well, you should have come to me first, before running off on another mission for Harding. We might have been able to deal with the boy before he was processed by the Watch. Now, there is no option but to have him stand before the magistrate. He will most likely be executed for his crime ..."

Kit thinks Father Hoarfrost has finished, but he clearly hasn't.

"All of that was bad, but then you dragged brother Powder into it. You had him give you prohibited potions; dangerous potions; potions, that if used inappropriately, could kill. He should have known better, but I know you. I know how you work people. I know how you ... *bend them* ... to your will. I know, because you've done it to me on multiple occasions. I don't know how you do it, but you do."

"I can't help it if I'm charming," Kit says with a small grin and a shrug. She tosses her long black hair over her shoulder, just to emphasize the point.

"Now is not the time for humour, Kit. You're not going to just bat your eyes and smile your way out of this."

Terror rips through her. Kit suddenly feels tightness in her chest. "What's to happen to me?"

"What indeed?" Hoarfrost leans forward, now drumming his fingers on his finely crafted desk. "We'll deal with that when you get back."

"Get back?" She can only imagine where he's going to send her.

The priest reaches into one of the many folds in his robe. He pulls out a map of Aarall and spreads it out on his desk. He points out two nearby villages, Ashcroft and Templeton. "The people here are in trouble. These self-proclaimed *nationalists* are bringing threats of violence to anybody who isn't a Berrat. They're even turning on the Gigas." He begins to shake his head in disbelief. "Those gentle giants harm nobody, they are pacifistic by nature, yet the nationalists' rhetoric targets them as well as humans."

"Have there been any deaths?" If there had been, Kit would not likely be able to bring the offenders to justice. Instead, she'd have to bring justice to them.

"Thankfully, not as yet – or at least not as of my latest report."

"I'll leave right now." Kit stands up briskly, not wanting to disappoint her mentor again. She stops before making it to the door, turning back towards the High Priest. "I'd like to bring some friends with me. Would that be okay?"

The High Priest shakes his head. "I'm sorry, I cannot spare any more acolytes for this task. Too many of them are working on preparations for the Feast of Titan. Besides, they're not as well *equipped* as you to deal with trouble. As for the priests, they are dealing with the problems here in the city. It's not just the outlying villages that are being targeted by these *people*."

Kit bows her head slightly, not wanting to look Hoarfrost in the eye. "My friends are neither priests, nor acolytes. They're Indie and Runt. I met them while I was dealing with the wolf problem ... for Captain Harding."

Hoarfrost continues to shake his head. "I'm sorry, but I can't risk civilians getting hurt on Temple business."

"Indie is a skilled fighter," Kit offers in mild protest. "Captain Harding offered him a post in the Watch. And Runt, well, he's a ... dog." She knows she should tell him that Runt's a dire wolf, but she's just not ready to go into a full explanation of how she's come to have a dire wolf for a friend.

The High Priest narrows his eyes, cocking his head to one side. "You're not telling me the *whole* truth, are you, little sister."

Titan's snowballs! How does he do that? Kit really hopes he isn't reading her mind. But Hoarfrost has been dealing with people for many years, and he knows her well. Kit thinks that she likely has a tell of some sort. "Yes, father." She casts her eyes downward and takes a deep breath. "I didn't lie, but I didn't tell you the whole truth either. Runt isn't a dog, he's a dire wolf."

When Kit looks up, the old man is grinning. "I know that. Brother Rime informed me when you and your *friends* came into the Temple. You caused quite a stir with him. Nobody else would verify his statement though."

Suddenly, the blood drains from Kit's face. "Brother Rime saw my wolf? That's impossible. Fenrir said that only people I allowed to see through her illusion would know that he's a wolf, and those people who are my enemies."

"Fenrir?"

Kit's mind races at the implications. Why would brother Rime be her enemy? Outside of seeing him on occasion during services, she's hardly ever dealt with him.

The old priest stands patiently waiting for an explanation. Kit decides that now is not the time to hold back, so she quickly recounts her adventures, describing in detail how Fenrir had helped her and how she had gifted Kit the suit of armor she was wearing.

"This is very troubling news, Kit. I am going to need to pray on this. I will ask Titan for his guidance." The old man again reaches into his robes and produces a handful of vials filled with red liquid, healing potions. "Here, take these with you. They're considerably stronger than potions you could brew yourself. I don't want any of your *friends* dying on me."=

"Thank you, father. I'll leave for the villages right away."

Again, the old man shakes his head. "Leave in the morning. The nearest village is several hours away, even by horseback. Have a good meal, and a good night's sleep. Visit the stables before you go. There will be two horses saddled and stocked up for your journey. When you're done, report back to me; immediately! Bring your friends with you. I want to meet them."

"Strength of Titan," Kit says while crossing her arms across her chest. "I will not stray from my duties."

"Titan's blessings upon you, child," the old priest says in reply. "Sleep well."

Chapter 6

IT'S WELL BEFORE DAWN. No light is coming in through the room's small slit-windows, making it pitch black inside. Kit's room, as usual, has a biting cold breeze flowing through it. She tries to pull her blanket up to her chin, but it won't move. She tugs again, this time putting considerably more effort into it. Again, her effort to pull the blanket up is met with abject failure. *What in Helja?* she mutters to herself as she reaches down toward the foot of the bed, trying to figure out why the blanket is pinned. It's then that she feels thick silky fur. "Runt?" Kit quietly calls out, hoping to rouse her dire wolf. "Runt, get down," she orders, but the mass of fur continues to lie motionless. "Runt!" she says again, this time more forcefully.

Suddenly, a large wet tongue scrapes across Kit's face. A good deal of saliva covers her cheeks, dripping down into her mouth. "Titan's snowballs!" she groans out as she wipes her face with the back of her hand. "Runt?"

It's only then that the mass of fur at the bottom of the bed begins to move, its weight shifting as it moves closer. A moment later, there is a large 'whump' as the animal crashes down beside her, its warm breath on her face. "Lump?" Kit whispers.

Lump rolls in towards her, pressing Kit toward the edge of the bed. Runt bounds up onto the bed, laying across Kit's legs, his sizable weight crushing her into the thin hay-filled mattress covering the stone-slab bed.

Try as she might, there is simply no room left for Kit in the bed, and neither Lump nor Runt are going to give up the space they've claimed for themselves. It's at that moment she realizes her night's sleep has come to an uncomfortable end.

"Alright, you two, let's get up. Let's get the day started." Runt immediately hops off the bed, followed shortly by Lump. "Ha!" Kit quietly shouts. "The bed's mine now. You two, go lie down." She's just starting to wrap herself in a cocoon when the blanket is being dragged off the bed, with Kit in it. Her butt meets the cold stone floor with an audible 'thud.'

Kit grumbles under her breath. "Okay, okay. Let's take care of 'business' and then get some breakfast." She's practically tripping over the two animals as she squeezes past them to get to the small chest at the foot of the bed. Kit quickly takes her clothes out of it and begins dressing. Her skin is covered in goosebumps as she pulls her tunic over her head. Kit figures she'll come back for her armor and the rest of her gear after the morning's ablutions have been taken care of.

She opens the door to her room and heads down the hallway. It's pitch-black here too, but Kit's been up and down these halls so many times that she has no difficulty in navigating the turns until she comes to a set of doors leading to the outside, to the Temple grounds. "Don't waste any time if you want to have breakfast," she says as the two animals make their way outside.

After taking care of her own duties, Kit returns to the door to find both Runt and Lump waiting patiently for her return. "Okay, I need to get dressed, then we can get going."

Both animals burst through the doorway and find their way back to the room. Once there, Kit quickly changes into her armour and fills her knapsack with essential items before heading to the stables to get Indie. He insisted on sleeping there, rather than in the Temple's guest quarters.

When Kit gets to the stables, Indie is already dressed and ready to head out. He has two horses saddled. Their packs are both filled with supplies and gear for the journey.

"We should stop by the kitchens for some food," Kit prompts Indie. "We can fill our bellies before we head out."

"No need," he smiles. "I've already taken care of it." He points to a side table that has a copious amount of food spread out on it. There are meats, cheeses, bread, and a large bowl of spiced oatmeal. "What we don't eat now, we can bring with us."

"I don't think the oatmeal is going to travel too well," Kit laughs. "But I'm guessing there won't be any left by the time we leave." Runt seems to nod his agreement.

It doesn't take long for the four to eat their fill. Indie packs the remaining food in the horses' saddlebags. There's enough food here to last nearly a week, but it's better to have too much than too little.

Kit mounts up and gets ready to head off. "Are you going to come along, Lump?" she calls out. She can't help but laugh to herself as she talks to the animals like they clearly understand everything she's saying. When Lump barks in agreement, she gives him a big smile. "Okay then, let's head out."

By the time they get to the city gates, the sun is just starting to break over the mountains to the east. Kit decides that since they're leaving so early, they're going to head to Templeton, the farthest village first. Indie expects that if they cut cross country, and things go smoothly, they'll make it there shortly after mid-day.

Indie immediately takes the lead since his skills as a scout are clearly far superior. Both Runt and Lump are running on up ahead, seemingly on alert for any trouble they might run into.

After several hours of traveling in a south-westerly direction, the terrain changes from rolling hills to heavy forests. "We should take a break on the outskirts of the forest," Indie suggests. "These forests can be dangerous, even at midmorning. I've been here before and they'll be slow to move through. The village is on the other side of them, near the Gaelinora Sea."

"I don't think the horses need a break, but my butt certainly could." Kit give her posterior and inner thighs a good rub down when she gets down off her horse. "I don't ride nearly as much as I should ..."

Indie climbs down off his horse with a simple grace. "If you want, I can shorten your stirrups," he offers. "If you use your legs more, it will take some of the pressure off your ... backside."

Kit's face heats up slightly at his comment. "I can do it myself," she blurts out. "I've been trained on how to take care of my horse's tack."

Indie promptly raises his hands defensively. "Whoa, no problem. I was just offering to help. I can get some food and drink out while you're doing that."

"Fine," Kit grumbles, suddenly aware at how foolish she must sound.

Runt and Lump are both keeping a close eye on the food that Indie is taking from the saddlebags. "You can go hunt for your own food, you two. This is for Kit and me." The wolf and dog both move closer. They're clearly more interested in an easy meal. Indie pulls out two sizable chunks of cooked goat and tosses one to each of them. "Don't tell Kit," he whispers as they both chow down on the tender meat.

By the time Kit has finished adjusting her saddle, Indie has taken out an assortment of food and laid out a sleeping roll for them to sit and eat on. "Picnic style," he says with a thin-lipped smile, causing Kit to chuckle at the comment before taking her seat on the ground. She's considerably hungrier than she realized, pretty much stuffing the food into her face, finishing her share in just a few moments.

When she looks up at Indie, his eyes are wide in amazement. "What?" she manages to muffle out, her mouth still stuffed with food.

"Nothing!" he says with a grin. "I don't think I've ever seen any- one with such a voracious appetite. Well, except for maybe Runt here."

"I was hungry!" the words coming out, along with some bread- crumbs. Kit's face begins to heat again, so she gets up and starts preparing her horse, even though there is nothing that she actually needs to do.

Indie tosses Runt and Lump the last few scraps of food he had taken out. "Okay, let's get going."

Kit's not sure, but she thinks she hears a bit of trepidation in his voice. Kit decides to head out first, but Indie quickly trots up next to her. "I'll take the lead." His face is grim. "I have a feeling I'll be able to see things faster than you will."

Kit shrugs your shoulders and gives him a coy smile. "As you wish, but the only thing I get to see from the rear is your horse's backside." And with that, the group heads into the forest.

As soon as they enter in the woods, the temperature starts to drop. The sun is barely making it through the canopy above, and it feels more like late evening than late morning. Everything looks like a tangle of branches and bushes, but Indie is having no difficulty finding a usable trail.

Suddenly he holds up his hand, motioning Kit to stop. Neither Lump nor Runt are within sight. "We're not alone," he whispers. His head is spinning about like it's on a swivel. "Follow me!" he yells as he digs his heels into his horse's ribs, urging it into a gallop.

Kit is about to do the same when a giant spider, a forest crawler, she thinks, lands on the ground in front of her. Her horse rears up, startled by the spider's presence, throwing Kit from her perch. She lands hard on her back, knocking the wind out of her. Spots are dancing in front of her eyes, and she can hear her horse screaming in pain. Kit quickly clamours to her feet, her battle hammer at the ready.

A second spider has landed on top of Kit's horse. She watches in horror as it sinks its fangs deep into the horse's neck. The first spider leaps up on the horse's head, repeatedly biting it on the face.

Kit's shield is strapped to her saddle, so she's going to have to fight without it. She runs up beside the spiders, taking a sideways swing at the one clamped onto her horse's head. She hits it squarely in the thorax, knocking it off the horse. It tumbles a few times before righting itself.

It quickly spins around and shoots a stream of web at her. The bulk of the attack goes over Kit's head, but she's hit by enough strands that her arms are tangled in the goop, making it hard to move them. Just as the spider is about to make itself ready for an attack, Lump jumps at it, catching it just behind the head.

A moment later Runt joins into the melee, his teeth burying deeply into the spider's abdomen. It screeches as Runt's teeth penetrate through his chitin exoskeleton into the soft flesh beneath. A quick shake of Runt's head rends a large piece of the spider's side away from its body. It's only when it goes limp that Lump lets go of his death grip on the spider's neck.

The second spider seems to be oblivious to the ongoing battle as it continues to suck the living juices from the horse's neck. Kit is about to try and pull it off the horse when a sword blade protrudes from its head. It shudders for a moment before releasing its grip on the horse and slides off to the side. As it does, Kit sees Indie standing there holding his short sword. A moment later, Kit's horse keels over.

"Get your gear off the horse and let's get going," Indie urges. If there are two of them, there may well be a nest nearby. They're usually solitary creatures.

"A nest?" Kit says with disgust. A lot of her gear is now under her dead horse. There is no way that she's going to be able to lift the beast to pull it out. Thankfully though, her shield is accessible.

Just as Kit finishes pulling one of the saddlebags off the horse, Runt starts growling, followed by Lump. As she turns, she sees there are three more forest crawlers along with a wolf spider. The wolf spider is nearly twice as big as the other arachnids.

"Back away, slowly!" Indie snarls. "They may be more interested in the horse than they are in us." Kit starts taking a few steps back, away from the horse. The wolf spider immediately jumps onto the animal, ripping it apart with its enormous mandibles. The three forest crawlers join in.

Unexpectedly, Runt unleashes a cold attack on the spiders. A funnel of frost comes from his mouth, encasing the spiders in a layer of ice. As they begin to move, the ice begins to crack. Kit immediately follows suit, releasing her own frost attack on the spiders. In mere moments, the spiders are again covered in a thick layer of ice. They're still moving slightly, so Kit wastes no time bringing her hammer to bear, crashing it down onto the head of the wolf spider.

Splinters of ice shards go flying on impact. The wolf spider shivers for a moment before going motionless. Indie, Runt and Lump each take on a forest crawler as they slowly try to get clear of the horse. They are stiff from being frozen and unable to defend themselves. They are each dispatched in quick order.

"Well, at least your gear is free now. The spiders seem to have done you a favour." Indie reaches for a now-exposed strap and pulls it from underneath the horse. The last of Kit's saddle bags is dragged out with it, along with some of the horse's entrails.

"That's just gross," Kit mutters as she starts trying to wipe off the leftover gore from her belongings. "It looks like I'm walking from here."

"We'll load up my horse with the gear and we'll both walk," Indie suggests as he leads his horse over. Kit throws her saddlebags over the horse's back, tying them to the other bags already attached to the saddle.

Kit calls to Runt and Lump as they make ready to head out. Lump has a wolf spider leg in his mouth and Runt is dragging the remains of one of the forest crawlers.

"Titan's snowballs! Where do you think you're going with those?" Kit makes no effort to hide her revulsion. Lump whines, hoping she'll let him keep his prize. "You two are both disgusting creatures. Do you know that? Absolutely disgusting."

Runt drops his carcass and begins to trot up beside Kit. He looks at her with the saddest eyes she's ever seen. "Sorry," she says as she scratches his ears. "I just ... I really hate spiders." He gives her a small lick on her hand. A moment later, Lump goes bounding past, the spider leg still in his mouth. "Go ahead," Kit says to Runt. "Go claim your prize." She'd swear he smiled at her before he runs back, grabbing the spider carcass, pieces of it falling off as he races past to follow after Lump.

"The smell of those spiders might actually keep predators away," Indie chuckles. "We're not the only things repulsed by them." He motions towards his horse, and the wild-eyed look it has.

Chapter 7

BY THE TIME THEY MAKE it through the forest, both Lump and Runt have lost interest in their prizes. Runt had found some wild game along the way, which was far more palatable than dead spider bits.

"Maybe on the way back we'll take the roadway, such as it is." Kit suggests, looking back at the forest with disdain. "The forest was more direct, but not what I would consider a scenic route."

"At least we didn't run into any wolves," Indie says with a grim face. "Even with Runt and Lump along, we'd have had a hard time dealing with a wolf pack."

Kit smiles, thinking back to her encounter with Fenrir and the wolf spirit. "I believe we'll be safe from wolves, wherever we go. I think Fenrir gave me a connection of some sort with them. I could feel them in the forest when we were nearly through the worst of it. While they were around, I felt safe. Like they were watching over us."

"Too bad they weren't around when the spiders attacked," Indie groused. "Then we'd be riding instead of hoofing it."

Kit gives her backside a light rub. "I'm not complaining about walking, but I wish my horse hadn't been killed."

Suddenly Indie's eyes light up. "Maybe we won't have to walk! Here, take the reins of my horse." He doesn't really wait for Kit to take them. He simply throws them at her and starts running through the tall grass. Not wanting him to get too far ahead, Kit breaks into a run, leading his horse behind her.

Kit gives chase for several minutes, barely keeping up with Indie's pace. When he starts to slow, Kit sees a small herd of horses up ahead. Very large horses. Chargers. These are prized war mounts, but they are highly unpredictable and incredibly aggressive. Kit watches in wonder as Indie approaches the herd, looking as though he's done this every day of his life.

A large black stallion breaks away from the herd, moving slowly, deliberately towards Indie. His long mane and tale are blowing in the wind behind him as he closes the gap between them. All the while, Indie is cooing at the horse, holding his hands out from his sides like he's forcing the animal to look directly into his eyes.

Without warning, the great horse bolts toward Indie, its eyes so wide that Kit can clearly see the whites. Just as he gets close, the charger drops his head in an attempt to bash him. With one swift motion, Indie sidesteps the attack and grabs a hold of the horse's flowing mane. Using the horse's momentum, he swings his leg up into the air, landing smoothly onto the horse's back.

The big stallion immediately rears up and spins around in a frantic motion. Indie's face is contorting from the exertion of trying to maintain his grip on the animal. He's slipping badly off to the side but manages to right himself. As soon as he's square on the horse's back, it takes off at a full gallop, weaving left and right, trying to rid itself of its rider.

Without notice, the horse skids to a stop and drops its head. With no saddle to hold on to, Indie's forward momentum launches him over the top of the animal, sending him careening across the grass. The charger then rears up and attempts to bring its hooves down onto Indie. Indie scrambles around on the ground, repeatedly dodging the horse's attacks. Time and time again, the animal rears up and crashes down onto the ground. Each time it does, Indie moves off to the side or quickly rolls away.

This continues on for what feels like several minutes when the horse finally runs out of energy, or it has simply lost its desire to kill Indie. When it does, Indie stands up and places his palms on the horse's muzzle. The charger's mane shudders, and he whinnies softly, seemingly welcoming Indie's touch. Indie slowly moves to the horse's side, all the while keeping his hand in contact with him. When he reaches the side of the charger, he grabs hold of his mane and hoists himself up onto the animal's back.

"I've never seen anything like that!" Kit shouts out. "How? How did you do that?"

Indie and the big charger calmly come walking up. "I challenged him, and he accepted my challenge. If I'd lost, he'd have badly injured me, possibly even killed me. But, since I won, he now willingly allows me to ride him.

"Connected?" Kit scrunches up her face trying to understand his meaning.

"You've never been taught this?" he asks. Indie truly looks surprised that this is news to Kit. "Nomad children typically learn this at a very young age. It's called *'binding.'* You single out a herd beast and challenge it. If it accepts your challenge, then you have a chance to bind with it. If you fail, well, the consequences can be bad." Indie runs his hand down the length of his horse's neck. "Chargers respect strength and speed. But, if you fail, they will do everything they can to maim or kill you."

"You're insane!" Kit shouts at him. "I was fine walking. We didn't need another horse."

"Yes, we did. If we take the roads, it will take us nearly a full day to walk from Templeton to Ashcroft. On horseback, we'll get there in a few hours."

Runt and Lump appear suddenly from the tall grass. The charger's eyes go wild with fear, but before he has a chance to react, Indie places his hands on him again. "Friends," he says. The animal immediately calms down, but he keeps a close eye on Runt. Runt, sensing the animal's trepidation, begins to bounce around, wagging his tale and rolling on his back. If Kit didn't know better, she'd swear the charger rolled his eyes at the oversized dire wolf puppy.

"I'm going to name him *Char*," Indie says proudly, continuing to stroke the neck of the great horse.

"Because he's a charger?" Kit scoffs. "Not overly original."

"No, because he's the colour of charred wood." Indie shakes his head. Without being asked, his stallion turns around and begins heading toward the village.

"Hey, are you going to have your new friend here carry some of the gear?" Kit's looking at the heavily burdened horse that she's leading. "He could use a break."

"You weigh nothing," Indie shouts back over his shoulder. "Your horse will have no trouble carrying you and all the gear." Indie's shoulders slump, and his horse turns back towards her. "Toss me the saddlebags. Char can easily carry me, plus all the gear. He's much faster than your horse as well, so your little roan is going to need all the help she can get."

After a few minutes of rearranging the bags, they're on their way.

Chapter 8

WHEN THEY GET WITHIN visual range of Templeton, Indie gets a sour look on his face. "There is an awful lot of smoke coming from the village. I fear it's burning."

"I don't see any smoke," Kit says, craning her neck to get a better view.

"We should pick up the pace," Indie says just before spurring on his mount. The little roan has to run hard to try and keep up. The boys move in along side of Kit, both of them running effortlessly beside her.

Several minutes into the ride, Kit begins to see the smoke Indie was talking about. She can't help but be amazed at just how much farther her friend can see.

Kit also sees a wagon train leaving the village. It looks like dozens of large wagons, with people and livestock walking beside them. When she meets up with the first of the wagons, Kit comes to a halt.

"Hail, friend! Titan's peace upon you." Kit pulls her horse up along side of the woman driving the wagon. "Can you tell me about the smoke we're seeing?"

"The Berrat have started a riot," she says. "We're getting out while we still can." She snaps her reins, urging her draft horses forward.

"Whoa, wait a minute if you will. What do you mean they've started a riot?" Kit tries to cut off the wagon, but it looks like the woman is going to run her over if she doesn't move.

"Some Berrat by the name of Pental showed up this morning. He started preaching at the Sea Gate, just as the fishermen were heading out to the docks. He pulled aside any Berrat who passed by, telling them to rebel against the human oppression." Her eyes were wide, like she was having trouble believing what she was saying. "He told them to kill the humans. That we were to blame for their problems."

"Surely the townsfolk weren't buying it," Kit responds, shaking her head.

"Almost every single one of them bought what he was selling. Those who didn't were either beaten up or hung." Her eyes were getting glassy at this point. "We're a peaceful community. We work our farms, cut lumber from the forests, and fish in the Gaelinora Sea. We used to live in harmony, humans and Berrat." She snaps the reins again, urging the draft horses to pick up their pace. "When they started burning the village, we got the Helja out of there."

"Strength of Titan to you," Kit says as she gets out of the way of the wagon. "Head for Aarall," she shouts to them. "Tell the City Watch what's happening here."

Just then Indie comes running up. His horse has no bridal or saddle, but he seems to be in complete control of it. "It sounds like every Berrat in the village has taken up arms against the humans. If we go there, we'll likely not make it out alive."

"I am a priest of Titan," Kit retorts, mustering as much courage as she can manage. "They'll listen to me."

Indie shakes his head. "I don't think they're going to listen to you or anybody else for that matter."

"We can't just leave them. Innocent people are being hurt." Kit's sense of righteousness is now kicking into full gear. "If they won't listen to me, then I'll deliver Titan's justice upon them."

"Are you going to kill every Berrat in Templeton? Is that your plan?"

"Well ... no. Not that." Kit is suddenly unsure of herself. She's never faced anything like this, and her training certainly didn't cover mass uprisings. Her shoulders slump as she feels the sting of defeat before she's even tried to do her duty. "Let's just ride up to the village gates then. We can make sure the citizens who want to leave can do so."

Indie nods in agreement, and before he says anything his stallion wheels around and begins to gallop toward the village. Runt and Lump immediately give chase, quickly leaving Kit far behind. "Okay, you go ahead. I'll catch up." She shakes her head as she spurs her horse into a dead run. Even at full speed, she's not able to keep up with her cohorts.

By the time Kit gets to the front gatehouse, Indie is being engaged by a number of Berrat. They look to be wielding gardening instruments. Even though they make poor weapons, they can still kill. Lump has a Berrat woman pinned to the ground and Runt is fighting off several others at the same time. The numbers are bad and if Kit doesn't do something quickly, she fears they are not going to survive the encounter.

She draws her battle hammer from its sheath and begins charging into the crowd of Berrat. "By Titan's name, I command you to withdraw!" Her cry seems to have gone unheard because nobody alters their actions. A moment later Kit and her horse crash into the crowd, sending a number of the Berrat sailing through the air. Those her horse did not overrun meet with the business end of her hammer. She quickly cuts through the mass like a scythe through winter wheat.

As Kit spins around to run through them again, the Berrat drop their weapons and scatter. Indie quickly pounces on one, pinning him to the ground. "You're staying with me," he whispers in a deadly voice. "You're going to tell me what's happening, or you're going to be joining the Great Cycle."

The crazed look in the Berrat's eyes vanishes and he begins to wail. "It wasn't my fault. I didn't want to do it. I didn't want to kill anybody." Those were the last coherent words before he begins to blather gibberish nonsense.

Runt is busy chasing the Berrat routing from the scene. "Runt! Come!" Kit calls out. "Lump! Come!" A moment later, they both come running back. Lump appears to be limping slightly. Kit hops off her horse to examine him. She finds a good size wound on his front shoulder. It's not life threatening, but she's not about to let it get infected. Kit quickly closes her eyes and calls upon Titan. Immediately, her hands begin to glow. When she places them upon the wound, Lump begins to whine as he tries to pull away. Kit speaks gently to him, reassuring him that she's helping. As she does, the glow from her hands spreads across Lump's shoulder, chest and back. In a moment, his entire body is bathed in the soft yellow glow.

"There," she says as she gives him a big hug. "Good as new."

Lump immediately begins to lick at the dried blood on his fur. Runt joins in, helping to clean him.

"Umm, Kit. We need to leave. Now!" Indie sounds like he's on the verge of panic.

There is a group of Berrat, several hundred strong, heading out from the gates. They seem to have human prisoners, dozens of them. At the head of the group is a Berrat dressed in solid-black attire.

"Hello, Kit Standing Bear," he yells out. "I wish to speak."

Kit has no idea who this man is, or how he knows her name. "I have nothing to say to you as long as you're holding prisoners," she shouts back. "Let them go. After you do, then we'll talk."

The Berrat in black puts his hand in the air, and then quickly drops it to his side. At his command, five of the human prisoners are executed, their necks cut wide open.

"Titan, no!" Kit shouts, righteous fury coursing through her veins. Kit's heart is pumping so hard that she can feel her ears starting to throb.

"Will you speak with me now?" he calls out, a hint of a smile on his lips, his eyes dancing with glee. Before Kit even has a chance to answer, he raises his arm in the air again.

"Wait!" she screams out, but he gives the signal again and five more helpless people are sent to join the Great Cycle.

"You're nothing more than a coward," Kit screams as she calmly pulls her battle ax from its sheath and begins walking her horse toward him. She can hear Indie behind her, begging her to stop. When she looks down, she sees Runt and Lump on her flanks. "Back to Indie," she orders. They pause for a moment before heading off.

"A coward, am I?" He begins to laugh with a high-pitched, squealing kind of laugh that makes Kit's blood curdle. "I am many things, little human, but I am no coward." He turns back to the crowd behind them. "Kill them all!"

"STOP!" Kit screams out. She quickly spurs her horse into a gallop, charging headlong towards the mass of people. In mere seconds, the Berrat carry out his order, executing each and every one of the prisoners. Kit swallows down the urge to vomit. Her actions have caused the deaths of innocent people. Dozens of them. Nothing she can do is going to turn back the hands of time.

Fury consumes her. She pulls hard on the reins of her horse, causing the little roan to skid to a stop.

"Now who's the coward?" the Berrat taunts. "Where is your fighting spirit, young priest? Where is your god to save these people, these innocents who have all died because of you? I hope you are feeling what I was feeling the day you caused my sweet Yenda's death."

"I have no idea what you're talking about," Kit replies. The Berrat man is slowly walking toward her now, the host of Berrat following only a few feet behind him.

"Yenda, the mother of Karim." Even from this distance, Kit can see the man's eyes go glassy as he mentions her name. "You did not kill her by your own hand, but it was your actions that caused her death."

"Yes, I remember her." Kit says calmly. She's managed to rein in her emotions, allowing her to think more clearly. "If it wasn't the guards who killed her, it would have been me." This last jab causes the Berrat's face to turn beet red.

"You could not have defeated her on your best day. She'd have ripped you limb from limb before she gnawed on your bones to suck out the marrow." Spittle was beginning to fly out of his mouth at this point.

"Maybe yes, maybe no," Kit says, keeping her face hard and emotionless. "But it was you. You poisoned her mind. You turned her against her own family. Her own blood. Isn't that right ... Pental." A smug look crosses Kit's face. Hopefully, calling him out by name will infuriate him further.

"On this day, I will kill you and the pathetic friends you have with you. Tomorrow, I will seek out everyone you have ever loved, and I will give them a slow, painful journey to the Great Cycle. Since your god has no intention of coming to your rescue, I suggest you make peace with him. Now."

With a wave of his arms, he directs the throng of Berrat to attack. Each and every one of them, without hesitation, starts running towards Kit.

"Titan, hear me," she says quietly, calmly. Even though the enemy will be on her in seconds, she manages to maintain her composure. "In your icy prison, I call upon you. In my hour of need, I call upon you. Rend open the earth. Unleash your fury." The head of Kit's battle hammer begins to crackle with energy, small bolts of lightning begin to lick the head of the weapon. Slowly the lightning begins to cascade down the handle and around Kit's arm. A moment later, her entire body is buzzing with energy; the sound turning to a deafening roar in her ears. Just when Kit thinks she's about to explode, she unleashes the full power of her spell at the feet of the oncoming horde.

There is an ear-splitting ka-boom when the lightning hits the ground. Those in the immediate vicinity of the strike are instantly vaporized. The ground splits apart. The crack begins to race toward Pental, widening as it does. Those Berrat who were not killed immediately begin to topple into the gaping hole in the ground, their cries echoing in Kit's ears as they plummet to their deaths.

Just as the opening reaches Pental, he levitates off the ground, a look of satisfaction crossing his face. "You now have the deaths of hundreds of innocents on your hands." Again, he begins to laugh in that horrible high-pitched wail. "It was by *your* actions that these innocents perished."

"They were hardly innocents!" Kit screams. The sound of the earthquake continues to fill the air. "They were all murderers, just like you."

"Perhaps yes. Perhaps no. Is somebody who is *compelled* responsible for their actions?" Seeing the look of bewilderment on Kit's face, he begins to laugh at her yet again. "I forced them to do what they did. Those mewling fools had no interest in my words, so I *compelled* them to do my bidding."

"You're insane," Kit screams at him. "A lunatic!"

"Perhaps yes. Perhaps no," he replies. You are certainly not fit to cast judgement on me, murderer." He continues to float towards Kit, until he is only fifteen feet away. "I think I have had enough of this conversation. It's time for you to die."

"Are you planning on boring me to death with your prattle?" Kit uses her hammer to motion for him to come closer. "I'd be more than happy to let you try."

"I have no intention of dueling with you," he says with a grin. "I'm much too busy for that. I want you to jump into the hole."

"And I want to crush your head with my hammer, but I guess we can't always get what we want." She swings her hammer menacingly as she speaks.

For a moment, just a moment, there is a look of confusion on Pental's face. But, as quickly as it came, it disappears.

The Berrat flies a bit closer still, his face a picture of concentration; his eyes, so intense, that it appears he's trying to look directly into Kit's soul. "You *will* jump into the hole."

Kit feels what could only be described as a wave of magic washing over her. "I don't know what you think you're trying to do, but you're looking more than a bit foolish right now. Come down from there so that we can settle this matter." Kit shakes her battle hammer at him to punctuate the statement.

Now Kit can clearly see confusion on his face. Was he actually expecting her to follow his command? Just as she's about to start mocking him, she hears the whiz of an arrow fly past her, striking Pental cleanly in the torso. His look of confusion changes to shock as he stares down at the shaft protruding from his chest. "What?" he sputters. Slowly, he grabs the shaft in his hand and begins pulling out the arrow, blood dripping off it as he does. Once he has it fully withdrawn, he examines it briefly. A look of disgust crosses his face just before he snaps the arrow in his hand and tosses it to the ground. Suddenly, he begins coughing. Sprays of blood spew from his mouth.

"Mark my words, priest," he says as he wipes the blood off his chin. "You will die. You. Your family. Your friends. Everyone you love, will die." As he speaks, it's clear that he's having trouble maintaining his altitude. His body is swaying, unsteady. Then, after uttering some incomprehensible word, he turns into a cloud of dust and blows away with the wind.

Indie, along with the two canine companions, comes up beside Kit. "Titan was surely with you today, Kit." It sounded like Indie was in awe. "It's the only explanation for why that vampire didn't kill you outright."

"Vampire?" She wasn't sure if Indie was joking or if he was in shock.

He raises his eyebrows, as if in total disbelief. "That was a full vampire. A blood sucking, spawn of King Faol. Are you telling me you didn't know?"

The way Indie said that makes Kit's skin crawl. "There are no vampires in Arnnor," she says with a dismissive tone. "He's a Berrat. Likely a mage of some sort, but he is no vampire. He didn't have fangs, or bat wings, or long hooked talons."

"What are you talking about?" Indie is looking at her now like she's an idiot. "Fangs, wings and talons? That's what you think of when somebody says vampire?"

"Sure," she shrugs her shoulders. "Everybody knows that."

Indie begins to chuckle. "I'm sorry, little sister, but that's just folklore. Well, except for the fangs." Kit watches as Indie walks over to the edge of the hole. "Vampires only have fangs when they're feeding. Otherwise, they're not visible. Vampires look like whatever race they were before they were turned. Often they become *beautiful* as a result of the transformation process, along with being exceptionally strong and agile."

Indie kicks a stone into the hole, watching as it falls. He waits several moments, listening intently. "I didn't hear it hit the bottom," he says casually as he turns back toward Kit. "That's one, deep hole."

"Forget the hole. Tell me about the vampires."

"Vampires are undead creatures. They are the spawn of King Faol, the first son of Demmall, the fourth son of Arcanus Illum. They can transform into wolves, bats and, as you saw, dust clouds." Indie gets a strange look on his face, something that looks like pity. "And they can control the minds of people using a power called *compulsion*. When someone is under their control, they have no choice but to comply with their commands."

As the words wash over her, Kit feels her stomach drop. "No control?" Suddenly, things start going dark. She can feel herself reeling in her saddle. She tries her best to control herself, but she can't hold back the vomit. "Titan, forgive me," she cries out as she falls from her saddle.

Chapter 9

WHEN KIT WAKES UP, her head is resting in Indie's lap. Lump is lying beside her, his head resting gently on her stomach. Runt comes padding around from the other side, concern filling his eyes.

"I murdered them," she says as tears begin to flow down her cheeks. "They were innocent, and I killed them. I murdered them all."

"Hush, you did no such thing." Indie's voice is calm and soothing. He is gently wiping the tears from Kit's cheek, but she could hardly tell. "You defended yourself. Pental is the murderer. He's the one responsible for every death that took place."

Kit begins to replay the earthquake in her mind. Every face, contorted in fear, is etched into her memory. Their screams echo in her mind. "I was arrogant. I thought I could save those people, the hostages." Her body begins to wrack as she tries to hold back her sobs. "I forced his hand. I made him do it."

Kit begins to wail, her grief and guilt completely consuming her. She turns her face into Indie, pressing it hard against his chest. Her sobs are now coming in waves, each one more desperate than the last. "I should have thrown myself into the hole when he told me to."

"What?" Indie says, as he lifts her up into a sitting position beside him. "What do you mean *he told you to jump in the hole.*"

"That's what he said. Twice. Two times, he told me to jump in the hole and kill myself." She uses her sleeve to wipe her nose. "I should have done it."

"You resisted his compulsion?" Indie takes a firm grip of Kit's arms, trying to force her to focus.

"I guess? I felt something, but I wasn't going to kill myself just because he told me to." She shrugs her arms, trying to break free of Indie's grasp.

"Don't you remember what I told you about vampires? They use compulsion to force people to do their bidding. You can't refuse it." Indie's eyes are wide in disbelief. "It's not possible to refuse it. It's what makes them so dangerous."

"I do what I want, when I want." Kit pushes away from Indie, standing up to put some distance between them. "I'm not going to just *let* somebody tell me to do something I don't want to do."

"Are you wearing a talisman of some kind? Did you drink a potion to protect yourself from it?"

Looking like Indie is going to start searching her, Kit shoves him away. "Hey, back off. I'm not wearing anything special and I certainly didn't take a potion."

"Maybe it's your sheer stubbornness that saved you then," he says shaking his head. "Nobody can resist a vampire's compulsion. It's as simple as that."

"Then it wasn't a vampire," Kit states simply. "Maybe he ... I don't know. I don't know why it didn't work on me. I just don't know. What I know is that I killed those people. As sure as I'm drawing breath, I killed them all."

"Stop it! Stop it right now!" Indie screams. "I know you. You would lay down your life to save others, just like you did for me. I know what you did for me. I don't know *how* you did it, but I know it."

Kit's mind races back to when she first met Indie. When he was attacked by the wolf and the venom from the wolf's bite was going to kill him. She offered her life in exchange for his. She expected to die for Indie that day, but she didn't. Indie's life was spared, as well as her own.

"Kit," Indie's tone is much softer now. His voice is calm and serene. "I don't know how you do what you do, but I know that you are the bravest, kindest, ... best person I've ever met."

Kit can feel her face beginning to flush. Indie is standing close to her. Very close to her. The intensity in his eyes is unsettling. Just as Kit's about to say something, Runt pushes in between the two of them, blocking Indie's progress.

"Thanks, Runt," Indie says. There is an edge to his voice. Whatever the look was in Indie's eyes, it vanishes. "Let's go check out the village. The smoke seems to have eased up since we arrived."

Chapter 10

THEY ARE FORCED TO walk around the gaping hole in the landscape. Kit avoids looking in, fearful she's going to see the death she brought upon the people of this village.

"How did you do that?" Indie asks. He's travelling right at the edge of the crevasse. His closeness to the edge is making Kit nervous.

"Do what?" she calls back. She knows full well what he's asking, but she's hoping he's talking about something different. "Get away from the edge. I don't need another death on my hands today."

"Make the earth open up like that?" He pauses his horse, turning back towards her. "I know priests of Titan can cause earthquakes, but I always thought you could just make the ground *shake*, not open up and swallow everything in the area."

Kit cringes at his words, which remind her of the mayhem she caused with her spell. "I don't know," she replies honestly. She's used the spell a few times in the past, but it was to knock down walls or to flush an enemy out of a fortified position. "I guess I was angry and that amplified the effect."

"Amplified? I'll say. I can't see the bottom of the hole you created." He was truly in awe of her power.

"Can we not talk about this, please," Kit's tone is more biting. Her emotions are barely hidden just below the surface. She digs her heels into her horse's ribs, urging her into a gallop. Lump barks with excitement, thinking Kit's playing some sort of game. Seconds later Indie is riding up along side of her.

As they get closer, the smoke is beginning to assault their senses. "What is that smell?" Kit crinkles her nose at the acrid scent. "It smells like roasting meat that's been left on the fire too long." Suddenly, she gets an ill feeling. "Oh, sweet Titan, they're burning people in there."

When they get past the main gate, there are a number of Berrat running about. They seem to be carrying buckets of water, trying to put out the smaller fires that are threatening to ignite other buildings. Several of the buildings, likely shops, have already burned down to their stone foundations. All about, people are wailing, clutching onto the bodies of the fallen.

As they move further into the village, the scenes repeat themselves. Buildings burned, bodies bloody and ruined, and the smell of death. The carnage Kit brought about outside the village is nothing compared to what transpired inside its walls.

"Sister, forgive us!"

Kit turns to see two Berrat women heading towards her. Their clothes are soaked in blood, their faces a picture of terror and remorse. "He made us!" one shouts. "We didn't want to, but he made us."

Kit climbs down from her horse as they approach. "Your actions were not your own," she says simply. Perhaps the words were as much for herself as they were for the grieving Berrat. "Titan does not punish the innocent." Her stomach lurches at her own words. Titan doesn't punish the innocent, but apparently, she does. "Pental is gone."

The women begin to shout. "Pental is gone! They killed Pental!" Others nearby begin to draw nearer. The shouts turn into a chorus of, "Pental is dead! Pental is dead!"

"No, he's not dead!" Kit shouts out. Try as she might though, her voice won't carry over the din of the growing mob.

"We've been saved! They have delivered us from evil!" some are now beginning to shout. Indie looks over while Kit's trying to get the crowd's attention. He seems almost amused.

Without warning, Indie stands up on the back of his big stallion. He holds his arms up, waving them slowly to the crowd. "Here me!" he bellows. "Here me!"

Slowly, the chanting slows down, and it becomes quiet enough that he can be heard. "My name is Indigo, and this woman with me is Sister Kit Standing Bear, a Priest of Titan!" As soon as the words leave his mouth, the crowd begins to cheer wildly.

"Here me!" he calls out again, and once again the people quiet down. "I need you to be quiet long enough that we can explain what has happened." The shouting dies off immediately, and the few people who were still talking are being shushed by those standing near them.

"Pental is not dead." Indie's voice is firm but sympathetic. The onlookers immediately begin to speak and shout, but Indie again holds up his hands for silence. A moment later the commotion dies down again. "We were able to drive him off, but we did not kill him," he says, looking out over the crowd from his high perch. "He was badly injured and likely won't return, but if he does, you need to be ready."

"How can we fight a demon?" one of the Berrat men near the front shouts out. Several others throughout the crown cheer their support for the question.

"He is no demon!" Kit shouts out. She's about to say that he is a vampire, but the look Indie is giving her tells her to keep that to herself. "He is a Berrat, just like you. A powerful man, yes, but he is no demon."

"He controlled our minds!" another Berrat closer to the back of the crowd yells out. "Only demons can do that!" There is a short pause before somebody else chimes in. "Demons and vampires," another person screams. "Pental is a vampire! Titan, save us!"

Gasps of terror reverberate through the crowd. The idea of Pental being a demon was not readily accepted, but him being a vampire could be a real, plausible explanation. Kit looks over at Indie, wondering if she should try to refute the claim. He replies by shrugging his shoulders at her.

"Yes!" Kit screams out, trying to be heard over the shouts and cries of the crowd. "Yes, he is a vampire!" No sooner do the words leave her mouth, than the Berrat begin to scream in terror. The crowd immediately disperses. Some of the people go running off down the street, while others run into the shops and homes, slamming their doors behind them.

"This entire village will be a ghost town in a matter of a day," Indie says shaking his head.

"Why?" Kit asks. "What's with their reactions? Sure, vampires are scary, but they can be dealt with."

"The rumors are," Indie begins, "that vampires are behind all the abductions of the people across Berrathia. Many of the Berrat migrated to Arnnor to escape the raiders. If they're abducting people here too, they likely fear that there is no place else for them to be safe."

"But Pental wasn't trying to abduct anyone," Kit says, still watching the Berrat scurrying about from building to building. "He was making them murder the humans. Why would he do that?"

"I have no idea." Indie drops down onto his charger. "We should continue to patrol the streets. Maybe there is more we can do."

Kit climbs back up onto her horse and spurs her into motion. They start heading up the street toward the village square. The smell is worsening as they get closer to the middle of the village.

The group approaches a tall stone archway. "This is the entrance to the square." Indie says, his hand covering his nose and mouth as he tries to cope with the smell. "I don't think we should go any further." He's looking at Kit, practically pleading that they stop.

"Whatever it is, there will be people who need our help." Kit's voice is full of resolve, but her gut is telling her that Indie is correct.

As they pass under the archway, the smell kicks into a whole new level of revolting. Indie tries to cover his nose and mouth with his sleeve. "Please, Kit, don't go in there. Nothing good can come of it."

"I need to see what's happening. If I return to Hoarfrost with incomplete information, he'll just send me back anyway. I'm going in. You can stay back with Runt and Lump if you want." Kit hears Indie say something into his sleeve. It sounded like he was swearing at her, but she decides to let it go. When he sees the look on her face, he lowers his eyes.

"I will stay by your side," he says with utter resolve. "Whatever you face, I'll be with you."

"Thank you." Kit gives him a small, thin-lipped smile in response.

The road reveals a large, open area. Typically, the first thing a visitor might notice is a very large statue of Titan. It's a close replica of the statue that looks down on the Temple of the Fist. At the foot of the statue are ruined, burning bodies piled up at its feet. There are hundreds upon hundreds of dead people, made up of men, women and children. From what they can see, they're all humans. The village square is otherwise completely devoid of people.

"Did they kill them all?" Kit questions to nobody in particular. "To what end? Why would Pental compel the Berrat to do this?"

"No, it's not everyone." Indie is still covering his face as best he can with his sleeve. "There were nearly two thousand people living in this village."

"Where are the others then?" The smell is making Kit gag, but she refuses to give in to it.

Runt is heading off past the statue toward what is likely the village's Temple. Like the Temple in Aarall, it is a large stone structure, but it is only a shadow of the Fist's size. Lump begins to bark frantically before chasing after Runt.

"I guess we're supposed to follow them," Kit says, hoping to lighten the mood slightly. Indie immediately takes off, happy to distance himself from the pyre. Kit quickly nudges her horse to follow him.

When Kit gets to the Temple, both Lump and Runt are at the top of the granite stairway, sniffing at the base of the doors. Runt jumps up, scratching at the wood. As Kit moves in beside them, they both take up positions behind her.

These doors look like replicas of the doors at the Temple of the Fist. They appear to be made of polished oak, bound with thick iron plates. They really did go all out, trying to make their own Temple resemble the Temple in Aarall. But, unlike the Fist, there are two massive rings present, one for each door. Kit tries pulling on one, but the door doesn't budge. She does the same on the other, but with the same result.

"Try pushing on the doors," Indie says with a chuckle. "Those rings are knockers, not handles."

Kit's face flushes at his suggestion. She keeps her face turned away, desperately hoping he doesn't notice. She puts her hands on the doors and begins to push. When they don't budge, she puts all her weight behind it. The door groans, barely moving at all before stopping. There are chains preventing the doors from fully opening. "Helja, why would they chain the doors?"

"Because they don't want to be burned alive?" Indie offers. "If the humans are in there, I'm surprised the Berrat didn't set the Temple on fire."

"Look at it," she says with a grin. "It's entirely made of stone. It's not the easiest thing to set on fire; unless you're a dragon maybe."

Indie seems to be ignoring Kit now. He pushes past to press his face into the crack. "Hello!" he shouts out. "Is there anybody in there?"

They wait for several seconds, but there is no reply. "If they're frightened, they're not going to come out because you yell *hello* at them."

"It was worth a shot," Indie says with a shrug. "Do you have any better ideas?"

Kit pushes Indie to the side, sticking her face into the crack. "I am sister Kit Standing Bear, a priest of Titan. It is safe to come out. We've dealt with Pental and the Berrat."

"Prove it!" somebody shouts from within. "We're not coming out unless you can prove that you are who you say you are."

"How do you expect me to do that?" Kit yells back through the crack.

"I don't know, but we're not coming out until we know it's safe." The man's voice is frantic, but there is a hint of hope in it.

"Do you have any wounded with you?" Kit calls out. "Bring them near the doorway so that I can touch them. I will heal their wounds as best I can."

"Kit, you can't," Indie whispers. "You've already used up your healing powers for today."

"Titan's snowballs," she curses. "I forgot that I healed Runt in the forest."

"Hello?" a voice calls out from behind the doors. "Are you really a priest of Titan?"

"Yes. Yes, I am, but I am not able to heal you." There is more whispering from inside. Kit pauses for a moment trying to find something encouraging to say. "I'm sorry. I forgot that I used my healing powers already today. But ..." her mind is racing, trying to come up with a way to convince them to open the door. "Do you have a weapon handy?"

"We have many weapons. We will defend ourselves until the bitter end," the original voice responds.

"Good. Good answer," Kit replies. "Look out the crack. You'll see there are only two of us, and our dogs. I will offer myself as a hostage." She stands next to the crack, with her back facing toward the doors. "If I am speaking false, use your weapon and take my life."

"There is no need for such nonsense." A new voice is at the doors. She sounds old. "You say you're a priest of Titan. Is that true?"

"Yes," Kit replies. "I am Sister Kit Standing Bear. I trained under the High Priest, Father Hoarfrost himself."

"Okay, priest. If you are, then answer me this. What is the name of the third book in the teachings of Ymir?" The old woman laughs as she asks the question. Clearly, she doesn't believe that Kit is who she says she is.

"It's been a while since I've studied the teachings of Ymir, the first *true disciple* of Titan." Kit stops and thinks, trying to remember her classes. She hated history lessons. What happened in the past was behind her. Who cared what people said or did so long ago? What matters is the here and now.

"You're no priest," the woman scolds.

"Wait!" Kit yells back. "Give me a minute. It's been quite a while since I sat through Brother Firn's history lessons." Kit begins to rattle off facts about Ymir, hoping that they'll jog her memory. "Ymir was the first Berrat to be raised to the level of divinity. He bested a great yeti in single combat. He used the bones of the yeti to craft the trident he wields. After Titan bestowed divine blessings upon Ymir and Fenrir, he told them to find somebody worthy to free him from his prison."

Suddenly, the answer to the woman's question pops into Kit's head. "The third book of Ymir's teachings is titled, *The Quest for Freedom*. It's all about the trials that would-be rescuers must endure before they can take on the challenge of freeing Titan from his icy prison."

"Well done," Indie whispers, nodding his head.

"You knew the answer?" Kit asks.

"Of course. I grew up worshipping Ymir."

"Then why didn't you just tell them the answer?"

"Because they asked you. If I answered, they might have thought something was up."

The conversation is brought to a halt when they hear muttering from beyond the doors. "I think that's right," the old woman says. "I haven't studied the teachings of Ymir in many years either." The mutterings continue for a while longer before the chains are pulled through the iron rings. When the doors finally open, six women dressed in heavy plate armor step forward. They hold the points of their pikes at chest height.

Kit takes a step back, dropping her hand to where her battle hammer hangs. "Titan's peace upon you," she offers. She's really hoping that this is not going to escalate.

"All clear," one of the women says as she lowers the tip of her pike.

"Are you sure it's safe?" says a man, stepping out from behind the guards. "Is that Pental person gone?"

"Yes, my lord," she replies. As she steps to the side, a tall ruggedly handsome man steps out from behind her. "I am Lord Aster," he says with polished ease. "Praise be to Titan, and those who worship him."

Kit bows slightly, her eyes never leaving his. "I am Kit Standing Bear," she says in response. "My cohorts are Indigo Montanya, Lump, and Runt."

Lord Aster nods his greeting to Indie. "Come in, please." As the four of them enter the Temple, the Lord orders the guards to seal the doors again. "I apologize for the way my citizens have treated you," he says with sincerity. "This day has not been one of my village's best."

"Can you tell me more about Pental, and what he was doing here?" Kit's trying to steer the conversation to anything other than what happened outside the village's main gate. "When did the problems start?"

"Two nights ago," the lord starts. "Pental showed up, insisting on having an audience with me. My people told him that I was not available, but he refused to accept anything short of an immediate, private audience." Aster's face goes dark as his memories go back to that moment. "My personal guard made it clear there was no chance of an audience that day or any day if Pental didn't follow proper channels." He then turns to the female guard standing next to him. "Xin, tell them," he says. "Tell them what happened."

The guard snaps to attention as soon as Aster speaks to her. Her response is rigid, like a well-trained soldier would speak to her superior. "There's not much to tell, my lord, but Pental's response was enough to warrant his immediate arrest. When I informed him that his request was denied, he said, 'Lord Aster will regret this decision. His days are numbered.' I ordered the guards to take him into custody, but he calmly told them to hold their position." The guard's face grows grim. "My people refused to arrest him." She then lowers her eyes, no longer able to hold her lord's gaze. "I should have recognized what he was at that moment. My guards would never refuse my order, under no circumstances whatsoever. I failed you, Your Grace."

"He compelled your guards?" Kit asks.

The guard's head begins to bob slowly as she raises her eyes. They were filled with pure hatred for Pental. "I failed my Lord. I imprisoned my own for refusing to follow my orders." Again, she drops her eyes to the floor. "I weakened my own position, all because I couldn't see what was right in front of me."

Lord Aster places his hand on her shoulder. "We've discussed this already, Xin. The fault was not with you, or your guards. We had no way of knowing there was a vampire among us." He then turns back to Kit. "The next morning, Pental began his preaching in the village square. He stood at the feet of Titan, telling anybody who would listen that humans were the enemy; that the Berrat must stand against the oppression the humans were imposing upon them."

"Why didn't you arrest him then?" Indie asks. "Surely you have laws against inciting public unrest."

"He was operating within the laws of my village, of this barony, and of this kingdom that we all live in," Lord Aster said with certainty. "We do not oppress the opinions of our community. All voices are welcome, even if we don't like what they have to say."

Indie begins to shake his head. "Perhaps if you had stricter laws, these sorts of problems wouldn't happen."

"Perhaps," Aster replies, raising an eyebrow. A small smile tugs at his lips. "But, if we followed the laws as you suggest, then you'd be executed for questioning my way of running my village."

Indie suddenly looks very uncomfortable, his eyes scanning the guards, looking to see if they were going to move on him.

"Relax, young man," Aster continues to grin. "You have nothing to fear for speaking your mind, and neither did Pental." The lord turns his attention back to Kit. "My citizens ignored Pental and his ravings. They simply walked on by, causing him to fly into a rage. Throughout the rest of the day, he continued his ranting, moving through the busiest areas as the day moved on." His face was now beaming with pride. "My community could not be swayed. A few Berrat had stopped to listen, but those who did clearly told him that he was wrong, and a fool, and that he was wasting his breath on them. Outside of his unending rhetoric, Pental caused no problems."

"But today that changed," Kit interjects, the lord nodding in agreement.

"This morning Pental stood at the sea gate, *telling* every Berrat who walked past to stand against the humans. Each and every one of them stopped what they were doing and began chanting, praising Pental and his radical ideas. At this point the Berrat were preventing anybody from leaving through the sea gate. Fights broke out between the Berrat and the humans. Before long there were several deaths. This only seemed to have emboldened the Berrat and they began moving on every human they saw."

"It was at that point that I deployed the full force of my military," Xin sounded almost remorseful at she spoke. "We forced back the Berrat, keeping them outside the sea gate. They were unarmed and untrained. Even though they outnumbered my people greatly, we held the line."

"If you were able to keep them back, how did things go so badly?" Kit asks.

"Pental," Xin starts. "He told the Berrat to kill us all or die trying. No sooner had he given his command, the Berrat swarmed my people. Our military fought them off as best it could, killing them as they encroached on the lines, but there were so many Berrat ... we were quickly overwhelmed. I called for a full retreat at that point. There was nothing more we could do."

Lord Aster takes up the conversation, saving Xin from having to describe the carnage further. "They picked up the weapons of the fallen guards," he said. "They moved through the streets in a giant mob, killing everybody who stood against them."

"At that point, I went to the Lord's manor to ensure his safety," Xin continues. "By the time I reached the village square I saw Renay, I mean Lord Aster, shepherding the people towards the Temple. My people took up positions, trying to give him as much time as possible to get the citizens to safety. While the Berrat concentrated on us, others were able to escape out the front gate."

"They saved us all," Lord Renay Aster says. "Against all odds, they held their ground, protecting the citizens of this village with their last dying breath." He squares his shoulders as he continues. "It was like they were all standing shoulder to shoulder with Titan himself! May he guide them to the Great Cycle."

"May he guide them to the Great Cycle," Xin and the other guards repeat in unison.

"When the lines broke, we sealed off the doors to the Temple." Renay's eyes are dark. "I had to save those I could ..."

"Your actions and those of your people are a testament to your rule over this village," Indie offers.

Xin moves close to the lord, placing her forehead against his shoulder. They both lost a lot of people today and they could not hide their grief.

"After a few hours, they began building a fire at the foot of Titan's statue," Xin begins. "They threw the dead into the fire like they were trash to be discarded."

"We didn't know what else had happened until you came to the doors of the Temple," Lord Aster continues. "Please, tell us how you came to drive Pental away."

Kit dreaded this moment. She knew he was going to ask, and she knew she'd have to speak. Pushing through her own grief, Kit goes on to describe the entire encounter, leaving out no details, no matter how small.

"You drove him off with an arrow?" Xin asks. "She seems somewhat doubtful of this part of the story."

"I was using a *blessed bow*," Indie says in the way of an explanation.

"Where did you get a blessed bow?" Kit demands. We had no such weapon with us.

Indie's face turns bright red at the question. "I *borrowed* it from the Temple's armory."

"You *stole* weapons from the armory?" Kit raises her eyebrows in utter disbelief. "How did you get past the guards stationed there?"

"Okay, so I didn't get it from the armory. Not *exactly* anyway." Indie is beginning to squirm, shifting his weight from foot to foot. "When you went to go see Father Hoarfrost, I had dinner with the dogs in the kitchen like you told me to. While I was eating, an old priest sat at the table next to us. He had a satchel with him, and this bow. Just before he left, he pushed the satchel toward me. 'You'll need this,' he said to me. I'm pretty sure he winked at me when he did. It creeped me out." Again, Indie's face is reddening. "After he left,

I took them and stowed them away. Before we left this morning, I packed everything in our saddlebags."

"Thank Titan somebody had the good sense to make sure you were well equipped this morning." The lord's voice was deadly serious. "Whoever it was that gave you that bow, well, he saved us all today."

"With Pental gone, I believe it's safe for you to leave the Temple now," Kit suggests, her eyes never leaving Indie as she speaks. "I need to report this to Father Hoarfrost and the City Watch. The High Priest is aware of the unrest being fomented by Pental and his followers, but this is far worse than anybody realizes."

"My people and I will see you to the front gate," Xin offers. Her voice is like steel. "*I* will make the decision if it's safe for our Lord and the citizens to leave this haven."

As the chains are being removed from the Temple doors, an old woman approaches Kit. "Forgive me, sister, for testing you. We had to know that you were who you said you were."

"You did the community a great service today," Kit replies, bowing to the woman. "Titan's grace upon you."

The woman replies with a wide, toothless smile. "May you forever walk in his grace."

When the doors open, Kit's nose is once again assailed by the smell of burning bodies. The bright light from the sun blinds her momentarily. When her vision clears, she can see that the stairs and the area at the base of the stairs are crowded with Berrat citizens. The guards immediately try to close the doors, but Kit manages to step out before they do.

"Please, Lord Aster!" somebody from the front of the crowd screams, "Please forgive us!" Kit listens as the doors of the Temple creak open behind her.

"You do not need my forgiveness," Lord Aster shouts back in reply. He is now standing beside Kit, casting his voice upon the throng.

"Your actions were not your own. Peace unto you." Even though his words are full of compassion, he grimaces when he sees the carnage at the foot of Titan's statue.

"Titan, save us," Xin whispers. She covers her mouth and nose with her hand. "I had hoped that more would have found refuge somewhere." The lord places his hand on her back, offering her support.

The Berrat begin to kneel on the stairs. Some of them are throwing themselves onto the ground, laying prone in the ultimate display of shame. Lord Aster walks toward those who were nearest to him. "Arise. Arise," he says as he places his hands on their heads. "We have much work to do to rebuild our village." Kit watches in awe as he steps among the Berrat, their eyes shining with adoration of the man.

"He really does love his citizens, doesn't he," Kit says to Xin who had moved in beside her. "I've never seen anything like it."

"You have no idea," Xin replies. She made no effort to hide her own adoration of the man. She was clearly deeply in love with him. "Seeing the dead is crushing him, but he won't let it show."

"We'll see our way to the main gate," Kit says quietly to Xin. Whatever pain she is feeling for the loss of life is nothing compared to what she is feeling for her lord. "The lord is in no danger. Titan's peace upon you." Kit looks back over her shoulder to ensure that Indie, Runt and Lump are following. When she does, she sees the look of grief and despair on the faces of those who were holed up in the Temple.

"You're going to need to address the human population's fears," she says quietly so that only Xin can hear. "Your lord may be ready to forgive, but they may not be so quick to follow suit. Those in the Temple likely lost family and loved ones this morning." Kit can't stop her own emotions from boiling over.

Xin squares her shoulders and straightens her back. "My Lord leads by example. Where he goes, the citizens will follow. He will assuage their fears. He will bind their emotional wounds." Xin's eyes continue to shine as she gazes at Renay.

"Then we'll take our leave. I'll speak to Captain Harding to see if he can send reinforcements, in case Pental returns."

"Thank you," Xin replies. Her eyes still firmly focused on Aster. "Have them bring us some of those blessed weapons as well," she says solemnly. "We may need them."

Chapter 11

AS THEY LEAVE THE VILLAGE, out through the main gate, Kit's once again reminded of the death she's caused. There are still bodies lying on the ground, with many more lying dead at the bottom of the crevasse she created with her spell.

"Are we going to visit the other village that Father Hoarfrost mentioned?" Indie's eyes are still trained on the hole, shaking his head at how big and deep it is.

"No," Kit responds. Her mind is preoccupied with replaying the scene in her head. She can still hear the screams. She can still see the look of terror on their faces as the earth opened up and swallowed them all, innocent and guilty alike. "I need to report what's happened immediately." She takes a deep breath, exhaling slowly. "I'll likely end up spending the rest of my life in a dungeon."

"Stop it!" Indie shouts at Kit. "Do you hear me, you stupid little girl? Just stop it!"

"I am stupid," Kit replies, her voice utterly full of defeat. "I didn't think, I just acted. Now innocent people are dead." She drops her chin to her chest and closes her eyes thinking that maybe she can just go to sleep and never wake up.

Suddenly Kit feels an iron grip on her wrist, and she's ripped from her saddle. She lands hard on the ground, practically knocking the wind out of her. A moment later, she's back up on her feet, weapon drawn, looking for her assailant.

"Good!" Indie screams. "That's the reaction I was looking for. You're a fighter, Kit. It's who you are. But you're also the most caring, most devoted person I've ever known. What you did was not your fault. Do you hear me? Do you? It was not your fault!"

Indie stands in front of Kit, waiting for her response, his eyes full of concern. "It's not your fault," he repeats.

"Thank you," Kit mumbles out to him. "If Titan wills it, I will do what I can to make it up to the villagers and to the families of those who died."

Runt and Lump come running up. Runt knocks Kit off her feet and the two faithful companions give her a heavy dose of 'canine therapy.' "Thanks boys," she says, rubbing them both about the head and ears. "I've got your back, too." It takes Kit a few minutes to wipe the slobber from her face and neck.

"Alright, let's head back to Aarall." Kit gives Indie a small smile. "Thank you. You're a good friend."

"I am," he replies as he hops back up onto the back of his horse. "Let's get moving."

For the next several hours they follow the road back to Aarall, stopping briefly to eat some food and water the horses. Indie keeps the conversation light, talking about anything just to keep Kit's mind off the day's events.

When the city comes into sight, Kit's stomach drops. She knows what's in front of her. Telling her sins to the High Priest won't be cathartic. It will be gut wrenching.

"I'm going to join the City Watch," Indie says so casually that one might think he was describing what he might choose to eat for dinner. He looks over at Kit, raising an eyebrow.

"Captain Harding would be pleased if you did, but it won't be the same travelling around without you." No sooner do the words leave Kit's mouth than she begins to blush. Hard.

Indie waggles his eyebrows at her. "You'd miss me?"

Kit quickly turns away from him, calling Runt and Lump back to her side, trying desperately to find something to do besides look at Indie.

"I don't actually plan on doing that," Indie says with a laugh. "I could see that you were upset when the city came into view. I just wanted to get your mind off things. No sense in worrying about things before you need to."

Kit's face is still hot, so she continues to look away. "Thank you."

"C'mon, let's get this over with," Indie shouts out just as his charger breaks into a canter. "The sooner you get it done, the sooner you can stop worrying about it." The two canines give chase, nipping at each other as they run.

Kit takes one more deep breath before pushing her horse into a gallop. In mere minutes Indie and the boys are well ahead of her, even though her horse is running at her top speed. "If I'm going to continue riding you," Kit says to her horse as she tries to stay low to the animal's back, "I'm going to have to put some speed enchantments on you." The horse whinnies at her words. It's unclear if she approves, disapproves, or if she is just making noise for the fun of it.

When Kit finally catches up, Indie and the boys are approaching the marketplace in front of the city. They look like they could run all day. However, Kit's poor horse is in a lather from being pushed so hard.

"If you're going to keep using that horse, you're going to need some serious speed enchantments if you want to keep up with us," Indie suggests.

Kit rolls her eyes, and her small roan whinnies in response.

"Can you take her back to the stables for me when we get to the Temple? She's going to need a good brushing, and an extra portion of oats." Kit runs her hand down the horse's neck, patting it as she does. "Thank you," Kit whispers to her. "Rest well. You've earned it."

When Kit gets to the stairs leading to the Temple, she dismounts and hands the reins to Indie. "Bring the boys with you," she says, as she gives them both a quick scratch. "If I'm not back before sundown, come visit me in the dungeons." She gives a smile and a small laugh. Kit's trying to be funny, but deep down, she's terrified that a trip to the dungeons may be in her immediate future.

As her companions head off, Kit gazes up the stairs to the Temple entrance above. She remembers back to the village, and the replica Temple they had created. "They really did a good job of it," she muses as she begins the climb to the top.

Chapter 12

AS KIT WALKS DOWN THE hall towards the High Priest's office, she can feel her feet starting to drag. There is no turning back, but there is also no desire to continue moving forward.

When she turns the corner, there are a number of acolytes standing outside Father's office. They scatter as Kit approaches. They were clearly trying to listen in on the conversation going on behind the closed doors. When Kit gets to the door, she quietly moves closer, straining to hear. There are voices, but she can't make out a word they're saying. She moves closer, pressing her ear to the wood. As she does, the door opens, causing Kit to lose her balance and tumble into Hoarfrost's office. She looks up to see Captain Harding staring down at her. "Hello, Kit," he says, his eyes looking back to Father Hoarfrost who is sitting at his desk.

"Hello, Captain," Kit says in response as she grabs his outstretched arm. The Captain lifts her easily back to her feet. "I was just ..."

"Eavesdropping?" the High Priest interrupts. Kit can't tell if he's amused or furious. "I gather you scared off the others who were milling outside my office?"

How does he know? Kit thinks to herself. She's lost count of how many times the High Priest has known she's been outside his office, without ever seeing her.

Kit is brought out of her musings by the Captain snapping his fingers in front of her face. "Are you okay, Kit? You disappeared for a few moments."

Kit blinks a few times, trying to clear out whatever it was she was thinking about. "Yes. Yes, Captain, I'm fine." She finally turns to address Father Hoarfrost. She decides lying is not the way to go. "Yes, Father, I was trying to listen in on your conversation. When I arrived, there were some people outside your office who immediately ran off when they saw me." Kit drops her head in contrition. "My curiosity got the better of me as well. Please forgive me."

"Thank you, Captain," the High Priest says without responding to Kit. "We can speak more of this later."

As the Captain moves to leave, Kit blurts out. "Wait! I think you need to hear what I have to say, too."

Kit watches as the Captain looks to Hoarfrost, waiting for his direction. When the old priest nods his head, the Captain closes the door and takes a seat. "What's so important, little sister?" he says. It seems his curiosity is getting the better of him as well.

Without warning, tears begin to gather. Kit quickly wipes them away, hopefully before anybody noticed.

"Please, Kit," Father Hoarfrost says, his voice full of concern. "Take your time and speak when you're ready."

Kit takes a deep breath, wiping her nose with the back of her hand. "There are vampires in Aarall!" The words come tumbling out of her mouth before she can stop them. Kit literally said the first thing that popped into her head. She had rehearsed what she was going to say as soon as she started climbing the stairs to the Temple. She was going to describe the events in detail, explaining everything she had seen, including the unforgivable sins she had committed, and yet, 'There are vampires in Aarall', is what pops out of her mouth.

Kit's taken aback when the Captain and the High Priest immediately stare at each other, their faces completely blank. "Explain yourself," the old priest says.

Thankfully, Kit manages to convey most of what she had rehearsed in her head in a reasonable order. When she describes the deaths of the people at her hands, Hoarfrost's gives her a look of pity. Meanwhile, Captain Harding has to cover his mouth to hide what was obviously a smile. "Titan's snowballs!" Kit shouts at him, "How can you find this funny?"

"Kit!" the High Priest scolds. "Language!"

Captain Harding now breaks out laughing at Hoarfrost's admonishment for Kit's use of Titan's *anatomy* as a form of cussing.

"There is nothing funny about this!" she screams at the Captain. "People died. By my hand, people died. And you sit there laughing at me and my pain?"

The High Priest practically jumps from his chair. "Kit! That is enough! Control yourself!"

The mirth from the Captain's face dies away immediately. He holds up his hand to the old man, indicating that he will handle this outburst himself. "I did not mean any offense, little sister. I was smiling because I was proud of you. What you did took more courage than I think you realize. The fact that the *outcome* was what it was, is most unfortunate."

"Unfortunate?" Kit's eyes are wide in amazement. "You think what happened to those poor people was unfortunate?"

"No, Kit. Their deaths are a tragedy, but not one of your own doing." Father Hoarfrost takes his seat again before clearing his throat, an unsubtle way of getting the Captain's attention. He nods slightly, as if to prod the Captain into finishing the thought.

"and ... I apologize for my laughter, but your choice of words in front of our esteemed *High Priest* was ... amusing." Kit's face immediately reddens, as she wishes she could crawl under a rock and just stay there. Forever.

"Kit, you did not cause the crevasse to open up," the Captain continues, completely disregarding any embarrassment that she is feeling. "Your use of the earthquake spell was pure genius. It was the perfect tool for the job. The unfortunate part, based on what you described, was that you called forth an earthquake immediately over what was likely a firebug warren."

"A what?" Kit had heard about firebug attacks happening lately, but they were pretty rare. From what she'd heard, firebugs are beetles about the size of a very large dog, and as their name suggests, they can spit a stream of liquid fire. She shudders as she thinks about it.

"That's the *thing* that my guards have been busy with lately. They've been hunting down these firebugs, destroying them when they can."

"It takes the entire City Watch to hunt down a few bugs?" Kit's raising her eyebrows in disbelief. She watches the Captain and the High Priest carefully, looking for a reaction to her question.

"It's not just a few," Hoarfrost responds. "The Captain's people have killed hundreds of them over the past few moons. People haven't seen much of the bugs because Harding and the City Watch have been doing a very good job of keeping it quiet."

"Those bugs live underground, as you likely already know." The Captain rubs the stubble on his chin as he begins. "They've always been around. The miners have, at times, encountered them while digging for whatever mineral or metal they're chasing. Lately though, the bugs have been coming up out of the ground practically anywhere. While investigating one of the attacks, my people found a tunnel beneath the ground. I sent a well provisioned party in to investigate. Eight of my Watch went in. Only two came back out."

"They found more tunnels, caves and *nests*." Hoarfrost continues. "When they tried to head back, their path was blocked. Not by firebugs. No, not firebugs at all. Something bigger ... much bigger and much more deadly."

As the Captain and the High Priest tell Kit of the bugs and the tunnels, it dawns on her. There were tunnels and caves under the ground where she summoned the earthquake. It must have been what caused the cave-in. She suddenly feels a weight lifting off her chest. It didn't mean it wasn't her fault, but she had feared that her anger had manifested in some horrible way, causing the giant crater. *I'm not the freak I thought I was,* she thinks to herself.

"What was the other creature?" Kit asks. "Do they spit fire like the bugs do?"

"No," replies the Captain shaking his head. "They launch spikes! Spikes that are half as long as I am tall."

Kit suddenly remembers her initial meeting with the Captain. His guards were in the training yard, practicing avoiding missile attacks. Suddenly, things start falling into place. "Does this have anything to do with the vampire, Pental?"

"No, Kit, I don't think so." Father Hoarfrost is shaking his head as he stands again. He moves slowly across his office to look out at the city below and the angry god staring down on that city. "Vampires in Aarall are a completely different problem. Possibly even more concerning than bugs that look to be building an army below our very feet."

"We have weapons to help fight against vampires," Harding says, his eyes darting between Kit and the High Priest. "We've been having them made ever since we learned about Faol's incursions into Berrathia. We figured that if the Vampire King is hitting Berrathia, it won't be too long before he turns his eyes toward us. Afterall, we're a much closer target than Berrathia. We literally share a border with the Kingdom of Faol."

"Why was I not informed of this?" Hoarfrost seems annoyed with the Captain. Kit would have thought this was good news.

"We didn't see it as a Temple matter," the Captain says with a shrug. "They're just weapons, and some armor, too." Hoarfrost's eyebrows rise at the mention of armor.

"Well, technically, what the Watch does is not a Temple matter, but had I known you were doing that, I wouldn't have been doing it as well. It seems we both had the same idea, and we've likely wasted resources in the process."

The big Captain smiles coolly. "It's not a waste. Not at all. I have enough equipment to outfit my men, but if there is more, we could also outfit a local militia. If we get any military reinforcements from the King, we'll be able to outfit some of them as well."

"Okay, so we've got plenty of weapons suitable for fighting vampires," Hoarfrost seems at odds right now, "but we're woefully short of gear suitable for fighting the firebugs, and whatever other creatures they seem to be teaming up with."

The Hight Priest and the Captain continue discussing the availability of equipment, how it could be best put to use, the training of personnel to use the equipment, and so on. Kit is surprised that they're having this conversation with her present, but more importantly, she's finding this whole conversation extremely *boring*. Her mind wanders off to Indie and the boys, wondering what they're doing. She then begins thinking about Templeton, the Lord who's running the village, and the sorrow that the people are being forced to endure.

"We need to do something for the village and the people who are struggling with everything that's happened." Whatever it was that the two men were talking about, Kit feels this is much more important. They both stop talking and stare at her, like they only just noticed that she is still in the room. Now that she has their attention, Kit presses the issue further. "They're going to need support. And I think we should find a way to set up a memorial of some kind for the people who died. And maybe some of the anti-vampire gear can be sent their way so that they can defend themselves if Pental comes back."

"We were just saying we should send weapons and armor to Templeton." Harding is looking at Kit like she's a bit dim.

She gives the Captain her best grin. "Oh, sorry. I guess my mind wandered off. But what about a memorial of some sort. We need to bring attention to what happened there. The people of Aarall and all of Arnnor need to know what's happening."

The High Priest gestures his approval. "A memorial is a good idea, but I don't think we'll need to spread the word about who Pental is, and what he's up to. That's the sort of thing that will travel across the entire kingdom within days. Nothing travels faster than bad news."

The Captain stands up, bowing slightly to the High Priest and then to Kit. "If I may, I'd like to start preparations for sending my people and some equipment to Templeton. We'll go by way of Ashcroft, just to make sure everything is okay there."

Hoarfrost is shaking his head in disagreement. "You need to keep your men deployed on the firebugs. That threat is happening *right now*. We have no idea if or when the vampires may move on Aarall."

"We need to check out Kit's crater anyway," Harding replies. His voice is now in commander mode, stern and sure. "This is the first report that we've had from that area as well, so it's important that we investigate it. From the sounds of it, Kit may have unearthed a nexus of some sort." The Captain gives Kit a bit of a wink with the last comment. He's clearly trying to help alleviate some of her anxiety over what she did. She's not exactly sure it's helping though.

"Fine, fine." Father Hoarfrost moves from the window back behind his desk. He offers him his blessing before taking his seat again. Just as the door closes, the High Priest's gaze falls upon Kit. "Now Kit, there is something I need to discuss with you."

Kit's heart starts to beat faster. Even though he didn't reprimand her for her actions in front of the Captain, she can only assume that he was waiting until he had her alone. Kit swallows hard and nods. "Yes, Father, how can I be of service?" The words come out more like a squeak. Kit curses quietly at herself for her lack of confidence. She tries clearing her throat to cover up her weak response.

"Kit," the old priest's face turns very serious as he begins to speak. She can't help but fidget under his scrutiny. "Your actions were exemplary." When he sees her look of shock and dismay, his face softens somewhat. "I know what you did hurt you. I know what you did cost the lives of many innocent people. But know this, you responded to an impending threat. You were willing to put your own life on the line in the service of people you've never met before. That, young priest, is the *Mark of Titan*."

"I did not enjoy taking a life, any life, even if it was in the defense of others. So many people died." Tears are beginning to well up in Kit's eyes. Again, she curses at herself for her weakness, as she tries to press on.

Before she can, Father Hoarfrost interrupts, his face a picture of pity and concern. "These are hard times, and it sometimes requires us to steel ourselves. How many lives have you saved through your actions? These zealots are a growing threat, and they're causing a great deal of division across our country. You had no way of knowing that these particular people were not acting of their own accord. Most of the zealots have fully bought into Pental's view of the world. They bought into it, and now they're spreading it, often with violence."

Hoarfrost stands up and moves out from behind his desk. He slowly kneels before Kit, placing his hands on her knee, his eyes now level with hers. "Know this, Kit, had you not acted as you did, we would not be having this conversation right now. You would most likely be dead, along with your friend Indie and your two canine companions." Kit nods quickly, the tears now flowing freely down her face. The thought of her friends being killed breaks her heart. "And every human in Templeton would likely be dead by now as well. Pental would have already moved onto the next village, repeating his actions."

Kit suddenly feels intense heat inside her chest. Whatever weight she was carrying from her actions is now gone. What remains is righteous fire burning from within. She stands up from her chair, looking down at the old priest. "I am the Hand of Titan. I stand for justice and law. The path before me is clear. If it is his will, I will root out Pental along with the hate and intolerance he is spreading. I will eradicate it from the lands."

The old priest groans as he picks himself up off the floor. Kit offers him her assistance, but he swats her hand away. He then takes a moment to consider what Kit said. "By your own words, you acknowledge that this is Titan's will and not a personal crusade." It was a statement, not a question, but Kit nods in agreement anyway.

A broad smile spreads across Father Hoarfrost's face, joy shining in his eyes. "I've always known there was something special about you, Kit Standing Bear. Sometimes you made me doubt that, but not today." He puts his hand on her shoulder and starts walking her to the door. "Titan's light shines within you. You have earned your place in this Temple and now it's time for you to seek Titan's Acknowledgement."

Chapter 13

KIT STANDS THERE, STARING at the High Priest, blinking while she tries to process what was just said. "I'm sorry, Father, I'm not sure I understand."

The old priest's smile broadens even further, his eyes full of compassion. "Not what you were expecting when you entered my office?"

"No, Father. I ... I was expecting that you were going to throw me in a dungeon or have me executed for murdering those people." Kit is still having difficulty supressing her emotions, even though she has no idea what she's feeling at this very moment. Bewilderment. Yes, that's it, she's feeling bewilderment.

"Kit, if you can succeed in the devotion challenge, you may well be the youngest person to ever be admitted, *fully admitted*, into the priesthood. You are a remarkable girl; a remarkably stubborn, willful, free-spirited girl. You have proven your strength in the face of adversity. You have proven your loyalty in the face of death. You have proven that your faith is strong enough to carry you through the roughest times in your life..." For a moment, the High Priest's eyes seem to go vacant, as though he was thinking back to a time long since past. "You are exactly the sort of person that Titan charged Fenrir and Ymir to seek out when he made them deities in their own right."

By the time the old priest has finished speaking so highly of her, Kit's face feels like it's on fire. She stammers for a moment, trying to find words. Words that are fitting for the accolades being showered upon her. Finally, she finds them. "Father, I am not worthy of such praise. Every day. Every single day I question my faith and my desire to be a priest. I crave the freedom to seek out my own path. I ... I fear the yolk that my pledge may put on me. I fear I will be resentful of that yolk."

Hoarfrost backs away from her and leans on the front of his desk. He crosses his arms and tilts his head, looking at Kit like he's seeing her for the first time ever. "To be a priest, to devote your life to Titan, or to anything for that matter, is never a yolk so long as you make the pledge for the right reasons."

Kit looks up at the old man standing in front of her. This was not the sort of reaction she'd have expected from a priest, let alone the *High Priest* himself. She expected a speech filled with energy and passion. A speech designed to embolden her and push her toward the goal of become an *Acknowledged Priest of Titan*.

"What if I decide that the priesthood is not for me?" It was the question on her mind. A question that has been on her mind for the past cycle. "What happens then?"

Father Hoarfrost stares at Kit while he considers the question. "Then you forfeit the grace of Titan and you live your life as you choose." When he sees the look of surprise on Kit's face he presses forward. "I am not aware of anybody ever choosing to leave the priesthood though, at least not here at the Fist." He takes a bit of a breath, looking like he needs to calm himself. "Some have left because they were excommunicated. Some have left to join the Great Cycle, but I don't know of anybody ever *quitting*."

"Why not?" Kit asks, more out of curiosity than for her own personal benefit.

Hoarfrost laughs a small laugh. "Good question," he replies simply. "Most people who join the priesthood do so because of the grand notion that they will be the one to free Titan. *One of the three*, as foretold in the prophecy, who would try to complete the mission." Again, the old man's eyes go distant, but this time it looks as though whatever memory he is recalling is dark. He shakes his head, like he's trying to drive that memory from his mind. He takes a deep breath, centering himself again. "Many join to have a place to live and to feel like they are a part of something bigger than themselves. But in truth, most are dropped at our door as children because their parents cannot afford to raise them."

"That's so sad." Kit had never thought about why other people joined. She had always assumed that they joined because, like her, they were called by Titan to serve.

"Not everybody is called by Titan. Very few, in fact." The priest's words make Kit suddenly feel uneasy. First, how did he know what she was thinking? Second, if she was called and most aren't, then that would make her *special*. Kit had never wanted to be special. She still doesn't.

"Kit," the tone of the priest's voice changes, becoming more serious. "The challenge is difficult. It will test your will, your resolve and your faith. Failing the test can be ... complicated. If you do fail, you can try again, but it usually gets even harder if you do. Many have tried, failed, and never tried again."

"When do I have to do this? Can I have time to think about it? Time to prepare?" If he expects her to do it right away, Kit fears that she'll fail."

"Whenever you're ready, Kit. This next challenge is between you and our god. Nobody else will attend. In fact, nobody will even know if you fail." The High Priest's words give her some comfort, but she's not sure she'll ever be ready.

"What if I succeed? How will you know that I passed the test?" Kit would never lie about such a thing, but with no witness, how would anybody ever know?

"I will know," Hoarfrost responds with absolute certainty. "Successfully completing the challenge changes you from without, as well as from within."

"Father?" Kit decides it might be best to seek some clarification on the challenge. "Forgive my question, but why is the challenge so difficult? All we are asked to do is to spend the night kneeling at the foot of Titan's statue." Her face scrunches up slightly as she considers the challenge. "Having to spend three nights in the mountains sounds like a much harder task."

The priest chuckles to himself. "Physically, the challenge is difficult. Kneeling on stone for ten hours gets painful, even for a highly motivated challenger. Doing it through the night when the temperature drops so low that your joints will seize doesn't make it any easier. But the pain is only a distraction. A distraction from the true test, which is opening your heart and soul to Titan, offering yourself to him, and waiting through the night for his acceptance, for his *acknowledgement*. If you fail, if he does not acknowledge your offering, it can be devastating. Knowing that he may ignore you sows a seed of doubt, and that doubt will gnaw at you when the temperature drops, and the north winds blow."

Kit shivers at the thought of it. Perhaps she had already heard of this during her lessons, but at the time, she was safe and warm inside a classroom. During her lessons, the opportunity to partake in the challenge wasn't before her, staring her in the face. Suddenly, this is all very real.

"Thank you, Father, for your understanding, your guidance and your trust in me. I will not fail you, or Titan." Kit gives him a small smile, mostly as a nervous reaction to the situation, but also in thanks for his support.

"May Titan's acknowledgement be yours, my child." And with that, the High Priest crosses his arms over his chest in the traditional manner of blessing.

As Kit opens the door to his office to leave, she hears the footfalls of somebody running away from the door. She chuckles to herself. It appears that there is always somebody eavesdropping outside the High Priest's office. If he knows they're out there, and it seems he always does, then why does it not anger him? Kit shrugs off the idea and begins her contemplations on whether or not she is going to take the challenge.

Chapter 14

KIT HEADS OUT FROM the High Priest's office. The next thing she realizes, she's standing at the bottom of the stairs that lead to the Temple. Her stomach is beginning to do flip-flops as she considers the challenge to receive Titan's acknowledgement. She's brought out of her trance when a cold nose is jammed into her neck, immediately followed by a wet, slobbery tongue.

"Runt! Get off me!" she scolds. He whimpers slightly and backs away. The sad look in his eyes breaks Kit's heart. "Sorry pal," she says as she reaches out and pulls him into a close embrace. The feeling of his thick neck fur against her face melts her worries away.

"Where have you been?" she asks him. A lick that covers Kit's face from chin to forehead is his response. She uses her sleeve to try and wipe off the drool. "Maybe you can cut down on the slobber, eh?" she laughs. "It's nearly impossible to get off my clothes." The big wolf breaks into a huge doggie-smile, his tongue lolling out to the side.

"Where are Indie and Lump, eh, boy? Did they ditch you?" Kit looks around, craning her neck, hoping they're nearby. Runt replies with a small woof. "Can you take me to them?" Another small woof. This time the pitch is much higher. And with that, he trots off toward the main gate. "Hey, not too fast!" she calls out to him. His gate immediately slows. He looks back over his shoulder to make sure she's following.

Runt leads Kit through the streets of the city. He seems to be heading toward the main gate. She continues to marvel at the spell Fenrir placed upon Runt's collar. An extra-large dire wolf is wandering through the streets of a crowded city, with nobody paying any attention to him. Well, except for those dog lovers who insist on petting any dog that comes within reach. At no point, however, does

Runt ever shy away from a friendly hand. Kit smiles inwardly, re-membering that despite his size, he's still a puppy inside.

As they pass by the City Watch barracks, Kit sees Lump in the open courtyard beyond the gatehouse. Three guards are playing monkey-in-the-middle with him, tossing what appears to be a ball of some sort. Lump looks like he's been running himself ragged trying to get the ball from the guards. Without warning, Runt breaks in-to a run and goes bursting through the guards manning the barrack's gatehouse. He goes directly for the guard holding the ball, taunting Lump with it. With one well-timed leap, he knocks the guard off his feet, dislodging the ball from his hand. As the ball tumbles across the ground, Runt takes a second leap, landing on the ball.

"Woof!" barks Lump. You'd swear he was congratulating Runt for getting the ball. The guard on the ground is cussing at him for his antics. With the prize in his mouth, Runt presents the ball back to the fallen guard. As the guard reaches out to take it from him, he turns his head at the last moment, denying the guard his prize. Runt then trots over to Lump and deposits the ball at his feet. When his furry companion doesn't pick it up, Runt uses his nose to roll it over to him, followed by a string of high-pitched barks.

"Bested by a pair of furballs!" The booming voice of Captain Harding rings across the courtyard. "Perhaps we should integrate them into our training regime. It might help you all to keep your sur-roundings in mind when you're going about your business." The big man slaps his hand across his thigh. He obviously thinks his remarks are funny. Some of the guards around him begin to laugh, likely be-cause he's their Captain and not because they actually found his joke funny.

Both animals break away from their games to run over to Hard-ing. Kit sees now that Indie is only a few steps behind him. When he sees Kit beyond the gate, he starts waving at her.

By the time Kit makes it past the gatehouse, Harding, Indie and the boys are just inside. "I'm surprised to find you here," Kit calls out to Indie. Both he and the Captain shrug at the same time. "You're not still trying to recruit him, are you, Captain?" They both shrug again in unison. Kit groans inwardly at the synchronized responses.

"I ran into Indie and your furry cohorts just after I left the Temple," Harding says with an easy smile. "After everything that happened to you two, I just wanted to make sure he was doing okay." Kit can't help but roll her eyes at the two of them.

"The Captain says I can help deal with ..." Indie scans the area, trying to see who might be listening in on the conversation. He drops his voice down to a whisper. "... the vampires! He said I can get special training to make me better at fighting them."

Anger flashes across Kit's face. She gives the Captain her very best death-stare. Runt, who is now standing beside her, starts growling. A very low, almost inaudible growl, but Kit can clearly hear it. She puts her hand on the ruff of his neck. "Easy boy, no need for that."

"I'm not forcing him into the Watch," the Captain says. There is an almost defensive tone to his voice. "But if you're going to continue on this path, having somebody trained in fighting ..." he lets Kit fill in the blanks. "Well, it's going to come in handy. You know that."

Kit toes the ground, feeling a bit ashamed of her reaction. Once again, she feels her face heating, but she's not sure why. "He's welcome to join the Watch, if he wants."

"I don't want to join the Watch," Indie says. There was a slight edge to his tone, but Kit's not sure why of that either. "I want to stay with you." He quickly looks between Kit and the Captain, like he's torn. When his eyes fall back on Kit, there is a strange look in them. "Unless you send me away, I'll be with you until the end." There was a sincere solemnity in his words.

"I'm just saying," Kit mumbles, her face continuing to heat. When she turns to the Captain, he's got a small grin on his face. "What?" she scolds. "What's with the face?"

"Whoa, little sister!" the Captain throws his hands up in defense. "Stay calm now." His voice is stern, but there is a hint of good-natured chiding in it. "The training will take less than a moon to complete. When he's finished, you can have him back."

Kit ignores the last remark. "When do you start the training?" She can't help the sound of resignation in her voice. This is happening whether she likes it or not.

"The Captain says I can start first thing tomorrow morning." Indie is looking over at the Captain as he answers, the Captain shaking his head in response. Indie suddenly looks crushed.

"We start at sundown. Tonight." The Captain gives Indie a hardy clap on the back. "They're most dangerous at night, so we train at night." This bit of new information makes Indie's eyes light up. He begins bouncing from foot to foot like he simply can't wait, even for just a few more hours.

"Okay then," Kit can't help but laugh. "How's about we head back to the Temple and have a big supper. I've got some things to look after tonight as well." She kind of let that comment hang out there. She's hoping for a reaction from Indie, but he's too wrapped up in his own joy to notice.

The Captain gives Kit a wink. "A good dinner is an excellent idea, but how's about we do it here at the barracks. Our cook, Mags, is pretty good, too, and she'll know what to feed you two to help get you through the night."

When Kit looks over at Indie and their two furry companions, they're all nodding in agreement. Again, she groans to herself. Kit can't help but chuckle at their antics. *Boys.* "That would be great, Captain. Thank you."

Chapter 15

THE FOOD PROVIDED BY the Barrack's head cook was a meal fit for a king. The Captain referring to her as a *cook* was a disservice to her to say the least. She was nothing short of a master chef. Kit had expected hearty food, which it was, but it was also a masterpiece of techniques, flavours and textures. When the meal was finished, Kit could barely move.

Kit looks down at Runt and Lump. The dogs slipped under the long family-style tables while they ate, gathering up *snacks* from practically every guard sitting at their table. Now, they are both laying on their sides, looking like they are in a food coma. Kit smiles, knowing exactly how they feel.

She looks over at Captain Harding. He is leaning back in his chair, picking at his teeth with bones from one of the several fish courses that were delivered. Indie, who is sitting next to him, has taken a similar position, but he is still nibbling at some of the fried pork skins. All meal long he never stopped pushing food into his mouth. Kit simply can't believe that he is still eating, even if it is at a leisurely pace.

"Captain, please be sure to thank the *chef* for this wonderful meal. If this is the way the Watch eats every day, I'm surprised you don't have ten times as many people trying to sign up to join." A small burp escapes as Kit speaks, eliciting a giggle from Indie.

"We do what we can to keep the members happy," the Captain says with a wide grin. "But truth is, Mags out did herself today." He pats his stomach. "Those corn-battered bacon bites were outstanding." Practically every person at the table cheers in response to the Captain's comment. Every other table joins in, even though Kit doesn't think they know what they were cheering about.

Kit pushes herself away from the table and stands up with a groan, thinking to herself that the fourth plateful was two platefuls too many. "I'm going to need to walk this off," she says with a chuckle, mimicking the Captain's gesture of patting his stomach. No sooner do the words leave her mouth than several of the guards practically jump from their chairs, offering to join her on a *walk*.

After a quick admonishment from the Captain, they all take their seats. All except for Indie who seems upset for some reason. Even Runt and Lump are up and ready to join her. Kit gives Indie a shy smile, telling him that she'll be okay on her own. She pats her hand on the haft of her battle hammer for effect. She gives both of the boys a big hug, telling them they'll have fun spending the night training with Indie. A moment later, she's wiping slobber off her face and neck. "I love you, too, boys," she whispers.

The sun is just ready to set as Kit exits the barracks. The temperature is already beginning to drop, but the cold isn't bothering her. In fact, after the heat from inside the barrack's dining hall, the cooler temperatures are a welcome change.

Her mind wanders off as she thinks about the challenge to gain Titan's acknowledgement. She thinks back to the High Priest's words, about how she is the exception to the rule; unlike others, she had heard the calling of Titan before joining the Temple. Before she knows it, she is outside the city's walls, making her way toward Titan's ice statue.

Once outside the walls, the winds become significantly stronger, forcing her to fully clip her armour's buckles all the way to the top. The soft interior fur of the armor is providing extra protection from the cold. Kit smiles, remembering when Fenrir gave her this amazing gift.

When Kit walks past the farthest point of the city wall, she can see Titan's statue in its entirety. The day's dying light, glinting off the ice, makes the statue look like it's been set ablaze. Titan's eyes, in particular, seem to be a dark shade of red, dancing with yellows and oranges. Deep shadows that are being cast across his face make Titan look even angrier than usual. Even though her armour is keeping her warm, Kit shivers at the sight.

Within an hour, the sun is fully set, and the temperature continues to drop. With no clouds in sight, the stars begin to light up the sky. The moon is barely more than a sliver, but Kit has no difficulty making her way toward the great statue.

She figures it must be midnight by the time she arrives at the base of the statue. Even though there are typically worshippers here day and night, she finds herself alone. Alone with her thoughts, her prayers, and her god. Kit feels the waves of cold coming down from the ice statue, but it doesn't dampen her spirits. Every now and then she hears drops of water hitting the ground around her. Kit looks up to see where the melting water is coming from, but it's impossible to tell. Occasionally water would fall in a pattern, making it sound like there were footsteps. She can't help but scoff at her overactive imagination.

Kit climbs up a set of stairs that take her to the main alter beneath the statue. They are not nearly as formidable as the stairs leading up to the Temple, but it still takes considerable effort. When she gets to the alter, she absentmindedly runs her hands along its cold, hard surface. Unlike the statue, which is hewn from ice, the alter is carved from one single, enormous block of marble. Even in the dim starlight she can see reflections coming from within the translucent stone.

"Okay, Kit," she scolds herself. "You're just wasting time. Either get on with it or start walking back." She takes a deep breath and looks up at the statue again. Its enormity reflects the size of the decision she's about to make. Suddenly Kit gets the sense that she's not alone. She feels a deep chill run through her body. Titan is with her!

She quickly makes her way to the front of the alter and drops to her knees. The ground is cold and rough, small bits of stone cutting into her knees. The pain seems to heighten her senses all the more. She feels welcome here.

Kit quickly knits her fingers together in front of her, dropping her chin to her chest. "Titan, hear me," she whispers. "I am not worthy of your grace. I have fallen from the path you set out for me; more times than I can remember. I often doubt my faith. I am lost in a sea of distractions." Images of Indie, Runt and Lump appear in her mind's eye, with Indie taking the forefront. She shakes her head, trying to chase them away, but they continue to linger.

She now sees Father Hoarfrost standing before her. His face is a picture of peace and serenity. A barely perceptible golden aura surrounds him, his eyes and hands upcast. Behind the High Priest Kit sees an image of Fenrir in her white wolf form. She moves slowly, calmly from behind the old priest. As she does, she shifts into the form of the old woman from the hut. Deep wrinkles and bright eyes speak of wisdom and experience. She shifts once again, this time to the form of the young Berrat girl she met in the market outside the gates of Aarall. Again, Kit can't help but smile at her. She's the picture of youth and innocence.

The vision suddenly shifts again. A tall warrior with skin that looks like it is carved from ice now stands before her. He wields a trident that appears to be carved from bone. He bows his head slightly to Kit. As he does, the ice melts away revealing Captain Harding. He gives Kit a coy smile before he simply vanishes, leaving her alone, kneeling in a dark void. The blackness feels like it's crushing in on Kit, pressing her down onto the ground.

"Welcome, Kit Standing Bear!" a voice booms in her head. "Prove your devotion to me!"

Kit feels her spirit lift from her body. Like a leaf on the wind, she travels to the northern reaches of Orth. She plunges beneath the surface of the turbulent sea, sinking into the inky darkness until she is so deep, she is engulfed in utter blackness. She is being tossed about in unseen currents. The ebb and flow of the salty water carry her in whichever direction they wish. Kit tries to swim, but it's hopeless. She doesn't know where to go, and even if she did, the current is so strong that she can't fight it. Kit allows her mind to clear completely and lets herself be taken by the sea. Even though she's under water, Kit can breathe normally.

She bobs and weaves in the darkness for what feels like hours, letting the current take her where it may. In the distance she begins to see a small glow. The current seems to pick up, dragging her faster toward it. The closer Kit gets, the brighter the glow becomes. Its light is now practically blinding.

Suddenly a huge shadow passes between Kit and the glow. The current shifts and she's now spinning, like she's trapped within a great vortex. When the shadow passes, Kit is no longer close to the light; its intense luminance is no longer blinding her. The current is gone, leaving her suspended in the water. Kit decides to swim toward the light. She is no longer passively letting the current take her. Kit is now paddling with all her might to reach it.

Once again, the closer she gets, the brighter and more intense the light becomes. Even with her lids shut tight; the light burns into Kit's eyes. She tries shielding them with her arm, but to no effect. Kit takes a deep breath, pulls away her arm and fully opens her eyes. For a moment, the pain is excruciating but it quickly passes.

Before her is what looks like a great vault. Kit's body is nearly frozen solid, but there is no fear of death. Her god is before her, yet unseen. There is another brilliant flash of light and Kit suddenly finds herself laying prone at the foot of a great ice Temple. It resembles the Temple in Aarall, but it's even bigger, and Titan's hands are bound by giant manacles with chains that run deep into the ground. Kit's mind is racing to keep up with what is transpiring. She's not certain, but she believes she can hear Titan himself speaking to her. "My child, I welcome you, and thank you for your service unto me. My icy prison prevents me from bestowing a more fitting gift upon you. But, if you can free me, I can promise unto you, life everlasting." When the voice stops, darkness falls upon her.

Kit opens her eyes to find that she is still kneeling at the alter. The sun is only just beginning to rise, and even though she's in shadows, she can see without difficulty. As her head begins to clear, Kit sees a nomad girl sitting on the step next to her. She is about Kit's age, maybe a few cycles older. Kit blinks at her, wondering if this is yet another part of her vision. This girl has been at the Temple with Kit since her arrival. But over that period, she's never taken the time to talk to Kit, and Kit's been too busy to seek her out. She's dressed in fine silks, and she has a very large battle-hammer strapped to her back.

"Have you been touched by Titan?" she asks. There is a hint of awe in her voice. "I do not mean to intrude, but I was watching while you were in prayer." Her eyes widen as she speaks. "It was as though you were in a state of rapture. Then, that mark appeared on your neck, glowing white. It was only there for a moment before it faded away."

Kit blinks at the girl. She can see clearly, but her head feels like she's still under water. She has no memory of the events, but this girl is surely speaking the truth. Kit does feel somewhat different now, somehow more aware of her surroundings. Kit touches her neck where the girl had indicated that the mark had appeared. The area is ice cold to the touch, and she can feel that her skin is slightly raised. She quickly pulls her hand away.

Kit continues to stare at the girl, completely confused. "Who are you? Why are you here?" The High Priest said nobody would be watching, and yet, here is this Temple girl sitting next to her, sitting much closer than Kit would like.

"If you have been selected by Titan, it is because he has great plans for you. I have been taught to worship my entire life, but I've never been called to his service." The girl clears her throat, noticing that she is somewhat fawning over Kit. "Oh, where are my manners?" She holds out her hand to Kit in greeting. "My name is Aithlin, servant to the High Priest. My friends call me Lin."

"Um, hello, Lin," Kit rolls over from her knees onto her butt, giving them a quick rub as she does. The pain and stiffness she's feeling in them isn't enough to fully bring Kit back to reality. She tentatively shakes the girl's hand, wondering. "Why are you here?"

Lin casts her eyes downward and she begins to fidget with her fingers. "I thought you might be going through the trials, and I wanted to watch." When she looks up, her eyes are wide and glassy. Kit senses fear coming off her. "Please don't tell Father Hoarfrost," she pleads. "I just don't think," she pauses for a moment and takes a deep breath. "I don't think he'd be happy if he knew."

"How could you know I was going to be here tonight?" Even as the words are leaving Kit's mouth, she knew the answer. "It was you who was outside Father's office when I came out, wasn't it?"

Lin nods slowly, her eyes once again downcast. She pulls her knees to her chest, wrapping her arms around them. "Yes, sister."

Kit places her hand on top of Lin's. "But why? Why would you eavesdrop on my conversation with the High Priest?" She scrunches her nose as she says this. "You like listening in when I'm getting scolded?"

"Oh no, never!" Lin blurts out, shaking her head furiously. "I ... I've been watching you since you joined the Temple; for nearly five cycles." Her eyes once again giant, glassy circles. "I've always known, from the day you arrived, that you were special. My grandmother even said so."

"Special? Me?" Kit practically chokes on the words. "If anything, I'm the least special person in the Temple. Truth is, I'm surprised I haven't been kicked out."

"Excommunicated? You? Never!" Lin is in shock. "You're one of the *three*."

"What? One of the three?" Kit draws her hand back, her brow furrowed.

Even as Kit pulls her hand away, Lin snatches it back up, pulling herself even closer to Kit. "From the prophecy, you know, the one that describes the freeing of Titan." Lin closes her eyes and tilts her head back slightly. "Three will try. Eight shall die. Three will go. Two shall grow. One will lose. One will choose." When she finishes reciting the prophecy, she opens her eyes. "You, Kit. You are one of the three."

"You believe that ... tripe?" Kit shakes her head. She's not sure if she should pity the girl or be angry with her. "They're just words. They make no sense, and even if it was real, I'm certainly not one of the three, or anybody else in that drivel."

"Drivel? Blasphemy!" Lin shouts at Kit. "Blasphemy! You, a priest of Titan, chosen by Him personally. How can you say that? How can you doubt the words of the *prophecy*?"

Kit's about to fly into a rage, but she manages to control herself before she does. "You listen carefully to me, *Lin*. I'm just a girl. I'm nobody special and I don't even know if I *want* to be a priest." As Kit says the words, she feels a tightness in her chest. Her internal conflict gnaws at her. "I'm nobody, and I like it that way."

"Nobody?" Lin starts to laugh. "I've been in the Temple since I was only a small child. When my grandmother gave me to the Temple, she told me that she had high hopes for me. She wanted me to be like her, a priest of Titan. She said that I was *special*." Lin's voice trails off as she speaks. "But I've never been able to commune with Titan." She quickly wipes her eyes. "I *want* to be a priest. With all my heart, I want to, but Titan does not hear me. He does not call unto me."

Kit's not exactly sure what to say to cheer her up, so she draws on some of the teachings that were drilled into her during the Temple's philosophy classes. "Who knows what is in Titan's heart? We are but a grain of wheat in the vast fields of his will."

"And unto him shall our insignificance be offered." Lin says in reply. She sounds utterly defeated. "I know the teachings. You don't need to remind me."

Kit shouldn't be surprised that Lin would be well versed in the Temple's philosophies. Truth is, Kit's surprised that she could quote anything from those classes herself, especially since she thinks she slept through most of them.

It's then they hear the sound of people coming. The sun is now cresting the top of Mount Toka, which means that the people who make their daily pilgrimage would begin to arrive shortly. Kit stands up, the stiffness now gone from her limbs, and offers her hand to Lin. "C'mon, let's head back and get some breakfast. I'm starving."

Lin gives Kit a small smile as she takes her hand. "Sure, I could eat."

For the majority of the walk back to the city, the conversation is light, idle chitchat. Most of the time, it's Lin asking Kit questions. Even though they've been at the Temple together since Kit arrived, she had never interacted with her until today. Over the course of the walk, it's like Lin is trying to catch up on everything Kit's done since her arrival. She occasionally steers the conversation towards what had happened during the acknowledgement ritual, but Kit's able to deflect her away from the topic. She simply isn't ready to discuss it with her, or anybody else for that matter.

By the time they reach the marketplace, just outside the gates to the city, one of the vendors begins calling Kit's name. Even in the morning din, his voice manages to carry all the way to her. Kit pushes her way through the crowd, to find Comden at his stall, his eyes filled with anticipation. "So, did you speak to Sister Miyuki? Would she like my prickle-berry loaves for the Festival?"

Kit's mouth begins to water when she thinks of the delicious, sweet bread Comden had given her. "Yes, indeed," she replies with a big grin. "She enjoyed them as much as I did."

"And?" Comden is leaning in on her, waiting impatiently for her response.

Kit begins to tap her finger on her chin, like she's having trouble remembering the conversation. "Let's see," she muses out loud. "I do remember giving her one of the loaves ..."

"Don't be cruel, Kit," the vendor's face is starting to turn red. He may actually be holding his breath waiting for her to speak.

A big smile crosses Kit's face. "She said she'd take it all! As much as you can make!"

At the news, Comden begins to dance around, his hands flailing in the air above him. "Oh, happy days!" he says in a sing-song kind of way. "Thank you so much, Kit. Thank you so much. Oh here, you have to try this. It's another one of my new recipes."

Just as Kit begins to follow Comden to the back of his stall, she feels a tug on her tunic. "Sister, I need to leave."

Kit's about to ask where she's going, but Lin has already started to head off. "What's the rush?" she yells to her. Lin is already a good distance away, the crowd enveloping her. She screams something back to Kit, but it gets lost in the crowd. It sounded like, "I have to tell the High Priest."

Kit gives her head a shake, thinking that she had better go see the High Priest herself before Lin blows the whole thing out of proportion. She's about to run after her when Comden gives her a small hand-pie. "Try it!" he urges.

She groans slightly. The idea that Lin is going to get to Hoarfrost before her is concerning, but it's not the end of the world. Kit takes a sniff of the hand-pie before taking a big bite. Her mouth is immediately on fire. She feels like she just swallowed a volcano.

"Holy Helja, Comden, what did you give me?" She starts sucking deep breaths, hoping the air will help dissipate the heat.

"Too many dragon peppers?" he asks.

"You fed me dragon peppers? No wonder it feels like I could blow flames right now." Kit's tear-filled eyes begin scanning his wares, looking for something that might quell the insane fire in her mouth. She sees what looks like muffins and quickly stuffs one of them into her mouth. In a few moments, the agony passes, and she can breathe normally again.

"Please forgive me, little sister. I guess I need to tone down the spice level." Comden grabs another hand-pie and examines it. He takes a big bite from it himself, chews and swallows. "I guess they do have a bit of a kick to them. Maybe I've been eating my wife's cooking for so long that I don't notice it anymore."

"You must be part dragon," Kit laughs as she watches him devour the last bite of his pie. "I don't think Miyuki would want to serve that. At least, not if it's *that* spicy." Kit quickly snags another muffin, giving Comden a shy grin as she does. "I'm going to need another if I'm going to survive the morning." And with that, Kit bids him a good day and begins her trek back to the Temple.

Chapter 16

KIT MAKES HER WAY THROUGH the Temple to the High Priest's office. Just as she arrives, she sees two acolytes standing outside his door. As soon as they see her, they scurry off. "It's rude to eavesdrop," she yells at them. Kit's just about to knock when she hears the priest call out to her.

"Kit? Is that you outside my door? Come in child! Come in!"

Opening the door, she sees that the High Priest's eyes are practically bulging out of his head. "I could *feel* your presence from outside my room. You are truly a miracle of faith!"

Kit's not sure how to react. Her gut instinct is to turn and run. Seeing the distress on Kit's face, the High Priest lets out a booming laugh! "Sit down, child. I'm only teasing you. Aithlin just left a few minutes ago. She could not stop gushing about your experience, so I thought I'd have a bit of fun with you."

"I don't think it's something to joke about," Kit says, almost as an admonishment.

"Sorry, Kit, but the way Lin was carrying on it was as though you actually experienced direct contact with Titan himself." The old priest could barely contain his laughter.

Kit cocks her head to the side, hoping that seeing the High Priest from a new angle will help explain his behaviour. "Your Grace, I fail to see the humour in this."

Suddenly the old priest's face blanches. "Tell me exactly what happened during the ritual. Leave out no detail."

Kit begins by taking the seat the High Priest offers her. "Well, Your Grace. I'm not sure what Lin told you, but my experience was very ... vivid." She continues to explain to him what she saw and how she felt during the ritual. Absentmindedly Kit puts her hand on the icy mark she felt when she awoke from her trance.

"Child! You ... you have been chosen by Titan!" The old priest sounds *proud* of her.

"I don't want to be anybody's *chosen one*," the words catching in Kit's throat, coming out barely more than a squeak.

The old priest looks on her with gentle eyes, and he again begins to chuckle. "You are not *the chosen one*, at least not in the sense that you are seeming to suggest, but you have been *selected* by Titan to take up the mantle of freeing him from his icy prison." The priest says a brief prayer before folding down his high collar. A mark on his neck begins to glow a pale blue, lasting no more than a moment or two. "I, too, was chosen by Titan, but I was unable to complete the tasks he set out for me. He has chosen many, but the trials to free him require *inhuman* abilities."

As Kit looks at Father Hoarfrost, she sees that he has become lost in thought. "Father, the experience changed me. I can't explain how, but I'm different now." Her words seem to bring him back from wherever he had gone.

"You *are* different," the old priest says. "For Titan is with you; now and always. This mark will allow you to call upon him in times of dire need. You will be able to draw strength directly from him."

Try as she might, Kit cannot fathom what the High Priest is telling her.

"Consider it a miracle that you can cast once a moon. You will be able to draw on Titan to significantly increase your physical strength." Father Hoarfrost leans in towards Kit, to make sure he is heard. "You must now wait for Titan's trials to be placed before you."

"What will these trials be?" This is happening much too fast. Kit's head is swimming. She's beginning to wish she had never gone to the statue or undertaken the challenge.

The High Priest thinks back on his own trials to free Titan. "Only Titan can divulge unto you what you will face during your journey to free him. Your trials may be different from mine. All I can tell you is, if you fail any of the trials, they will all be reset, and you will need start from scratch. I tried twice. The second attempt nearly killed me. It killed most of my cohorts, including my best friend and my elder brother."

The old priest was becoming emotional, thinking back on what had happened to him. He then dismissively waves his hands about as if to chase away the sad memories.

"But I don't want to be responsible for anybody's death." Kit remembers how Indie nearly died while he was helping her, and from the sounds of it, that was a simple task compared to whatever these trials might entail.

"Kit, we will all return to the Great Cycle one day. It's what we do with our time that matters. If we die in the service of Titan, then we would die knowing that we were doing something worthwhile." The old priest's face darkens, and his eyes get a far-off look to them again. Kit's just about to speak when he seems to return from wherever his mind went.

Suddenly, Hoarfrost raises his eyebrows. "I almost forgot." The severity of the conversation is now gone, and he heads over to a large cabinet at the back of his office. From Kit's position, she can't see what's inside when he opens the door, but she can hear him muttering to himself. "No, no, that won't do. Ah yes, here we are." When he turns, he's holding a small stack of clothing. He holds them out, presenting them to her. "Here, here," he says. When he sees Kit standing there staring at him, he beckons to her again. "Come, take them."

She walks over to the priest, accepting the gift of clothing that he's offering her. Kit hadn't noticed initially, but there is a small leather bag on top of the pile.

"Since you passed the Rite of Abandonment, you have officially become a Priest of Titan. I should have issued this to you days ago. All Priests are issued a new cassock, a new tunic and a blessed holy symbol." He gives her a small grin. "I know, you were likely expecting a ceremonial presentation for this, but things have been a bit hectic lately. After this morning's revelation, Titan's Acknowledgement, I simply couldn't delay any further." The old man runs his fingers through his long black-grey hair. "I will be sure to give you a proper presentation during the Feast of Titan's Bounty."

Kit bows her head slightly. "Thank you." She can't help but beam with pride.

"Now that you are a priest, and you've received Titan's acknowledgement, I think it's time I give you your first *official* duty."

Kit can't believe her good luck, her first official duty. She's so excited that she's practically vibrating with anticipation.

Father Hoarfrost clears his throat and raises his chin to her. "For your first official duty, I want you to go to the kitchens and find Sister Miyuki. She has work for you to do."

"What?" Kit can't believe what the old priest has asked her to do. Before she has a chance to think about it, she blurts out. "I am now an *official* Priest of Titan, and you're sending me to the kitchen to *scrub pots*?"

Father Hoarfrost calmly takes his seat behind his massive wooden desk. "Perhaps, little sister, I should send you to Windward Harbour to mine for salt. It might teach you some humility."

"But I'm a Priest of Titan!" That comes out much whinier than Kit would have liked.

"Yes. You are a *priest* of Titan and I am the *High Priest*," Hoarfrost puts extra emphasis on his title, "And as High Priest, I am sending you to find Sister Miyuki. She has a task for you."

Kit lets out a long sigh. This is not going anything like the way she had expected. "Yes, Your Grace. If that is Titan's will ..."

The old priest drops his face into his hands. Kit can hear him grumbling to himself. Finally, he lifts his head up and begins speaking slowly, as though she is no more than five cycles. "Why must you be so ... you? Sister Miyuki asked me to send you her way. She has a gift that she wants to share with you. If you weren't so headstrong, you'd have just done as I asked and not ruined the surprise." The old priest then slowly raises himself from his chair. Placing his hands on his desk, he leans in toward her. A shadow crosses over his face and the room suddenly becomes as cold as a winter storm. "And the next time you disobey my orders, I'll have you thrown into the dungeons until you learn some respect." He then plops back into his chair and the room again returns to its normal, but somewhat frosty, temperature.

"Yes, Father. Thank you, Father." Kit adds an extra acknowledgement for the clothing before heading out of his office as quickly as she can.

Chapter 17

KIT QUICKLY HEADS TO her room and changes into her new clothes. Now in her *official* priestly attire, she watches her new, holy symbol swing from its chain across her chest as she walks. She smiles happily to herself. As she's heading down the stone stairs on her way to sister Miyuki, she finds herself running her hands along the highly polished, surprisingly smooth stone walls. Unbidden, memories of lessons from Temple classes come surging up in her mind.

The Great Dining Hall, along with its attendant kitchens, storerooms, and other areas which require heat, such as an herbarium, had been designed with artistry and economy by a rare design partnership between two famous architects: the half-dwarf Quartz Rockvein and the half-elven Evan Stargazer – half-brothers who shared the same mother.

The hall was built under the Temple, to make the best use of the modest land that the Church of Titan had been able to purchase. It provided heating to both the Temple and the dining room by using the heat from the kitchen fires and clay ovens. It also made the Hall usable as a dining hall, private chapel, meeting room and winter classroom through the use of sliding walls, circular wall displays, changeable wall decorations and candelabras.

Sunlight was brought downstairs by the clever use of mirrors located in the Temple above, which shone reflected light onto the lesser - though still quite beautiful - glass windows in the Hall; they gave the illusion of the Hall being at ground-level, rather than being below. Two long tables flanked each side, small fires in alcoves behind them. They could accommodate up to fifty novices, seated on equally long benches. Between the novice's tables, were six more rows for the Temple's acolytes. In front of these eight rows is a slightly raised table, intended for Temple priests. Behind that, raised considerably higher, is a beautiful table carved from the huge trunk of a Berrathi-

111

an Pine tree, which seats the High Priest, six senior priests and up to five guests.

Behind the High Priest's place of honour, on a circular platform, is a roaring fireplace, flanked by a statue of the Blessed Fenrir on the right, and one of the Blessed Ymir on the left. The sculptor, an Arn-norian named Janek, had only thousand years-old legends, and not the subjects themselves, to go by when he crafted them. No one living had ever actually seen them. But the Great White Wolf and the Frost Giant looked so real that they gave many novices nightmares if they got close enough.

Kit gives her head a shake. *Where did that come from?* she muses to herself. First, she's quoting philosophy lessons to Lin and now she's remembering her *history* lessons. *Apparently, I listen while I'm sleeping*, she laughs to herself. And, having actually seen Fenrir herself, she can say with certainty that the statue of Fenrir is flawless.

When Kit makes it to the kitchens, she looks around for Sister Miyuki, but she doesn't seem to be anywhere in sight. Standing in the middle of the dining area, Kit yawns deeply and rubs her eyes. They feel like they're filled with sand. *Another night with no sleep,* she thinks to herself. *After I finish up here, I really need to catch a few z's.*

At that moment, the smell of fresh brewed coffee greets her nose, waking her up before she's even had a chance to take a sip. She wanders over to the large stone carafe being kept warm by one of the many fires and pours herself a mug. As the sides of the mug begin to warm her hands, Kit inhales the aroma deeply, letting it sink in. After just a small sip, she can feel some life seep back into her tired body. Continuing to cradle the mug between her hands, Kit makes her way to a table with some empty spaces.

She takes a seat and begins waiting patiently for Sister Miyuki. Moments later she comes waddling into the dining hall. She's carrying a small crock and a loaf of what looks like wintergrain bread. "Good morning, child," Miyuki offers, with her warm, robust voice.

"It seems like only yesterday you were but a small, dirt-covered waif at the city gates. Today, you are an *acknowledged* priest of Titan."

"You heard?" Kit says, somewhat shyly as she looks over the top of her steaming mug of coffee.

"Oh child, nothing of any consequence happens in this Temple without all of *us priests* hearing about it." Her eyes are beaming with pride. "And when something as truly remarkable as being acknowledged happens, well now, that news spreads like wildfire."

"I really don't want any extra attention." Kit puts the mug down on the table; the heat from the cup was now making it too hot to hold onto.

Miyuki's face suddenly becomes distressed. "Oh," she says, looking down at the small pot she has in her hand. "I guess you don't want this crock of prickle-berry honey?"

Kit's eyes light up when she hears what's in the crock. She quickly thrusts her hands out, her fingers practically convulsing, as she awaits the gift.

Miyuki begins to chuckle to herself, causing her rotund body to shake in a comical way. "Here," she says, handing Kit the crock with a small wooden spoon, "In honor of your new rank! Let's keep it our secret!" Miyuki begins to waddle off, but before she gets too far away, she turns back to Kit with a very stern look on her face. "You best bring me back a clean crock, do you hear?"

Kit looks into the small crock to find it's full of prickle-berry honey, something usually saved for the Feast of Titan's Bounty. Equal parts sweet and tart, it's a rare delicacy, as prickle-berry bushes blossom only once every four years, and harvesting the flowers is labour intensive and often painful work. Impulsively, Kit drops the food on the table and races across the hall to give Miyuki a crushing hug. "You're the best, Miyuki!"

Miyuki gives Kit a big smile and a quick kiss on her forehead before continuing back toward the kitchens. "Mind what I told you.

I want that crock back clean!" She gives another laugh and waddles off.

Kit's slathering a slice of bread with a generous dollop of honey when someone sits opposite her. As he sets down his bowl of what looks to be broth with vegetables, he grins broadly at Kit, showing a few missing teeth. His cassock is shimmery white with many thousands of green threads woven through it, creating an intricate, almost mesmerising pattern. Amidst the white and green, thin strips of dark brown leather hang from his waist down to his toes. It makes him look like a snow-covered evergreen with a human head. It also marks him as being part of the delegation from Jotunheim's Frost Forest Monastery, one of the oldest factions of Titan's Priests. This small but very social sect dedicates itself to bettering relationships among family members, especially fathers and sons.

Kit watches his gnarled hand shake a little as he brings a spoonful of broth to his lips. He manages to get most of it into his mouth, but a bit spills onto the table. He has no napkin. Kit thinks that he must have left his in the kitchens.

With a small smile, Kit offers him hers. Her own meal of bread and honey can be sticky, but she won't mind licking the honey from her fingers when necessary.

The old priest looks at Kit and smiles warmly. "Thank you, young one. Although I have always loved hot soup, eating it these days has become troublesome. My hands are like wayward children – they mean well, but they don't always do what they are told!" They both laugh at the priest's joke. Kit watches intently as he slowly pats the table dry, and then extends a shaky hand.

Kit grasps it, only to be surprised by how firm his grip is. "I am Brother Snowbank, archivist at the Frost Forest Monastery."

"Sister Kit Standing Bear," she replies, her new title sounding strange but wonderful. "It is a pleasure to meet you. It is rare, I am told, for you and your brothers to travel so far from Jotunheim. What brings you here, if I may ask?"

Snowbank looks at Kit as if he's taking her measure. Leaning forward, he inquires, "Is it always this mild this early in the season, Sister Kit?"

"It seems Gaia is in a hurry this cycle," she replies staring up at the ceiling as though she's gazing up into the sky. "It's unusually warm, even for the final week before the beginning of the Thaw. And the oaks budded weeks ago."

"Gaia?" states Snowbank, sharply. "How is it that you mention her name?"

"Forgive me, Brother," she quickly replies, "I am from Berrathia, and the Old Ones are still worshipped there."

"Child, you need not apologize," he sighs. "Titan is a demanding god, and he is the one who would not be pleased – even if he does not deem growing things to be worth his attention. Don't look so shocked! I do not discount the possibility that there are other gods. Nor do you, I think."

The turn of this conversation unnerves Kit. "I only serve Titan," she declares, and Snowbank chuckles. His laugh is weak and rheumy, making it sound like he might have trouble catching his breath.

"I do not doubt your current fealty, Kit Standing Bear. You bear Titan's mark. But your Berrathi gods have also marked you. Hoarfrost may not have the eyes to see it, but I do. How you can bear *both* marks though, that sweet child, is a mystery to me." The brother's eyes narrow as he inhales deeply through his nose. "And you smell of wolf!"

The old priest stares back down at his bowl of soup. "But, to answer your question: The Frost Forest brothers are here because the melt is early in Jotunheim as well. It is a cause for concern. It is not unheard of, such great warmings. Hmmm, that reminds me..."

He pauses. It seems to Kit that he's either lost in a memory, or he's fallen asleep. Warmer weather means more snowmelt, and too much brings the danger of flooding. Oddly, Kit can't help but wonder why he said, '*The Frost Forest brothers*' and not '*We.*'

Concerned, Kit says in a louder than normal tone, "Reminds you of what?"

His eyes snap open. "No need to shout, Sister Kit. No need to shout." No sooner does he finish than his eyes once again get that far off look to them. But, before Kit has a chance to try and wake him up again, his mind returns from wherever it had disappeared to. "Does the Fist of Titan still have the Mad Monk's manuscripts? Perhaps they hold some answers." Kit furrows her brow and scrunches up her face at the question. She has no knowledge of any special manuscripts or of any Mad Monk.

"Not that I am aware of, brother, but truth be told, I only very recently became a *priest*, so there is likely much that I have yet to learn."

"Hmph!" Snowbank snorts. "I see Old Hoarfrost keeps the Temple's Old Tales under wraps. Do you have a moment to hear it?" Kit's about to say no when he presses forward anyway.

"The short version, then," Snowbank says with a wink. "Many hundreds of years ago, a farmer in Aarall was digging in his fields and found bones and skeletons, thousands of them actually. Well, these bones were unlike anything anyone had ever seen before. The Fist of Titan sent Brother Edur to examine them, dispose of them, and then bless the farmer's fields. Edur spent days drawing pictures of each type of skeleton. He imagined them belonging to giant crabs, hybrid human-horses, winged humans, wolf-headed bears, and so on. The bones were eventually ground up and used to fertilize Aarall's fields. This tale would have ended there, but for an unseasonably warm spell, much like the one we're having now. While Edur was out checking the Temple's livestock, a monk came running from the direction of Titan's Trail, the path that leads through the mountain behind the great statue. He told Edur that he'd seen something inside the great ice statue. Something that looked like a door."

Sister Miyuki sticks her head out of the kitchen's archway and says, "Can I get you anything, Kit? We're about to send Sister Nevara this morning's leftovers."

"No, no food," Kit replies, "But maybe some water for the brother, here?"

"Expecting someone, are you? Oh, you must mean one of those Frost Forest brothers. Yes, of course." She returns in a heartbeat and sets the glass down in front of Kit. "You tell him I'll get him anything he likes." And with that, she walks away, humming, "When Titan's Breath Doth Blow."

"Where was I?" Snowbank ponders. "As Edur walked the Trail, he had to be careful to avoid the sudden rush of ice water running downhill. Luckily, he had a staff, or was it a cane, to help him keep his balance. He saw, sparkling in the sunlight, an area that once comprised the *buttock* of Titan. It had melted partway through, revealing what indeed appeared to be a door. He inched nearer to get a closer look, but the ice beneath him broke, sending him arse o'er teakettle, depositing him right in front of the door! He tried the handle, but it was still frozen in place. He was about to give up, when a silly whim made him knock three times on the door. The sound of ice cracking was ear-splitting, and the door swung open, followed by a whoosh of stale air that practically knocked him off his feet."

Snowbank chuckles dryly, then drains the entire glass of water. "Before you ask, I don't know what he found. But, according to the tales that have been passed down, whatever he found in that room drove him mad. In his haste to return to the Temple and tell his story, he apparently slipped and fell off the path, sending him careening down the mountainside. When they found him the next morning, he was near death and well beyond any magic that might have been able to heal him. He was clutching onto a wooden box, raving about a Library that was filled with books that spoke of mass murders and strange creatures, much like the skeletons he'd found. He died the next day."

Snowbank watches for Kit's reaction, and mysteriously adds, "At least, that's the story the *High Priest* told, and that's what's been passed on. Who knows what really happened?"

"That's an incredible story! And you think we still have those papers?" Kit doesn't know why, but the thought of finding and reading those papers has awakened her curiosity. *Why would they drive someone mad?* she thought to herself.

Snowbank rises, and leaning across the table, beckons for Kit to come closer. "What I think, Sister, is that the High Priest at the time, Hoarfrost's distant ancestor, had that box and it's contents burned."

"But what about the room? The Library? Didn't others investigate? What else was inside?" Kit's excitement is bubbling out of her, words coming out much faster than they should.

"Funny you should ask," says the brother. "A fierce snowstorm hit on the very night Edur fell, restoring Titan's ice statue." He pokes Kit in the stomach with the tip of his tall, white, bone cane. "Now, fancy that!"

"The Library, what happened to the Library? Is it still there?" Kit's practically frantic at this point.

The old priest laughs, not the rheumy rasp that Kit had heard earlier, but a rich, deep laugh that fills the kitchen. "Here," he says, handing Kit his cane, "You'll need this, I think. Ask Hoarfrost about Edur and the Secret Library. Tell him that Brother Tyr sends his regards! And that he expects his due on the Feast of Titan's Bounty!"

While Kit is busy examining the cane the priest had given her, the old man had walked away, heading toward the stairs up to the Temple. As he does, she hears him say, very quietly, "We'll meet again."

"Wait!" Kit screams at him. Just as he turns back, a tall column of fireflies appears beside Snowbank. At that moment, Kit suddenly realizes that she is unable to speak, and unable to move.

"There you are, Eris," Brother Snowbank says to the fireflies, "We've underestimated them. Again. You especially underestimated this one." The old priest's eyes are twinkling, practically sparkling with mischief.

"Hmph!" the lights say. "Well Tyr, you've certainly taken a liking to her. To what end, I wonder?"

Kit decides that whatever the column of fireflies is, it's definitely female, and obviously jealous. And then it hits Kit; *Brother Snowbank likes me. But I wonder why she called him Tyr. Perhaps it was his name before he took Brother Snowbank as his priestly title.*

"You're just jealous," Snowbank says. "And why shouldn't I like her? She's young and comely. She's smart, and kind beyond her years. Kinder than some of us; if that's even possible. And she's twice god-touched, which means she's one of the three."

"Fool! She can hear us!" Eris is livid.

Snowbank laughs. "So what? Are you frightened? She isn't! Look at her – she's magnificent! Now, off with you!"

"How dare you! What are you scheming?" Eris' voice had become shrill.

"She's a free agent, Eris. She cannot be controlled, only influenced. She needs information. Remember the Rear-End Library?"

"That's against the rules!" Eris shrieks. The fireflies are coruscating wildly.

"This is the Great Game we're playing now, not some winner-takes-all child's game! We five wrote the rules, and we can change them if necessary!" It was Snowbank's turn to be furious. "Goodbye, Eris!"

The fireflies vanish.

If she could, Kit would be shaking. Snowbank turns and walks back to her. She still cannot move or speak. As he moves in behind her, he places his warm, large hands on her shoulders and massages them. All tension in her body immediately disappears.

Kit's trying desperately not to blush.

Her chair turns by itself to face brother Snowbank. "The Secret Library," he tells her, "is hidden inside Titan's statue. Climb up to the arms at dawn's first light and wait for the sign to show you the way. Do not linger. The light will show you the location of things containing knowledge that will interest you. Take them with you and go. Otherwise you will die when the Library collapses. And I do not want you to die, Kitten. Against all odds and reason, I am your friend." He bends down, and kisses Kit on the cheek, where it burns briefly.

"Until we meet again, Kitten." His release of her body and speech is so sudden that Kit barely has enough time to leap at him, demanding more answers. But she only finds empty space and the sound of his faintly arrogant, but intoxicating and delightful laughter. When it stops, she hears a coyote howl in the distance. It's now late afternoon, and in spite of how warm her whole body feels, a chill runs up Kit's spine.

Her mind races with what she's been told, and she desperately wants to know more. She stifles the urge to scream. Instead, she grasps the cane Snowbank had given her, and raising her left knee, she slams it across her thigh, hoping to snap it in two, only to have it bounce off as if it were made of yew. It springs upward, carried by the momentum created by her frustration, and whacks her in the jaw. Her head snaps upward and she loses her balance, falling backwards onto the table. Kit ends up sitting in Snowbank's bowl, wetting her newly acquired priestly clothes with broth.

The broth, which she could have sworn had been consumed, is also somehow miraculously still hot, sending her shrieking into the kitchens. Kit practically bowls Miyuki over as she rushes to plunge her posterior into a tub full of blessedly cool but dirty dish water.

"By Titan's Snowballs," Miyuki cries, "What has gotten into you, child? Are those your brand new ...? Oh, my. Oh, my, my, my, my!" Her brows crease with worry.

Kit, still sitting in the tub of dishwater, looks up at her rotund friend. "I've just met with the most exasperating, annoying old fool of a priest you're ever likely to meet! Miyuki, what's the matter?" Miyuki's face is white as new-fallen snow, as she's pointing over Kit's shoulder.

"WHAT...is that?"

Kit picks herself up out of the wash tub. When she turns, she sees it. It's the bone cane brother Snowbank had given her. It's floating, and its exquisitely carved sky-dragon's head, with two blue jewels for eyes, is level with hers. Those deep blue jewels suddenly *blink*, startling Kit, knocking her backwards, back into the tub of dirty water.

From her soggy, seated position, Kit attempts to make light of the floating cane. "It's a, well, a graduation gift," she answers with a small shrug. After picking herself back up from the tub, she continues. "From Brother Snowbank of the Frost Forest Monastery."

"Did you say, *Brother Snowbank*, young lady?" asks Miyuki, "I've never known you to lie before, but that's impossible. You see, he passed away last year. I know because my cousin is with the Jotunheim Order. I don't know what sort of trouble you're in young girl, but if it involves magic and lying, I can't help you."

Kit looks at Miyuki, completely perplexed by her comment. "Lying? What? Why do you think I'm lying?"

Miyuki's face is dark. She's practically scowling at Kit. "Hoarfrost wants to see you. He came in while you were eating, looked in at you, and then practically ran out using the delivery entrance. He looked spooked. Now go! And take that ... thing with you!" She grabs an armful of baskets. "I'd ask you to help me with the delivery of these breakfast leftovers to Sister Nevara, but you've got that cane to tame and Hoarfrost to visit." With that, she quickly makes her exit.

Ki turns to face the cane, only to find it's not there. Suddenly, Kit gets rapped on the back of her head. When she spins around, she sees the cane once again floating, giving her a steady, unwavering gaze; a knowing gaze, almost as if it's waiting for something.

Then it hits her. If it really is alive, and aware, and intelligent, and if the dragon head isn't just an arbitrary shape chosen by the craftsperson, what would it be waiting for? And then she remembers Snowbank.

Kit's eyes quickly scan the area, happy to see that she has this part of the kitchen to herself, because if she's wrong about this, she doesn't need the kitchen staff thinking she's lost her mind.

She gives the cane a slight bow. "My name is Sister Kit Standing Bear, and I am honored to make your acquaintance. I'm sorry for what I did, trying to break you in half. Truly, I am. If you are made from dragon bone, then you are the closest thing to a dragon as I have ever encountered. If, by some arcane chance, you have the mind of a dragon, I am doubly honored that you have been placed in my care. And one day, if I should meet your kind, I hope we might meet as friends."

The dragon head's blue jewel eyes blink again, this time slowly. Kit smiles lightly, choosing to believe that this was the cane's way of acknowledging acceptance of her apology. It floats a bit closer to Kit. When it comes within an arm's length of her, Kit gently takes hold of it.

Remembering that Hoarfrost was here to see her, Kit leaves the kitchens and makes her way to Hoarfrost's office.

From outside his office Kit sees the High Priest looking through his bookshelves, pulling one volume, glancing at it, returning it to the shelf, then pulling another. Kit catches her reflection in a glass case outside the office entrance. Her clothing no longer appears to be wet or stained. When she looks down at them, she confirms that the reflection was not an illusion or some trick-of-the-eye. *What the?* Kit says to herself, startled by the change in her clothes.

"You're welcome," says her cane. "We couldn't go in to see the High Priest dressed the way you were."

"Come in, sister!" calls out the High Priest, still looking at a book in his bookshelf.

Before entering, Kit looks down the hallway to see if there are any acolytes milling about. She can see that the door to the rear bell tower is open, revealing the stairwell within. The bell has a high-pitched peal and is used to sound the city alarm. Luckily, it hasn't been rung in many years. Not since the Gizmo uprising ...

Kit gives her head a shake, once again, scaring away the unbidden memories from history class that are inexplicably called to the fore-front of her mind.

"You took your time, Sister Kit." Father Hoarfrost calls from his office. "By my reasoning, you finished your breakfast a long while ago. Where have you been? What have you been doing? Who have you seen? Come in! Sit down!" Hoarfrost had moved from his book-shelf to his window that overlooks the city and the great statue of Ti-tan. He voice has never sounded so stiff, or cold, or on edge.

"I met someone today, your Reverence, from the Frost Forest Monastery. He was disagreeable at first, and perhaps not always in his right mind. We spoke a while, and when he left, he bade me ask you about Mad Brother Edur and the Secret Library." Kit sees his whole body start to tremble.

"He said that, did he? Did he give his name?"

"Yes, your Reverence. He introduced himself as their head archivist, brother Snowbank."

The old priest practically winces at the sound of his name. "Con-tinue, Sister Kit."

"He said the Library was in *Titan's icy buttock*. And that..."

The old priest turns and looks at Kit, his eyes seemingly full of pain, and terror! He walks stiffly to his desk, where a highly polished, wooden box sits. He grabs it and shoves it towards her. "Take it and go!"

It seems that it's only at that moment that Hoarfrost sees the cane Kit is holding. What little colour there was in the man's face immediately disappears. Kit has no idea what is happening but feels it's a good time to go back to her room and look through the box. As she's about to leave, she remembers something.

"Father, brother Snowbank also said to tell you that brother Tyr sends his regards and expects his due on the Feast of Titan's Bounty!" Kit bows slightly to the High Priest and takes her leave. She doesn't see Hoarfrost falling to his knees, his mouth open in a silent wail.

Chapter 18

KIT STEPS INTO HER room, her bed desperately calling to her, when a chorus of voices breaks out from behind. She is quickly surrounded on all sides by fellow acolytes, as one after another congratulates her. There is the unmistakable POP of a bottle of wine being opened. The half-elven acolyte, Silverleaf, gives her a broad grin as he raises the bottle in toast. When Kit smiles back at her friend, he starts filling glasses for everyone to share. Kit thanks Silverleaf for the wine with a small kiss on the cheek, and he blushes scarlet, a trait no doubt inherited from his human father. Most leave after one glass, but a few of Kit's best friends stay behind.

Amara the Gigas explains that the glasses are a graduation gift from her. She'd made them in the shop where she's been taking classes. They're exceptional, made of crystal, each etched with remarkable renderings of Berrathi folk tales. Before Kit can ask, Amara tells her that Danny designed and carved the etchings himself. Kit promptly looks around and wonders aloud why Danny Fox-Dancing, a true-born Berrathi, and her best friend since her arrival six cycles ago, is not here.

Slate the Dwarf laughs, and answers in his recently deepened voice, "Our boy was on a hot date last night! We haven't seen him since."

"What poor fool has fallen under his spell this time?" Kit enquires, her eyes full of mischief. She waits, watching, as her friends all look at each other, and burst out laughing.

"It's Rodrigo, son of Hanzo, the Bear-Clan trader," states Amara, who spits into the fireplace. "He lives and woos dangerously, does our Danny."

"No way! It's Tuneful Songbird, the Shaman's daughter," says Silverleaf, a worried expression on his face. "He'd best not make her sing, or he's married for certain!"

Kit laughs, and the day's craziness fades into the background. She raises her glass for a toast.

"That's our Danny! Say what you will, but truly; everyone loves Danny, and Danny loves everyone! To all of you, I wish you all have a Trial as memorable as mine, and as successful or better! May we all serve Titan with pride!" and the glasses are drained as another bottle is opened. Kit thinks back to one of the many adventures she's shared with this lot, back when they were lowly novices in a class of forty-two. "Say, do you remember..."

"...that time we helped the Walrus woo Moshitoyo's niece?" roars Amara, slapping Kit on the back, nearly sending her flying across the room.

"Now, there was one for the storybooks," says Silverleaf. "Who'd have thought that the heart and soul of a bard beat inside the body of that ill-mannered hooligan?"

"Is that what you think of that sweet young man?" Kit asks the half-elf, "I'd have thought that you, of all of us, wouldn't be so judgemental!"

"His parents are Slavers, and his siblings are Boreal Mariners. What are we to make of him, then?" he retorts. The Boreal Mariners started off as a street gang, but when they got into the slave trade, they became one of the most powerful factions in all of Aarall.

As the group talks about romance and writing poetry, Kit quietly wrestles with the recent events; the slaughter and vampires in Templeton, the firebug invasion, and the completion of the first of Titan's trials. She wants to share them with her friends, but the weight she carries feels like it's crushing her. Kit chuckles quietly to herself, thinking that keeping Runt's secret from them was going to be hard. Kit watches her friends enjoying their revelry. Just the sight of their happiness makes her feel better. Suddenly, all the conversation, the laughter, the good-natured rough housing, suddenly stops. They're all now staring at Kit.

"Hey, what's up? You're awfully quiet, for someone who's the talk of the Temple!" Slate says, his voice filled with concern.

Kit decides that there's one thing she should make them aware of – at least, a little bit.

"I took on some work for Hoarfrost, and ran some errands for Captain Harding…"

"You worked for 'hard-ass Harding'?" teases Amara, "Oh, tell us everything! Sweet Titan, he's so dreamy!"

"I can't tell you everything. But I want all of you to be on alert…" she begins, telling them about the firebugs. "Now, I want you to keep your eyes and ears open. If you can, get the Gizmos involved as well. Listen for any news of strange droppings, or empty shed carapaces, animals going missing, that sort of thing. When you're outside of town, look for any suspicious holes, fires or scorch marks. If you hear or find anything, bring it to Captain Harding's attention. Do *not* hunt them. Stay away from them."

"And just where are you going to be, *Sister Kit*? Are you off on a mission for Titan already, with your *good-looking new friend*?" jibes Amara.

"Sooner or later, you're going to have to introduce him to us. It's not often we get to meet someone who's been *resurrected!*

"Resurrected? Who's been resurrected?"

"Why your friend, Indie, of course," says Amara, waggling her dark shaggy eyebrows at Kit. "Word around the Temple is, that you brought him back from the dead."

Kit let's out an audible groan. "What fool started that story; I wonder?" Kit's eyes study each and every one of her friends, but none of them are willing to 'fess up.'

"Okay, everyone," she calls out. "You've all had a good night's sleep, but I've been awake for over a full day now. You'll meet the good-looking Indie soon enough. I need to get to bed!"

A honeyed baritone voice says seductively, "You were saying it was time to go to bed?" Danny Fox-Dancing stands in the doorway, his normally immaculately styled red hair a tousled mess, his clothes rumpled, and akimbo, his broad-shouldered physique chiseled to perfection, with that damnable infectious grin beaming at them all. "And before any of you ask, I'm not revealing anything about last night, so don't even bother asking! I'm far too polite to speak of such things."

He leaps into the room, and after looking around proclaims, "The same, I'm afraid, cannot be said of all of you! Back to your business, kiss Kit goodnight, and leave the good sister alone with me." There are both protestations and cheers. "I'll get all the info on this *handsome new friend* and tell you all later!"

Kit falls dramatically onto her bed. Danny follows suit.

Kit turns her head towards him. 'Does it get any better, growing older?"

Danny, a full two cycles older, turns to her and replies, "I'm told the first 30 cycles are good. After that it's all downhill."

"That can't be right." Kit says, propping herself up on her elbow.

"Well, for us it is. Elves, Dwarves, Gigas, Shifters, Vamps, Gizmos, Dragons – add a couple hundred."

"That hardly seems fair. Why would Titan only give us forty good cycles?"

"Don't know, Kitten. What I do know is, it's not how long you live, it's how well you live in the time you have."

"How'd you get to be so wise, Foxy?"

"Who are you, and what have you done with Kit?"

Kit can't help but chuckle as she feigns innocence. "What ever do you mean?"

"I mean, in all our years as friends, you have never once, not once, called me wise!" He screws up his face at her, looking both infuriating and irresistible. "You've called me a lot of *other* things, some kind, some cruel, but never wise!"

Kit sticks her tongue out at him. "I don't see the point of stating the obvious!"

"My point exactly!" he exclaims. "You're different!"

Kit gets up off her bed and points at Danny, looking down her arm as she does. "I passed not one, but two trials in what, three days? I've changed from acolyte, to Priest, to *Acknowledged*, in less than a minute. I ate breakfast with someone. I think he was pretending to be a dead brother from the Frost Forest Fathers Monastery. He told me an absurd tale about a Library hidden in Titan's frosty butt and then he gives me a bone cane as a gift. After that, I met with Hoarfrost, who goes psycho on me before he shoves a box, full of who-knows-what, at me and now you're telling me I'm *different*?"

"What do you mean he was pretending to be a frost brother?" Danny props himself up on his elbows, waiting to hear more of this story.

"He said his name was brother Snowbank. When I spoke with Miyuki about him, she said I was lying. She said brother Snowbank was dead and she wanted to know why I would lie about talking to him."

"That is very strange," Danny says with a furrowed brow. This puzzle had too many missing parts for him to figure it out.

Kit plops back down on her bed. It feels like a damn has burst inside her as all of her emotions come flooding out. "Yesterday, I...I watched hundreds of people *killing*, and *being killed*. I killed scores of people, innocent people, while trying to save other innocent people! Titan lent me his power and I called up an earthquake! I fought off a vampire and lived! I almost died today, Danny, oh gods, I almost died today, I almost..."

Danny wraps his big-muscled arms around Kit, squeezing her tightly. As she begins to shake uncontrollably, he draws her in, trying desperately to give her comfort.

"Some were children, Danny. Oh, Titan forgive me, children, Danny..."

"*Shhhh,*" he says, stroking her hair as she buries her face into his shoulder. She's now practically wailing as the flood of emotions utterly consumes her. After what feels like an hour, the sobs finally subside.

As Kit looks up, Danny gently wipes the tears from her eyes. He pulls out a handkerchief from his pocket, offering it to her. As he does, he says quietly, with deadly seriousness, "You know, Kitten, when I said you were different, you could have just told me that you'd simply changed your hair, and I would have been good with that." And they both laugh themselves silly for a few minutes. When the laugher stops, Danny's face once again gets serious. He looks at Kit while holding her at arm's length. "Better?" he smiles.

"Much."

"So, where's this box that Hoarfrost gave you? Have you looked inside? Can I see it?"

Kit finds the box and places it on the bed between the two of them. The size of a large tome, it's been polished to mirror-brightness. It's made of some wood so dark red, that it's almost purple. There appears to be no obvious lid, lock, keyhole or latch mechanism of any kind. They each try to open it, but to no avail. An idea occurs to Kit, "Old magic," she says with a shrug, "simple but very precise. I'm going to try something. Promise you won't laugh!"

"I promise nothing," answers her best friend, "*especially* if it involves nudity." Kit gives him a stern look and shakes her head. "You know, as an acolyte, you're supposed to be chaste."

"That only applies to the *sisters*," Foxy says with a wide grin. "We *brothers* have no such *limitation* put on us." Kit promptly kicks him in the shin. Hard.

While Danny rubs his bruised leg, Kit turns the box so that it faces her, and says with all solemnity, "My name is Sister Kit Standing Bear. You have been given to me in good faith by High Priest Hoarfrost, your previous owner, so that I might learn from what knowledge you may contain. I entreat you, open for me that I might do so."

A silver line shimmers around three sides, a 'click' is heard, and the box opens toward Danny. "Foxy, you're not laughing," she notes.

"If you were looking in the box, Kitten, neither would you be," comes his reply. He turns the opened box toward Kit. Laying on top of sheaves of paper is a small, human skeleton no larger than her hand. There are thin gold wires holding it together. The wire atop the skull has a small loop, which Kit uses to lift up, and delicately place the skull on her pillow. The page below it has a sketch of a skeleton set to one side and writing on the other. The title on the page says, 'Homme Minuscule,' which neither of them can read or understand.

They look through the papers, occasionally coming across other skeletal remains: a tooth, a hand, claws, and notes all written in the same strange script. Many of the pages have drawings of creatures that stand upright, some that walk on four feet. Notes in Jotunnish, which Kit can barely understand, are scribbled with dates and locations. There is, at the bottom of the box, a small book, full of nothing but words in the same foreign tongue. There is also what appears to be a flute, no bigger than a cat's forearm, made of bone with six holes.

"Do you remember SouSou, the novitiate from the East?" asks Danny.

Kit remembers a reed-thin young girl of sixteen cycles, with beautiful gem-shaped eyes and blue-black straight hair.

"She taught me a tune or two," he adds, gently taking the bone flute from Kit's hand.

Kit can't help but wonder why Brother Edur would write in a forgotten language. The thought occurs to her that the notebook may be from the secret Library itself. As she considers this, the strains of a sad, haunting tune fill the air. A tune both gentle and yearning.

The pages in the box begin to shimmer, and suddenly the writing is clear. Kit reads the first few lines and cries out. Danny stops playing, and the translation immediately disappears. Kit tells him what happened, and he begins playing again. As he does, Kit reads the words aloud.

"*The first recorded Game of the Gods, by Anan Noano Berrabbithi. This marks Game number forty-four. The Sea and Land Giants are at war, and the Great Worms churn the ground and have killed the Elk-folk, the Eagle kin and the Bunnikers. The Lion Bugs are advancing, but the Dogmen are fierce. We cower in our caves and wait for the worst to pass. We endure. Sometimes we fight. Often, we defend. Mostly, we patiently avoid the conflicts altogether, and we wait. Sometimes the ones who claim themselves to be gods, help. Sometimes they hinder, but often they simply betray. In the end, the gods wipe out all they have made, leaving the rest to simply die off. Those who do survive have their memories stripped from them before it all begins yet again.*"

Danny continues playing, while Kit turns the page.

"*My family does not forget, for we are the Berrabbithi, and our god, Gaia, has made us strong, so we alone remember. The true Berrabbithi grow fewer in number, as other survivors join us and find love, creating families and offspring of their own. The gods create new peoples, and it all begins again. Such destruction, so much death, and why? We asked Gaia, and for many Games she was silent. Then came an answer: 'They are but bored children, and not to be trusted, or worshipped. You must teach them and help them grow, or this cycle will continue.'*"

Kit sees that many pages have been torn out, and of the remaining final pages, many are stained black with old blood mixed with ink. The final page has seven lines, of which only the first three and the last one is legible:

Three will try. Eight shall die. Three will go.

The last line written in the book reads 'The Library holds the key.'"

Kit closes the book, places it and the skeleton into the wooden box. She holds out her hand, asking Danny to hand over the bone flute. He's about to hand it to her when it simply vanishes beneath his skin. He looks at Kit in astonishment!

"Somewhere inside me, Kit Standing Bear, is a weird bone that's also a magic flute, very possibly thousands of years old. And to think *I* was calling *you* different! You know, Sister, that what we've just read smacks of blasphemy. That if it's true, and Anan Noano was sane when he or she wrote this, it changes everything we know about...well, maybe, everything?"

"Yes." Kit replies, nodding her head. "And I'm going to find that Secret Library tomorrow. The last lines of the book; those were the words of the prophecy, and it said that the Library holds the key!"

"You mean, we're going to find it."

"This isn't a child's game, Foxy," Kit cautions him.

"On the contrary, Kitten, I think it's all a very old game. And we're no longer pieces to be played. We're now players. Or, at least, you are." Foxy leans back onto his elbows and waggles his eyebrows at her.

Kit punches him in the stomach. Hard. While he's holding his gut, feigning severe injury, Kit drags him by the heel off the bed, dropping him on the cold stone floor with a resounding thud. She points to the door, making her point clear. "I need my sleep."

"Sleep tight, Kitten," he says as he exits, closing the door behind him.

Chapter 19

BOTH HER MIND AND BODY are utterly exhausted, but sleep eludes Kit. She lays in bed, staring up at the wooden beams above. As she does, she is reminded of a time, back when she was ten and still living in Berrathia. As the memory takes hold, Kit is no longer a priest in the Temple; she is but a child sitting under the night sky, a star-filled tapestry, with her mother at her side.

Kit looks up at the stars, startled to see the Hunter, the Healer, The Wise One and the Warrior, each in opposing directions to their opposite. For the Berrat, it is the night called Rite of Way, a time of spirit guides and pathfinding.

This is the night all children who are the age of ten, must be accompanied by their fathers to a place in the mountains, the forest, or the meadows. Any place which is special to their family. After having fasted for a full day, each child is taken to this special place and left alone, with their father watching from a safe distance. Through the night, each child must wait for the Great Spirits to show them which path in life they are to follow.

"Ananak," a term of endearment used by Berrat children when speaking to their mother or grandmother, "why do I have no father?" Kit had asked her mother this question before, but she would never answer. "All the other children have fathers with them."

Kit's mother, Riva, looks at her, her eyes filled with sadness. "I have not wanted to share my secrets with anybody," she says slowly, carefully choosing each word before she speaks. "But on this night, your rite of way, I will answer whatever question you ask of me."

Kit watches as her mother's lower lip begins to quake and her fingers fidget while she tries to find the words. With a hitch in her voice, she begins. "Not long before you came into my life, our village was raided by slavers. They killed many of us, and many more were taken into captivity. I was one of the those who were taken."

Kit sits and watches carefully as the pain of recalling the memory takes hold of Riva. "Ananak, if the memories cause you pain, I don't need to hear them."

"They are painful," she responds, taking a deep breath to help steady herself, "but you do need to hear this." Casting her eyes up to the heavens, she continues the story. "While in captivity, one of the vampire guards decided that he found me attractive. Rather than let me be sold off, he decided to turn me and take me as his mate. Sweet Gaia, he was so strong. He easily overpowered me, sinking his teeth into my neck. At first, it hurt. A lot. But a moment later the excruciating pain passed and in its place was a profound sense of peace and belonging. I thought that's what happened when somebody was turned, but when the guard pulled himself away from me, my blood dripping down his chin, he looked terrified. His eyes were wide, and he began to babble nonsense at me. A moment later, he rushed from my cage, leaving the door wide open. I bolted from my cell, along with every other person in there with me. We were immediately set upon by guards, but I managed to escape. I was too afraid to see what was happening to the others. I just ran, as fast as my feet would take me."

"Ananak, are you ... a vampire?" Like so many other times in Kit's life, the words came tumbling out of her mouth before she had a chance to consider what harm they may cause. But, in this instance, her mother just smiled and let out a thin, nervous laugh.

"A vampire? No, I was not turned that night. I don't know why, but I wasn't." Riva began to run her hands over her pant-legs, as though she was trying to remove wrinkles that weren't actually there. "When I made it home, I told my tale, exactly as it happened, to the village elders. They sent me to the shaman to be *inspected*. She took me into a sweat tent, where we stayed for what seemed like hours. I told her the tale, and while I did, she prayed and called to Gaia to protect me. Just before we were done, she told me that my experience had left me barren, but before the moon was full, I would have a child."

Kit was only ten cycles, but she understood the significance of the shaman's words. "How could you have a child if you are barren?" she asked. Her mother had never spoken so openly to her and she was afraid to break the spell, but again the words were out before she could stop them.

"I didn't understand either," Riva laughs. This time her laugh is genuine. "But, as predicted by the shaman, it happened." Before continuing, Kit's mother closes her eyes. "It was a moonless night. I was laying in my cot and I heard the cries of a baby outside the door to my hut. I opened it, to see what was happening. There was nobody there. Again, I heard the cries, but now they were further away. I walked between the huts, following the cries as they continued to move away from me. Panicked, believing a child was being abducted, I ran through the darkness. Before I knew it, I was a good distance away from the village, at the edge of the forest."

Kit's mother's eyes are still shut, but her expression changes to that of pure joy. Kit could swear that she could actually *feel* what her mother is feeling.

"When I entered into the forest," she continues, "I saw a light. It was warm and inviting. It drew me to it. As I got closer, the light got brighter. I was filled with peace, tranquility and, most of all, love. A voice, so sweet and caring said to me, *'On this night, I entrust unto you my child. Where I must go, and what I must do, she cannot come. But know this, good Riva, she will change the world, for Gaia has foreseen it.'*"

Kit can barely breathe. Gaia, the earth goddess, the great spirit, spoke of her to her birthmother? "Ananak, what happened next? What did my birthmother look like? Did she actually speak with Gaia?"

"I don't know what your mother looked like. She was bathed in light, making it impossible for me to see her. I can't say for certain if she spoke with Gaia, but she told me that she had." Riva is looking up at the sky as she finishes the tale. She then looks back at Kit. "The next thing I remember, I was walking into the village with a bawling baby in my arms." She smiles warmly at Kit. "That would be you, Kitten."

"What happened next? Did you take me to see the shaman?"

Riva's face suddenly goes dark. "No, Kitten, I didn't. I didn't get a chance to. By the time I had returned, many of the villagers were awake. You were making enough noise to raise the dead." She laughs lightly at the comment. "When the elders saw me, they took you away from me, stripped you of your clothing, and examined you from head to toe. Because you were not Berrat, they did not want you in the village. And ..."

"What, Ananak? What?"

"They claimed you were an abomination. You had 'growths' between your shoulder blades, thin, nearly imperceptible ridges. They were about to take you away when the shaman came out from her lodge. She insisted you be returned to me, at once. There was a heated discussion, but in the end, I got you back. Reluctantly, they allowed us to stay in the village."

"Oh, I see," Kit replies. Her heart is breaking. She could hardly breathe. "That's why everyone hates me?"

"No, my sweetness, my Kitten. They do not hate you ... they fear you."

"But I'm just a girl! Why would they fear me?" Kit's practically shouting at her mother. Her blood boiling with rage.

"Hush now, my Kitten," Riva takes her child's hands in her own. "Almost everyone fears the unknown. The circumstances of your arrival were, well, unprecedented." Suddenly Riva ends the story. "It's time to end the questions. I must leave you now so that you may continue with the rite."

"Ananak, please don't leave me. I'm ... afraid."

Riva reaches into the small satchel that she carries over her shoulder. She produces an ulu, a wolf-bone utility knife, commonly used within the tribe. "Here," she says as she offers it to her daughter. "Keep this with you. It will keep you safe."

Kit holds the knife in her small hands. Surprisingly, it fits perfectly. As she examines it, she sees that it's old. Very old. "Thank you, mother. Was this your knife when you were young?"

"It is the very knife I held when I went through the night of my own Rite of Way," she says. There is a tinge of, something, in her voice.

"Tell me about your rite, mother." Riva shakes her head in reply. "But you said I could ask you anything this night and that you would answer me."

"After. After you have completed your rite, I will tell you."

"Now! Tell me now, please, Ananak. You promised."

"Okay, I'll tell you, but only because I promised ..." Riva takes a deep breath, tears almost immediately welling up in her eyes. "My experience was, difficult." She looks back at Kit, almost pleading her not to ask for more information. When she doesn't stop her, Riva reluctantly continues. "During my rite, I, too, was frightened, and my father gave me an ulu to hold onto; that very same ulu I just gave you. I took the ulu and clutched it close to myself, while my father moved away, watching me from afar. I waited and waited for my spirit guide to come. I waited for so long that I fell asleep. I was awakened by the sound of a bleating sheep. It startled me, and when I jerked out of my sleep, I cut my hand on my ulu. Deeply. A moment later, the sheep was standing before me, its face only inches away from my own. I took her face in my hands, accidentally smearing my blood all over it.

The pain in my hand vanished immediately. When I looked, the cut was gone and so was the sheep."

At this point, Riva is deep into her story. Her eyes have practically glazed over as she continues. "My father came running to my side, his eyes wild. 'A blood covered sheep!' he yelled. 'You were visited by a blood covered sheep!' I tried to explain what had happened, but my hand was healed. The cut was gone. When we returned to the village, he forced me to tell the elders. I tried to tell them what happened, but my father interrupted, continuing to present the story as he had witnessed it."

When she looks at Kit again, there is fire in her eyes. Hate. "My father. My own father would not believe me. The elders would not believe me. My father's version spoke of an omen, an ill omen and that my life would be forfeit. I was to be slaughtered, and with me, many of my family and tribes-people."

"But why? Ananak, why wouldn't they listen?"

Riva drops her chin to her chest. It seemed that she had resigned herself to the fate that they had decreed. "We are a superstitious people, Kitten. We believe in many things. Some are true, some are the ravings of lunatics."

Kit wraps her small arms around her mother's neck, taking her in a warm embrace. "I'm glad Old Sky Eyes let you come with me tonight."

"You have no father," her mother says. "If he didn't let me come, you'd have missed out." She pulls away from Kit's embrace, lightly brushing the hair away from her eyes. "Old Sky Eyes, he's the wisest elder in our village. Perhaps the wisest in generations. He sees what others do not. He sees *you*, Kitten. The others did not want you to partake of the ritual, but he overrode them all, for you."

Riva stands up, and smiles. "Enough stories. The night is nearly over. Dawn will be upon us soon and you have not yet begun the ritual. Little piece of my soul, my little Kitten, when in doubt, listen to your heart. It will always speak the truth, even if it isn't what you want to hear. Now, may your path be revealed unto you, and may it lie straight and level before you." She presses a small stone into Kit's hand. "Last night, I dreamed that I gave you this stone." She gives her a quick kiss and runs to a location far enough away for Kit to be alone, but close enough that she can keep an eye on her.

Kit watches her mother as she takes up her position. She can barely see her in the distance. Knowing that she is looking over her, Kit thinks of all that had been said tonight. What path does she want to take? Will it be one of the Great Four, or will it be one of the many paths in-between? Kit leans toward the Warrior, and yet part of her yearns to help, like the Healer. She decides to put her worries aside. She quietly listens to her heartbeat as it mingles with the quiet of the cool midsummer's night.

What felt like only moments later, the full moon emerges from behind the clouds and bathes the clearing in a soft glow. Kit hears the beating of strong wings. She spots an eagle perching on a rocky cliff, looking down at her. A slight rustle to her right draws her attention away, revealing a hare eating from a small bush of bearberries. Hares are never active at night, Kit thinks, and she feels a shiver run down her spine. There's a soft scraping of leaves and bark, far in front of her, and as she turns to see what's making it, Kit catches a glimpse of a sizable black shadow moving in the shrubs to her left.

Suddenly a stoat, a large weasel-like creature, launches towards the rabbit.

Without a second thought, Kit throws the stone in her hand at the hare, who, startled at the sound, runs off and vanishes just before the stoat lands on the now-empty space. It swivels it head towards Kit and hisses.

A chorus of shrill cries causes the stoat to dash back from whence it came. As it does, it is set upon by a wolverine, who swipes at its belly with a wickedly clawed paw. Without thinking, Kit jumps onto the animal. Using her ulu, she slashes open its throat. It's dead within seconds. She's about to pick up the wounded and unconscious stoat when the eagle launches itself towards it. Kit hears more cries. She instinctively knows that what she's considering is perhaps the stupidest thing she could ever do. But she hears Riva's voice in her head, *"listen to your heart."*

Without further hesitation, Kit throws herself over the stoat, shielding it from the eagle's attack. Pain blossoms in her left arm as the eagle's claws find purchase. Kit slowly raises her head, to see the eagle staring back at her. Intently. Intelligently. What does one say to a Spirit Eagle?

"This stoat has hungry children. I do not want them to be without a mother; without someone to care for them. They'll die otherwise."

The eagle cocks its head slightly.

"I would have died without a mother, without anyone to take care of me." Kit's not sure if that was the right thing to say, but the eagle continues to stare at her, so she continues. "I don't know if the wolverine also has hungry children, and if it does, I'm very sorry. But the stoat's babies are here, and it would have eaten them, too. If you are hungry, there is the wolverine." She moves her head towards the dead animal.

To her surprise, the eagle flies over to the wolverine's carcass and slowly begins to feed, all the while keeping its eyes trained on Kit.

The stoat stirs beneath Kit. It has been gravely wounded. She has no herbs, no poultice; Kit knows no spells. She goes to the bearberry bush, hoping to feed the baby stoats a berry mash. But the bush is covered with moths. Bear moths, by the dozens! They swarm past Kit as she approaches, and then cover the dying stoat. They stop its bleeding, vanishing into the wound. For a few moments, the stoat appears to float above the ground, and then it awakens, standing on its four legs.

It looks at Kit, and then back at the eagle. It appears to be waiting.

The hare appears before Kit, holding the stone in its mouth, which it drops at Kit's feet. It then stands on its hind legs and bows to her, before crossing over to the stoat. The stoat immediately kills it, shredding it into small pieces. With care, it carries the pieces to its babies to eat. Kit drops to her knees, filled with a sense that a great lesson has unfolded before her. Even though she can only understand a small part of it, she's confident that one day it's meaning will become clear to her.

The spirit animals vanish, one by one, until the eagle lands in front of Kit. It picks up the stone with its beak. Tossing it into the air the stone is briefly enveloped by bear moths, and then falls into Kit's hand. The eagle vanishes in a blinding flash of moonlight. Kit turns to find Riva behind her, shaking badly.

"Ananak," Kit says breathlessly, "Did you see that?"

Her mother grabs Kit firmly by the wrist, giving her a shake. "I saw nothing. You saw nothing. You will not speak of this. Do you hear me? Do you? You will not speak of this."

Kit yanks her arm out from her mother's grasp.

"I will NOT be silent," she states, challenging her mother. "The Blessed Four – all of them – came to me! All of them! I deserve to know what this means!" Seeing Riva cast her gaze to the ground, Kit adds with sincerity, "Don't you want to know what it means, Ananak?"

"I know what it means, child. You think the gods have blessed you. That's what you think, but you're wrong. They didn't bless you; they've cursed you! I have seen so many futures for you, Kitten, and there is blood and death awaiting you in so many of them. Let others give themselves to the gods to play with! You will say that nothing happened, do you hear me? Nothing happened!" Riva shakes with fear, and sorrow, and anger.

A strange chill runs through Kit, blowing upon her heart, and awakens her own cold anger. Old hurts surface. Slights that she's suffered from childhood acquaintances and neighbors. "I can't ever be the Berrat child you've wanted me to be! You took me in. You gave me your love, and for that I will be eternally grateful! But this tribe hates us both! Do you think my experience is going to make it worse? Do you want me to lie to protect me, or to protect you?"

Riva slaps Kit so hard that she staggers backwards, loses her balance and falls awkwardly to the ground. Tears stream down her face, and she looks deeply wounded, as if her mother had stabbed her in the heart with her ulu. It occurs to Kit that, in a way, her own words were sharper than any knife could ever be, and it is too late to take them back. She wishes that she could. *Where did that anger come from?* she thinks to herself.

"You ..." wails Riva, "are not of my womb. But you are my heart and my soul, even if you hate me. I cannot stop you from telling the truth. For your own sake, leave. It may keep the tribe, and you, safe. Go! Being god-chosen does not mean your every step is blessed, or that your path will be painless. I will tell the elders that I fell asleep, and that when I awoke you were gone."

Kit watches in silence as her mother leaves. She's torn. She doesn't know what to say or do. Her words taste like ash in her mouth. After a few minutes Kit begins to chase her down the mountainside, wailing for her to stop and wait. In the distance she sees fathers and children walking back towards the Elder's camp, torches flickering like tiny fireflies in the darkness.

She continues racing hard to catch up with her mother. Regardless of how Kit feels, Riva is her mother. She saved her. Raised her. Nurtured her. Kit would do anything for her.

When Kit finally catches up to Riva, she takes her hand in her own. "I'm sorry, mother. I love you. I will do as you say. I will remain silent." She looks up, waiting for a reaction, something that says that everything is alright, but Riva keeps her eyes forward. Kit can feel her heart breaking, but she knows that she's only getting a small piece of what she deserves.

When they reach the Elder's camp it's still night, with the Blessed Four still shining in the sky. The Elders sit in a row, Old Sky Eyes in the center, and two others on each side of him. The fathers and children, seated in front of the Elders, all look at Kit and Riva, who are the last to arrive. The young are called by name, and their fathers walk with them. Each child is asked about what had happened to them, their fathers there to verify their stories. Many of the children were chosen to be gatherers, several to work in crafting, a couple to teach and one to be a storyteller. Three of the children were chosen to be hunters, and finally, one to be a warrior. A warrior who was apparently needed elsewhere.

The warrior's father limps slowly forward, tearfully reporting that the Bear Spirit had taken his son this night. He had watched as they ascended to the stars. Old Sky Eyes looks with pity on the man, feeling the pain he is enduring. "The Bear is the most powerful of the warrior spirits," he says with reverence. "If he needed a sacrifice, your son, then he took him with cause. Something is coming. There is no other reason for this. Your son's life is the price for the Bear's protection over us. We thank you for the great service your son has provided to our community this night." The rest of the elders echo the sentiment.

At last, it's Kit's turn. Old Sky Eyes motions her forward. She wastes no time, taking her place before him, getting down on one knee. Kit bows to each of the Elders, and finally to Old Sky Eyes himself. She feels the warm, reassuring hand of her mother on her shoulder, offering Kit her love and support.

Finally, Old Sky Eyes speaks. "Kit Standing Bear. You have been raised as one of our own, yet you are not Berrat by birth. I would be lying if I didn't say there were some who did not think you *worthy*

of taking part in the Rite of Way, but I overruled them. All of them."
He chuckles as he eyes the other Elders. "So, tell us, child. What happened tonight? What path has been opened to you?"

When Kit lifts her head to speak, her mother clears her throat. "She is ashamed to speak, O Wise One, so I will speak for her," states Riva, "Nothing happened. Nothing at all."

A murmur works its way around the assembled Berrathians. The other elders grin smugly. "Quiet!" shouts Old Sky Eyes, who coughs and looks at Kit. She could swear his eyes hold a glint of laughter. "Is this true, Kit?" he asks.

If Kit says yes, then she lies, and it will insult the spirits who manifested to her. If she says no, she will disobey her mother, potentially causing her undo pain and suffering. With no answer seeming to be the *right* answer, Kit chooses to say nothing at all, clamping her mouth shut before words, unbidden words, come spilling out of her mouth. She's about to stand and walk away when she hears the sound of wings.

An eagle made of moonlight lands on Kit's knee. She is soon joined by the hare, the stoat and the wolverine. Hovering above Kit's head is a cloud of bear moths. Behind her, Riva sinks to her knees, sobbing quietly.

A warm wind blows, taking the moonlight spirits with it. Those assembled are quiet. Except for Old Skye Eyes, who claps his hands and steps out of his chair to embrace Kit. "Anyone who still thinks this child here is no true Berrat can leave right now."

"What does it mean, Wise One?" Riva asks.

Old Sky Eyes considers the question, as he lets his gaze fall upon the other elders as well as the gathered community. "Never have I heard of a child being chosen by the Healer, the Wise One, the Hunter, the Warrior and The Great Spirit herself. What does it mean? It means that all paths are open before Kit Standing Bear. Her path is her own to choose, and she is not bound to any. They show a remarkable faith in you, young Kit."

"She will leave us. I have seen it." Riva can barely contain her anguish.

"Maybe she will, maybe she won't. The choice is not mine, nor yours, nor the Spirits. It is hers and hers alone."

"Riva," asks Sky Eyes, "are you still having visions?"

"They have never stopped."

"Visit me tomorrow," he says with a slight bow. "We can speak of it at length."

Kit rises and wanders among the other children. They all keep their distance from her. "Spirit-touched," some of them murmur, making the sign against evil. This was the night when Kit's life changed, everything bringing her here, to this moment, under the signs of the Blessed Four.

When the memory comes to its end, Kit closes her eyes. At last, she falls into a deep and dreamless sleep.

Chapter 20

WHEN KIT AWAKES FROM her sleep, it's nighttime. She lies in her bed, staring up at the darkness, wondering how long it's been since she closed her eyes. Suddenly, she begins to panic. The sun's first light will show her the way into the Library and it's a long hike to the statue, plus there's the climb up the mountain ahead of her as well. She jumps out of bed, her feet landing squarely on Lump's tail. He barks and leaps to his feet, practically knocking Kit off hers.

"How did you get in here?" she asks him. It's not like he's going to answer, but she's always talked to him like he was human. "Did somebody let you in while I was sleeping?" He whines softly, nuzzling up against Kit's thigh. "We've got to hurry, my furry friend!"

Kit quickly lights a lantern and throws her armor on, before choosing a pair of heavy hiking boots to wear. It's not like there are a lot of choices available. Priests and acolytes alike are afforded two pairs of footwear, light boots suitable for indoors and good weather, and hiking boots suitable for practically every other occasion. In this case, Kit had the fine pair of boots that the villagers had given her for saving a boy, but for now, the heavier boots are what she'll need.

Hearing footsteps outside her room, Kit pokes her head out the door, seeing Amera and Silverleaf heading towards the Temple. "What time is it?" she calls out to them.

Amera looks at her and smiles.

"Just waking up, Kit? You must have been exhausted from your trials."

When Silverleaf sees the impatient look on Kit's face, he quickly answers. "About thirty minutes past sundown."

Without so much as a thank you, Kit pulls her head back into her room and slams the door shut. She's got plenty of time before she needs to head out. Sunrise isn't for at least ten hours. Lump must have known it wasn't time to leave. He's curled up in a ball on Kit's bed, peacefully snoring away.

Kit takes a deep sigh as she pulls the box out from beneath her bed. She's a Priest of Titan who's in possession of blasphemous articles that should have been destroyed by High Priest Hoarfrost. The Secret Library is the ravings of a lunatic, the papers in the box must have had hallucinogenic powder on them, and on the cane as well!

Kit opens the box and starts flipping through its papers, which are indecipherable without Danny playing the strange bone flute. The flute that is somehow now inside him. Convinced that the box, and all its strange contents are evil, Kit tosses it into the room's small fireplace and prepares to start a fire.

In moments, flames blaze all around the box, and with a satisfied sigh, she waits. And waits. And after she has relit the fire for the third time, she realizes that it's useless. She's startled by a grumbling "ahem" coming from the corner of the room. The only thing there is the dragon bone staff, which she spoke to yesterday as if it were alive. Which it isn't, of course. It's evil.

She's thinking this as the eye-jewels come ablaze and it says, "Ordinary fire doesn't seem to harm it. Shall we try dragon flame?"

Speaking to enchanted, and possibly evil objects is not a course taught at the Fist of Titan. Kit learned how to enchant weapons and armor at the local smithy, but those were ordinary things that lacked awareness, much less possessing the ability of independent thought.

"Or do you plan on wasting more kindling?"

The temple didn't teach sarcasm either, but she has no trouble recognizing it when she hears it.

"What may I call you?" Kit respectfully, yet sternly, asks.

The cane's sky-dragon head appears to grin. "You ask my name? Well," it says with deep solemnity, "you offered me yours in good faith. You may call me Fury, though I am but a part of Fury. Let's give dragon fire a try, shall we?"

Fury lets forth a gout of flame, hot enough to force Kit to back away from its intense heat. But the box stubbornly remains intact. "Well," he says, "Unsurprising, but it was worth a try."

"Someone wishes the mighty Titan's honor besmirched, and his legacy defamed. They will pay dearly!" Kit declaims, her voice full of righteous fury.

"Titan was a fool, with no discernable honor and no legacy except his dreadful gameplay. And," adds Fury, "he was a truly awful father to his sons."

For a moment, Kit is speechless. Only a moment, though, as the implications of what was said sinks in. "You knew Titan? And his sons? Impossible! Titan is the All-Father, the Creator, the..."

Two pairs of eyes, one Elven, one Gigas, peer into the room, their owners safely hidden from view.

"Titan fathered two sons, but you could hardly call him a father. And he is one of many creators." As Fury retorts, there is a cold harshness to his tone.

"Blasphemy!" Kit screams as she begins smashing the cane against the wall.

"Kit, for Titan's sake, stop that!" yells Amera, running from behind the archway, followed by Silverleaf. "You'll..."

"No, she won't," reply both Silverleaf and Fury simultaneously.

"SPIES!" Kit cries out, as she starts taking swipes at both her friends. Kit backs Amera into a corner and is about to crack her skull with the sky-dragon cane when she's struck on the back of her skull.

Kit awakens to Silverleaf holding an ice compress to her head, and Amera deep in discussion with Fury. On her lap is the hated box, with all its damnable contents.

"I'm sorry for cracking you in the head," Silverleaf says, wincing at the bump that he gave her. "You kind of went nuts on us. When you just left after asking for the time, we ... umm ... wondered what you were doing. When we overheard you talking with ... someone, we decided to stop and listen."

"Eavesdrop, you mean!" Kit scolds, causing Silverleaf to blush badly.

"You know Titan?" Amera asks Fury.

"No," Fury replies, "but I know his sons."

"How the heck, and more importantly, why, did his sons trap him?" asks Silverleaf.

Before Fury can answer, Kit gives her friend the same answer that Sister Caribou gave her, the day she asked that very same question in class: "Firstly, Titan allowed his sons to *think* they'd caught him unaware, letting them trap him underwater and sealing him in an icy prison."

Fury laughs, but Kit presses on, "But the mighty and loving father, Titan, did not see how deeply his sons' resentment ran. The spells they had bound him with were hate-filled and reinforced with the fear that they would never live up to his expectations. And so, Titan is calling upon us, his faithful, to show his sons the power of self-reliance and unconditional love. He gives us trials to overcome, that we may be worthy to free him from the bonds placed upon him by his thankless and loathsome children."

"Spoken like a true believer," Amera says cautiously. Kit senses she's about to ask a loaded question.

"Thank you, Acolyte. How else may I enlighten you?" Kit asks with a wink and a smile.

"Why are the all-mighty Titan's sons' names not mentioned anywhere?" asks Silverleaf, in a very condescending tone.

"They shall remain nameless until they have repented their actions, at which time Titan himself will reveal them, so that they, too, may be revered." Kit gives Silverleaf a smug smile as, once again, unbidden memories from her theology classes come bursting out of her.

"Their names are Bael and Ollin." Fury says in a matter-of-fact tone. "I don't know what has become of Ollin, but Bael is trapped in Helja." Fury pauses. "We've doddled for too long, Kit, if you want to get to where you're going on time, we need to leave. Now."

Kit quickly apologizes to her friends for running out on them, as she grabs her knapsack, her weapons, and Fury, and bolts for the door. As she races down the hallway, Lump stays close on her heels.

Chapter 21

KIT TAKES A QUICK TRIP down to the kitchens to pick up some supplies for the journey. She's utterly famished, and she thinks she's going to need some extra energy to get her through the night. As she rushes into the kitchens' dining hall, she sees Miyuki sitting at one of the tables, chatting with a few acolytes and some of the kitchen staff.

"I don't know if you're coming or going," Miyuki says with a laugh, "but if you don't slow down, you're going to slip and break a leg. The floors were just washed and they're still wet!"

As though Miyuki had predicted it, Kit skids across the wet stone floor, slamming into one of the benches.

"What's the hurry, sweetie?" Miyuki laughs, as she excuses herself from the table.

"I'm, um, taking a hike up to Titan's statue." Kit doesn't want to say too much, but if she's going to get what she needs, she has to tell Miyuki something close to the truth. "I'm going to be taking Titan's Trail."

"Titan's trail? In the dark? This time of year?" Miyuki whistles at the prospect. "With the strange melt that's going on, the trail's going to be dangerous."

Kit gives her friend a look of desperation. "Can you pack me some food for the journey?"

Miyuki gives Kit a quick wink. "Of course, I can. Follow me."

Kit and Runt follow Miyuki back into the kitchens. Miyuki heads over to one of the larger clay ovens, and pulls a large iron tray from over top of it, pouring its contents into a sizable cloth sack.

"Here you go," Miyuki says, as she hands Kit the sack of warm wayfarer's muffins, filled to bursting with sweet-tart snowberries. She's also prepared a large flask with strong cocoafee, a mixture of strong black coffee and hot cocoa.

Without another word, Miyuki, the sister, goes back to her work.

Kit just stands there, watching carefully. There's significant skill required to properly knead dough, and Miyuki is recognized as someone who has not only mastered it but has elevated it to an art-form. She could have been fabulously wealthy had she opened her own bakery. But the untimely deaths of her firstborn and her husband from a wasting sickness sent her seeking solace here at the Temple, and here she stayed.

Kit walks up behind Miyuki as she's rolling out the last of the bread dough for the next morning's mixed berry and nut loaves and wraps her arms around her. "I love you, my *very* big sister!" Kits says, meaning it with all her heart.

"My hands are full of flour and bits of dough, dearie, or I'd be hugging you back. Where is this coming from? I mean, it's sweet and all, and I love you right back and more, but what brought this on, if you don't mind my asking?" She grabs a small boar sausage from a plate, and throws it to Lump, who possessively carries it somewhere secluded to devour it. "Don't you have an adventure to run off to?"

"Oh, Miyuki," Kit says as she continues to hug her friend. "The last few days have been crazy. Really crazy. Things have happened. Some important things, I think. And I just think my life is, you know, *changing*."

"Ah, sweetie, don't fret. Life is like traveling down a fast-flowing river, riding in a tiny boat. It's going to take you where it takes you. You might be able to steer it one direction or another along the way, but ultimately, you're going to go in whatever direction it's flowing."

Kit gives her friend a strange look. "I have no idea what that means," she says, grimacing somewhat while trying to figure it out.

Miyuki starts to laugh, causing her ample rolls to jiggle in multiple different directions. "Me neither! It sounded really good in my head before I actually spoke the words though." Miyuki gives Kit another big hug, "You should get going, you know, down to wherever the river is going to take you." She pulls back and brushes a wayward lock of hair out of Kit's face. "Danny was here before you, and he's been waiting for you on that Trail for quite a while. I know that you are best friends and all, but even *his* patience will grow thin."

Chapter 22

AS KIT MAKES HER WAY to Titan's ice statue, she thinks back to the contents of the box, the words of Anan, and the revelations gifted to her. One part of her want to dismiss the ideas, but the doubt is now there, in the back of her mind.

Before she knows it, Kit has reached the statue and navigated her way past Titan's massive feet. Looking to the east, Kit figures there are about ninety minutes, give or take, until sunrise. She's cutting it very thin.

Just as she's rounding the corner, Kit finds Danny Fox-Dancing sitting on one of the two large rocks that mark the beginning of the trail that leads up the mountain, behind the great Statue of Titan. Lump covers him with wolf-doggy kisses, and from somewhere in his rucksack Danny produces a musk-ox thigh bone. How he knew the dog would be with her was a mystery, but that was one of his odd quirks. Often, he'd bring things you'd have forgotten you might need.

Kit shows him her flask, and of course he produces a mug, which Kit fills halfway with cocoafee. She looks upwards to see the stern, cold face of Titan, almost half a league above.

"Magnificent, I must admit," Danny says, "but it does make you wonder..."

"Wonder what?" Kit asks, putting the flask away.

"How the heck, and more importantly, why, did his sons trap him?"

"Danny!!!" Kit shouts admonishingly, "That's blasphemy!"

"No, it isn't!" he says, shaking his head. "Don't you go all high-and-mighty, Priestess, on me! C'mon, Kit, think! Was he being a jerk? You know how dads can be a jerk sometimes, eh?"

"No, *acolyte* Fox-Dancing, I don't! Or have you forgotten?" Lump-on-a-Log bumps against Kit's waist, softly whining. Kit reaches down, and absentmindedly scratches his head.

Danny *had* forgotten that Kit grew up without a father and apologizes.

"Let's start. It's a long way up, even for a trip to Titan's waist. And look," he says, holding up his lantern and pointing at wet snow patches, iced-over patches, and some mud-slick sections, "this sort of path is going to slow us down." Kit follows his gaze, watching tiny rivulets wending their way downwards.

They have only been climbing for a few minutes when Danny grabs Kit by the arm and hauls her to the side of the path. Two bucketsful of water smash into the path where she had just been standing, washing away rocks and mud, along with a good six inches of the ledge the path occupied. "Where...how...?" Kit stammers.

Danny carefully sticks his head over and looks up. "That water probably came from Titan's elbow, but I'm guessing it may have come from higher up, possibly his head."

"That's impossible. There's no snow up there, no mountain. That's just, impossible."

"Why? Because it's magical ice?" asks Danny. Meanwhile, Lump rolls around in the mud, enjoying every filthy, wonderful moment.

They start climbing again, and although the small party is in darkness, it is indeed quite warm. Kit unclasps the top of her armor, to an accompanying whistle from Danny. Lump thinks the whistle is for him, of course, and bounds between the two of them. He also chooses that moment to shake wildly, ridding himself of any mud clinging to his long, red fur, spraying both Kit and Danny in the process.

"You haven't answered my question. Why can't magical ice melt?"

"Magical ice," Kit states, as though she's speaking to a child, "doesn't melt. It's *magical*!"

"Not even," asks Danny with a sly grin, "if it meets *magical fire*?"

Kit's only beginning to see his point when she hears a deep, rumbling laughter. She looks around frantically for its source when Danny shrieks, "Your cane! Your c - c - cane!!" Kit holds it in front of herself to see its mouth wide open, tongue curled back, teeth exposed, laughing hysterically.

"Oh," Kit giggles slightly. "Danny, meet Fury. He's the *gift* I told you about, the one the guy pretending to be Brother Snowbank gave me. He's a dragon spirit stuck inside this dragon bone cane. Pretty awesome, eh? And he knows Titan's sons...which makes him really, really old..."

Suddenly, Lump grabs the cane from her hand and starts running up and down the path with it.

Kit calms Danny down, and explains the strange gift she received from the demented old Brother Snowbank. "Lump, come here, boy!" The retriever returns with the dragon cane, dripping with saliva. Upon Kit grabbing hold of it, its jewel-blue eyes rake her with a critical gaze.

"*That was the most...*" he begins, blowing a drop of wolf-dog spit away from his snout, "*...the most humiliating thing to happen to me in eighteen hundred years!*"

"I apologize for Lump, he thought you were a..."

"*I know what he thought, young human. He thinks highly of you, and very highly indeed of your friend.*" The sky-dragon's head appears to grin. "*Hello, friend of Kit. You may call me Fury.*"

"Fury?" repeats Danny, "Where have I heard that name? Didn't Silverleaf mention a mythical Dragonlord named Fury?"

"That would be me," Fury says with a grin. "Or perhaps, more accurately, I am a part of that mythical dragon lord, named Fury."

As the group climbs another section of the trail, reaching just above Titan's knee, Danny asks, "Fury, why were you laughing earlier, when I said magical fire might melt magical ice?"

"Because, despite your being human, you actually had the answer you were looking for. It takes magical heat to melt magical ice."

Danny watches as Lump laps up several mouthfuls from a small pool formed by the water dripping down from Titan's arms. "Is that going to…"

"Hurt him?" says Fury. "Maybe, maybe not. Will it change him, or you, for that matter, should you drink it? Probably."

Suddenly an angry growl issues from Lump. A swarm of fireflies suddenly appears on the path before him. He begins barking frantically. The fireflies coalesce into the rough form of a robust woman. "Your journey ends here," she says, with a maniacal laugh. As she finishes saying the words, the fireflies disappear, only to be replaced by four ravening wolverines.

"Lump, come!" Kit screams at the dog, but two of the wolverines have already descended on him. Lump manages to grab one of them by the throat, ending its life immediately. The second has a secure bite on Lump's tail, as he starts dragging him towards the others. Before Kit even has a chance to reach for her hammer, an arrow strikes the wolverine holding Lump just behind its shoulder. The wolverine bellows in agony for a brief moment before falling limp on the ground.

"Lump, come!" Kit calls to him again. This time Lump is able to comply. His tail is badly mangled, but he's ready for more.

The two remaining wolverines team up on Kit. As they do, Kit swings her hammer wildly at them, missing with every attack. Lump breaks past Kit, once again grabbing one of the animals by the throat, dragging it away from her.

As the fourth wolverine launches itself at Kit, an arrow strikes it cleanly in the chest. It's badly wounded, but it's not dead. It tries desperately to attack Kit again, but this time she's able to bring her hammer down on it, finishing the animal off.

"What in the name of Helja is Eris doing here?" Kit screams frantically, her question not aimed at anybody in particular?

"Eris? Who's Eris?" Danny asks, as he puts his short bow away.

"It seems she's someone who does not want you two to make it to the Library," Fury shouts. "And she's not done with you yet."

Lump bounds ahead, growling ferociously at two bear-sized white spiders, mandibles dripping with greyish venom.

"Ice Widows? What in Helja's name are they doing so far from Jotunheim?" cries Danny.

Even though these enemies were unexpected, Kit is still in full battle mode. "Healing Aura!" she cries out, as she charges at the pair of spiders. Immediately her body is surrounded by a bright green glow, extending out in every direction by about six feet.

While running at full speed, Kit launches herself into the air and brings her hammer down in a two-handed overhead smash onto a spider's head. The creature lurches backward, seemingly stunned by the impact.

The second spider spins around, exposing its spinnerets toward Danny and Lump, firing a glob of sticky webbing in their direction. Lump deftly avoids the attack and launches himself at the second spider. Danny unfortunately takes the brunt of it, and he's covered with a dense, sticky web.

Lump, with the spider's hind leg securely caught in his jaws, starts dragging the spider away from Kit. It tries desperately to shake Lump loose, but he's able to maintain his grip.

"Help!" Danny calls out, through the goop that has covered him from head to toe. "Help!"

Suddenly, Danny is bathed in a bright blue flame. The webbing slowly begins to melt enough that Danny can free himself.

"Help requested. Help given," says Fury, who manages to have a smug look on his carved face. He's lying face up on the ground, right where Kit had thrown him when she attacked the wolverines.

"I could use a little help, too!" Kit calls out as she strikes the dazed spider a second time. The spider quakes again on impact, as it holds tenuously onto its life.

There is the sound of a bowstring and an arrow strikes the creature in the middle of its eight eyes. A moment later, the light goes out in all of them.

Meanwhile, Lump continues to drag the second spider around by its back leg. It's trying to use its mandibles to get a hold of him, but Lump continues to evade the attacks. There's yet another twang from a bowstring, just before an arrow strikes the spider in his thorax, causing it to screech in agony.

With the spider reeling from the arrow-strike, Lump releases his grip on the spider's leg and moves to take a death-grip between the spider's head and thorax. Not wanting to accidentally hit Lump, Kit attacks the spider's massive abdomen. Her hammer-strike cracks the animal's exoskeleton like a giant egg, spilling its insides all over the ground.

Danny tosses his bow to the ground and switches to his longsword, and stabs it into the spider's thorax, sending it immediately off to the Great Cycle.

While Lump continues to wrestle with the lifeless body, Danny plunges his sword into a snowbank, ridding it, somewhat, of the spider's innards.

Lump rips off one of the spider's legs and starts shaking it as if it were a stick. Kit can't help but laugh a little, despite the fact that they were twice set upon by creatures that did not belong on this mountain.

"What were creatures like that even doing here?" Danny asks.

"Maybe," Kit thinks out loud, "Titan is telling us he doesn't want us to go any further!"

"This has nothing to do with Titan, Kit Standing Bear. Nothing at all. It's about someone very powerful not wanting you to reach the Library. And someone who disagrees with them. It's a game," explains Fury, "And someone is overplaying their hand."

Danny screams at the sky, "We are not playthings put here for your amusement!"

"I will not be denied my prize," Kit shouts out, ignoring Danny's cries. "Dawn's first light is going to break over the mountains very soon."

It takes the group a while to finish the last leg of the climb. As they get higher up, the streams of melting ice become more numerous, more dangerous. Just as they make it to the final stage, where they are now within sight of Titan's frozen buttocks, their way is suddenly blocked by the same swarm of fireflies.

"Out of our way, Chaos Witch!" Blue flame spews forth from Fury's mouth as he screams at Eris.

"Your lives end here," booms the seductive female voice. "Come and play with your shadows!" The firefly swarm flies in an ever-widening circle, until it rockets skyward, leaving in its place four creatures never before seen, nor heard of: not in paintings or stories. They're black as midnight, red burning eyes, tattered wings and horned heads. Their hands and toes have claws that resemble stilettos.

"Foul! I cry foul! Arbiter Mephitis stop this!" shouts a cracked and rheumy voice. The four shadows' swift advance, and Fury's gout of flames, are frozen in blue light, streaming from the hands of none other than Brother Snowbank, the brain-addled, ill-mannered loon who started this whole thing!

Kit almost shouts an obscenity at him, but halts as the air shimmers not ten feet above her head. Encased in a bubble full of brilliant green gas is a creature of stunning but bizarre beauty.

Thick green hair, comprised of hundreds of small water snakes, hangs from an alligator-skin covered human head and neck. Her hands are those of a swamp rat, and there is a long rat's tail swishing behind her. From her back spreads an enormous pair of green, leathery wings. She takes one look at Kit and rolls her eyes.

"Eris," she says in a sibilant but commanding voice, "I know you're here as well. Show yourself, now, or I'll let Tyr have whatever he asks for." In the time it takes to inhale, 'Eris' appears opposite Brother Snowbank, who Kit can only assume, is Tyr. She's voluptuous, perhaps a bit on the heavy side. Her form pulses in a mass of patchwork flesh and writhing black clouds. The other, lizard-like rat-thing, must be Mephitis, the 'Arbiter.'

Kit looks past the frozen form of Fury, to see Danny watching the three *wizards*. His face is contorted with pure, unadulterated rage. Strangely enough, Lump is calm. His eyes are trained on Eris, but he otherwise appears in control of himself.

Eris on the other hand seems to have lost all command of her emotions, sounding more and more like a petulant child as she rails on. "He's besotted with this human, Meph. He's breaking all sorts of rules. He brought her, this stupid little girl, here, to the Library. It's my right to forcefully stop this worthless piece of refuse from learning its secrets! Our secrets! The Travelers' secrets!"

"She can still hear us, you know," Tyr says as his entire aspect changes from an old monk to a broad-shouldered, powerfully built, middle-aged Nomad.

"What the?" Kit asks, as thoughts come rushing to her mind, faster than her mouth can keep up. "Who are you three? What the Helja are those things? Who's besotted with whom? This is Titan's domain! How dare you?"

Suddenly, Kit finds she's unable to move, or speak, or hear. Danny rushes to her side. She can see his mouth moving, but Kit can't make out a word he's saying. Tyr and Eris are shouting at each other; Mephitis says something that enrages Eris.

Danny spins away from Kit and begins screaming at the three wizards, his face growing redder by the second. Eris raises her hand toward Danny. An unseen force sweeps him from his feet, sending him off the mountainside, plummeting to the ground far below. Unable to move, Kit can only watch in horror as her best friend plummets to his death. In a wink, one of the four shadow demons disappears.

Something deep inside Kit breaks open, filling her with white-hot purpose, allowing her to test the unseen bonds that hold her. In her mind's eye, she seeks out a weak point and starts bending the restraint through the pure force of her will. Her hearing is the first to return, followed shortly by some control over her hands. She pushes with all her might against the bonds, painstakingly bringing one of them, inch by inch, closer to her weapon.

Mephitis proclaims her Arbiter's verdict: "I see no merit in your choice of final combatants, Eris. Your argument is with the one called Kit. I absolve the other three from combat."

"Two," Eris says, her patchwork body shaking with laughter.

"Yes, of course. I absolve the creature called Lump and the cane possessed by Fury from battle. They may watch, but none may interfere. This is my arbitration's judgement. The anger of Four will obliterate anyone who goes against it. We, too, may not interfere."

Kit finally moves her hand to her weapon, just as Mephitis says, "Commence!"

Without a second thought, Kit springs from her position, much faster than anyone would have expected, swinging her hammer at the shadow demon's head. Just before impact, Kit pulls the hammerhead away from her target. It is no longer a shadow demon, it's Kit or perhaps a shadow of herself.

Failing to strike, shadow-Kit screams as it makes its first move. Like Kit, it is equipped with what appears to be Fenrir's armor, a battle hammer, and a wooden shield. Except shadow-Kit is holding its weapons in opposite hands.

The creature swings with its hammer, and Kit instinctively blocks the attack, knowing exactly where it would be.

Kit changes levels and tries to swipe the creature's feet out from under it. But it, too, seems to know just what is happening, jumping easily out of the way, avoiding the attack altogether.

This game of cat and mouse continues for several minutes. Kit is beginning to breath hard from the exertion, but shadow-Kit seems completely unaffected.

Gasping for air, Kit takes a step away from the creature. "What are you?" she asks her shadow-self.

"What are you?" the creature answers in Kit's voice.

Kit drops her hammer and shield on the ground, and slowly starts to walk toward her shadow-self. "I am Kit Standing Bear, Acknowledged Priest of Titan. I am reborn!"

The shadow-Kit starts to mimic Kit's words, but somehow cannot. It pauses, as though confused. It looks to Eris, as though it's asking for her help. Not wasting a moment, Kit smoothly pulls her dagger and plunges it into the heart of the shadow-demon. The creature's eyes go wide with surprise. It seems unable to decide who to look at, Kit or Eris. A moment later, it falls to the ground, transforming back into its shadow-demon state.

Kit stares at the fallen creature, not fully trusting that it's dead. Fury and Tyr begin cheering, and Lump bounds over to her, his tail wagging. There is a moment of joy, as Kit realizes that she's defeated the creature, but it quickly turns sour as Danny's death comes bursting into her conscious mind. In an explosion of emotion, Kit leans her head back and wails, a howl really, but stops when she hears Lump starting to growl. She turns to him, just in time to see the shadow demon, taking a swipe at her with its talons.

"Eris, she's won the fight against herself! Call off your pet! This breaks the arbitration!"

"What is the meaning of this, Eris?" shouts Mephitis.

Kit quickly slashes at the demon with her dagger. It throws its arm up in defense. Kit's blade slices through the demon's arm, just above the wrist. The creature's hand disappears in a puff of noxious black smoke. It opens its mouth in a soundless laugh, as the clawed hand reforms at the end of the bloodless stump.

"It's a newly bred type of shadow demon." Eris boasts, arrogance and pride in her voice. "You must have assumed it was the *old* kind. And the rules of combat are simple. One dies, one lives."

The demon manages to rake Kit's ankle with its newly formed claws. Blood sprays from her leg as Kit tries to regain her balance.

"Your own arbitration binds *you*, as well as it binds *us*. No interference, remember? Semantics was never your strong point, *Meph*." Her laugh is cruel and mocking.

The demon knocks Kit's dagger from her hand. As it raises its claws to behead her, a high-pitched screech echoes off the mountainside. A bird-shaped fireball suddenly erupts from the demon's chest. It circles the creature, which opens its mouth in a silent scream before exploding in a cloud of ash. The firebird lands in front of Kit, and collapses. In seconds, Kit is staring down at Danny, naked but very much alive.

"Impossible! That bird is extinct! That boy is dead! Cheaters! The terms of the arbitration..." Eris is silenced by Mephitis, who glares coldly at her.

"...have been followed. I did not state that this boy could not participate, nor did I say *he* could not interfere." The Arbiter folds her hands, her serpent tongue darting between her lizard lips.

"You said…"

"She said none of *us* could interfere. And the boy was obviously dead, so he *was not included*," adds Tyr with a very satisfied smile. "You really should brush up on *your* semantics, Eris."

"But the human boy…"

Tyr continues, "Is obviously more than what he seemed to be? Somewhat like your shadow demons, I think."

Eris, enraged, turns into her firefly swarm and quickly flies south. Mephitis tells Tyr, "I have not decided what to do about your recent behavior, Trickster." Tyr flinches under her scrutiny. "Oh," continues the Arbiter, "have I hit a nerve? Look, what you plan to do here, with this girl and her companions, is unorthodox, but it does not break any rules. See that they, and you, do not break any while inside the Library. Be careful. Eris is becoming even more, *unstable* these days."

Tyr smiles, a sad little smile. "This world, it's changing us Meph, in ways we cannot yet fathom. You be careful, too, my friend." Her strange, hard beauty softens at Tyr's words.

"That name sounds pretty when *you* say it. Gather your people and take them inside, their time is running out." And with her final comment, Meph soundlessly vanishes.

Danny begins to stir. Kit, kneeling over his body, simply can't stop crying.

"Hey, Kitten, why are you crying? And why am I naked? Why am I not cold? What the Helja? Last thing I remember, I was falling…" Danny's questions are cut short as Lump pounces on him, covering him with slobber. "Good to see you, too, pal!"

"Titan be praised," Kit says to herself, but only half-heartedly.

Tyr walks over, handing Kit the dragon bone cane. He looks down at Danny and snorts. "I think we've had quite enough of the Berrat anatomy lesson." With a wave of his hands, Danny is once again wearing the clothes he had on before his fall.

"Who are you?" Danny asks, as he looks down at his now fully clothed body.

"His name yesterday was Brother Snowbank," Kit says, in no way hiding her contempt, "But today he's called Tyr. Who knows what his true name really is? He's a wizard, I think, like those two women."

"That's a very poor name for what I am," Tyr comments, "But it will suffice. We'll talk about you later," he says to Danny with a wink. "For now, we need to go there," and he points to a corridor of shining light, leading to a doorway where Titan's backside should be. "We have until midday." He approaches a simple doorway, and steps inside.

Kit helps Danny to his feet and gives him a bone-crushing hug.

"Hey, hey, hey!" he laughs, "How am I still here?" he asks as they walk down the shining corridor. He looks back over his shoulder. "Next time, though, please remind me never to tell a lady wizard that she smells like a bag of fermented sheep dung!"

Fury laughs. "The fact that she didn't obliterate you suggests that she likes you, firebird man!"

"What did you call me?"

Kit pushes Danny inside, as Lump bounds ahead.

"You and I are the first of our kind to ever set foot in this place." Fury whispers, just as the door closes behind them.

Chapter 23

WHEN THE DOOR CLOSES, the group is left standing in pitch-blackness. Seemingly not bothered by the dark, Lump moves deeper into the room, using his nose to help him find his way. As Lump gets further inside, a ball of light appears, illuminating the entire area with a soft yellow light. The Library is cavernous. The walls are smooth, polished wood. As Kit's eyes trace over the walls and ceiling, she can see no seams, no joints, not even a single nail mark. It's as though the room was carved out of a single, enormous piece of wood.

From the group's vantage point, they can see a long hallway before them, leading to a large circular table in the middle of the room, surrounded by eight finely crafted wooden chairs. Kit chuckles to herself when she sees that Lump is busy sniffing the table legs and rubbing his body against them. He's either trying to spread his scent, or he likes what he smells, and he wants the scent on him.

Danny sets his shoulders back and presses forward toward the center of the room, joining Lump. "It's incredible!" he calls out, his voice echoing throughout the room. You half expect to hear somebody *shush* him. Everybody knows you don't make noise in a library. But there is no reprimand. There is nobody in this room but Kit and her friends.

Kit looks over at Tyr. Even he seems to be in awe of the room. "First time in the Library?" Kit questions him.

Tyr scoffs at her. "Certainly not Kitten, but it has been a very long time." Tyr slowly spins as he takes everything in. "A very long time, indeed. Well!" Tyr exclaims, clapping his hands together. "There are rules in this Library, and those rules will be followed, whether you all like them or not."

Fury laughs. "Here we go," his jewel-eyes begin to swirl, eliciting a laugh from Kit as well, as she thinks that this is Fury's version of rolling his eyes. "Please enlighten us, oh wonderous Tyr. What are the rules of this *Library?*"

Based on the look on Tyr's face, he doesn't find any humour in the cane's question or his mannerisms, but with all eyes on him, he decides to ignore the cane's antics.

"The Rules," Tyr begins with a flourish, "are simple. You are allowed to select and read only three books."

"So, one for each of us?" Danny asks. "One for me, one for Kit and one for Fury."

Tyr furrows his brow as he stares Danny down. "You are *each* allowed to read three books. Once you open a book, it means that you have selected it. Even if you don't read it, it counts as one of your selections."

"Hey!" Danny yells out, interrupting Tyr again. "These words are nonsense. I can't read any of them." Suddenly, the book Danny is holding 'lights up,' casting a pulsating golden glow on his face. "Well, I'll be ..." he laughs. "I can read it now!"

"And Danny has made his first selection!" announces Tyr. There is more than a hint of annoyance in his voice. "I wasn't finished with my description of the rules!" he yells at Danny. But Danny is already sitting on the floor, staring intently at the book. Clearly, he is no longer listening to anything that Tyr has to say.

"Okay," Kit says, interrupting Tyr yet again. "So, we get to read nine books in total? Three for me, three for Danny and three for Fury?"

"Unless Tyr is going to open the books, and turn the pages for me, I don't see how I can read anything. Look ma, no hands!" Again, Fury rolls his eyes, causing Kit to snort-laugh.

"Perhaps I can change you to your *draken* form. Would that allow you to read your own books?" Tyr is looking completely exasperated at this point. He is still trying to finish the description of the *rules,* but nobody will let him get a word in edgewise.

"So, I won't be a cane anymore? You'd do that for me?" Fury almost sounds like he is pleading for the change.

Tyr waves his hand toward Fury. There is a bright flash of light and the cane form of Fury is replaced with a draken form, something that resembles a human-dragon hybrid.

Kit's jaw drops open, as she makes a weird gurgling sound. "Fury?"

In draken form, Fury is resplendent. He is nearly seven feet tall. His skin-scales are an iridescent blue, the blue of a mid-day sky. As he turns his head to Kit, she watches as his colour shifts, reflecting different colours within the room. Fury's head is bobbing with approval.

"Oh, yes, that is so much better." He gazes down at his clawed hands and clawed feet; a large wicked, toothy smile crosses his scaled face. His eyes sparkle and dance, looking very much like his jewelled eyes when he was in cane form. His forked tongue pokes in and out of his mouth as he *tastes* the air in the room.

"Okay, as I was trying to explain," Tyr once again begins, making no effort to hide his annoyance. "twelve books will be read."

"Nine," interrupts Kit. "There are only three of us who can read."

"Twelve," responses Tyr. His face is turning red with frustration. "Will you deny Lump the opportunity to partake of this wonderous opportunity?"

Kit begins to giggle, raising an eyebrow at Tyr. "You do realize that Lump's a *dog,* right? Sure, he's very smart, but he's still a dog."

Tyr again waves his hand, but this time toward Lump. There is another bright flash of light, and in place of the gold-red haired Lump-on-a-Log, is a young man. His shaggy, golden-red hair falls in his eyes and he brushes it away with his hand. He stares down at his hands and smiles. He blinks a few times as he looks around the room. When his eyes fall on Kit, he says, "H-h-hello f-friend Kit."

Kit stands there, staring at her furry friend, now in human form. "Holy Helja, Lump, you're beautiful." Lump responds with a wide grin.

Kit spins around to face Tyr. "What in Helja did you do? You didn't ask his permission. You didn't check to see if he wanted to be changed. You just *changed* him." There was a threatening edge in Kit's voice. She was not going to allow anybody, especially not some self-important, pompous mage, transform her *friend*, not without permission, anyway.

"The change is not permanent, especially not for Fury here. We can't have him running around loose in his draken form." Tyr seems to be speaking to Kit like she is just a child, incapable of understanding the significance of what he's given her. "Lump here; I've made it so he can change between dog and human form at will."

He turns to Lump who is licking the back of his hands. "Stop that!" scolds Tyr. "Do you understand what I just told your friend, Kit, here?" Lump continues licking the back of his hand. "Lump! Stop!" Tyr yells again.

"I am l-l-listening," Lump replies as he takes a break from licking his hand. "I don't have any f-fur. I smell f-funny."

Kit walks over to Lump, taking his hand in hers. "Lump, do you understand what Tyr is saying to you? He's made it so that you can change from you to human, and then back to you again."

Lump's form shimmers for a moment, as he transforms back into his golden retriever dog form. His paw is still in Kit's hand. A moment later, he shimmers again before returning to human form. He squeezes Kit's hand in his. "I understand, pack-leader f-friend. I am *happy*."

"When are we ever not happy?" Kit says, as she gives him a big hug. "I have so many questions for you, like how can you already speak the common tongue?"

Lump is about to respond, but Tyr cuts him off. "You two can talk until the sun comes up, but not right now. We have limited time in here, and I still haven't finished explaining the rules." The Library begins to quake as he finishes.

"We get it Tyr. We get it." Kit places her hands on her hips to help make her point. "Three books. That's what we each get to read. When we're finished, we have to leave. Does that about sum it up?"

"Well, yes, I suppose it does," Tyr says with a bit of a sulky voice. "I wanted to tell you that you're not just reading the books, but they are also reading you."

"And does that matter to us? Does it affect our choice?" Kit continues on with her scolding tone.

"No, I, um, suppose not." Tyr suddenly seems less confident. "But there are nuances, details about how this works," he tries to continue. "Understanding the details will enhance your experience."

"I just want to read the books," Kit continues in the same, scolding tone. "If we have questions, we'll ask you."

Lump interrupts, "I have a question." He holds up a book that he pulled from the shelf. "What's a deity?"

Kit furrows her brow and walks over to the shelves where Lump is standing. He hands her the book.

"Primordial Deities and Their Socio-Economic Effect on the Universe?" Kit stares at Lump, and then at Tyr. "What sort of books are these anyway? I thought we were going to get to read some really cool stories."

"Had you let me finish, I'd have told you exactly *what sort of books* these are." There was no hiding Tyr's sarcastic tone. "You know the rules. Figure it out for yourself." And with that, Tyr storms off down one of the many hallways between the bookshelves.

Kit gives the tome back to Lump. "Maybe find something a bit easier to read," she offers. "This looks pretty heavy."

As Lump takes the book back, he smiles at Kit. "It's okay, pack-leader, Kit. I will learn." And with that, he cracks open the book. A moment later, his face is bathed in the same golden light that Danny experienced. "Interesting," Lump mutters.

When Kit turns away from Lump, she sees that Fury has also made his selection. He is holding a massive tome in his clawed hands, slowly turning the pages, staring intently at the book.

"Well, I suppose I should pick some books for myself," Kit mutters, suddenly feeling alone in the room.

As Kit begins to walk around, she sees that the shelves are divided into sections, a gold nameplate hovers over each. She sighs deeply, wishing that she could pick more than three. While she was in Berrathia, she never had access to books. The Temple's library had many books, but they all read like instruction manuals, and she was never afforded much time to read them, except as a part of her class assignments.

As she cruises past each section, she reads the name aloud, perhaps hoping that it will help her decide. None of them hold any interest to her until she comes across a section names *Indigenous Pantheons*. "Titan's snowballs, what's a *pantheon*?" she mutters.

"A pantheon is a collection of all gods worshipped or revered by a group of people, or as it pertains to a specific religion."

Kit spins about, looking to see from where that voice had come. "Who said that?" she asks as she continues to spin.

"I am the Librarian," replies the voice, decidedly feminine. *"What topic do you wish to explore? Art, History, Science, interspecies steamy romance?"*

"I don't know what I'm looking for," Kit replies. "But I can say with certainty, not *interspecies steamy romance*."

"Oh, that's too bad," the voice replies. *"There is a whole section on interspecies relationships."*

"Gross!" Kit replies with disgust. "Leave me alone. I want to look for myself."

"I will be here if you need me," the voice says. There is a hint of sadness, no loneliness, to it.

Kit's voice softens when she hears the emotion in the librarian's voice. "Sorry, I'll let you know if I need some help."

"Don't forget, young Kit, your time in the Library is limited."

Kit nods, understanding the significance of the librarian's comment.

As Kit walks down the aisle, she sees books with strangely named titles. Nothing makes any sense to her. Nothing, until she comes across a book titled, "Orth." As her hand brushes the spine, she feels a tingle in her fingers.

"A book about where *we* live?" she questions out loud as she takes the book off the shelf. There are no other words on the red leather covered book; just the word Orth in raised, golden script. She was about to put it back when she hears the librarian's voice again.

"An excellent selection. I couldn't have chosen better myself."

Kit shrugs her shoulders and opens the cover of the book. Just like the others, her face is bathed in a soft golden light.

As she begins to read, she sees a list of gods that are considered 'native to Orth.' It speaks of Gaia, Pele, Triton and Medeina. Their stories are told in great detail, and she learns much more about some of the races which they favor. These names are of the gods of the *Old Religion,* those worshipped by the Berrat. Kit's mother had told her stories about each of the gods: Gaia, the earth mother, Triton, god of the seas, Pele, god of fire and rebirth, and Medeina, goddess of winter and death. Gaia was the goddess who Kit knew best. She was the goddess their tribe worshipped. She was the goddess Tyr said had blessed her.

The final passage in the book made no sense to Kit. She read and reread it, trying to understand its meaning.

When the Travelers Bael and Ollin forced Orth into the planet, it is believed her consciousness merged with, and was nurtured by Gaia. This is speculation on our part, as Gaia is unwilling to answer our questions. She has been silent for many millennia; ever since she gifted us with the Library seed, which we were led to believe had been borne by the Great Oak, the Tree of Life. She bears watching. She still has worshippers among the cursed Berrathi.

It's only then that Kit notices that Titan is not mentioned at all. He is the one, true god of Orth, and his name is not mentioned once in the entire book. Kit furrows her brow as she considers the meaning of this. The consideration both intrigues and infuriates her. She quickly slams the book shut and heads out of the section.

Kit's mind is racing as she wanders down the aisle marked, "Languages." She scans the room, not looking for anything in particular. Across the Library, she can see Danny and Lump both sitting in the same section, each with a book in his lap. A few sections over, she can see the head of Fury towering over the top of the bookshelf. Whatever he's reading, he seems to find it entertaining.

While Kit continues to contemplate the significance of Titan's name being absent from her book, without thought, she pulls a book off the shelf and opens the cover. The first page reads, *The Languages of Orth*. "Ah, Helja! Why did I open this book?" She's about to slam it shut and return it to the shelf when she remembers Tyr's words. *"Once you open a book, it means that you have selected it. Even if you don't read it, it counts as one of your selections."*

With a sigh, Kit plops cross-legged onto the floor and begins to read. The first chapter is titled, "Berrat and their Regional Dialects." As she begins to read, she instantly gains a complete understanding of each and every dialect of the Berrat language, even the ancient, long forgotten dialects of the Berrabbithi. Before she realizes it, she's flipping through the book's pages so fast that she can barely see the words on the pages. But the information contained on each page is being etched into her memory. When she finishes the last page, she slams the book shut. "Sweet Titan, it feels like my head is about to explode."

"You have consumed a great deal of information, Kitten. I would suggest that you take a break, but your time in the Library is quickly coming to an end."

Kit jumps up from her seated position. Her head swims and she's feeling a bit dizzy. She manages to push past it, after returning the language book to its place on the shelf.

She leaves the section she's in and sees a section marked, "History."

"I don't have much interest in History," Kit says, with a hint of distain in her voice.

"A person who does not know her history is doomed to repeat it," the disembodied voice says, as if in reply to Kit's comment. Kit's eyes dart around. She's starting to think the librarian is following her around, even though she can't see her.

"Fine, I'll check it out." Kit runs her hand along the spines of the books, letting it touch each book in succession, while her eyes scan the shelves above and below where she can reach. As her fingers cross over a book titled, *History of the Travelers,* she once again feels that now familiar tingle.

It is a vast tome that is so heavy she can barely hold onto it. Struggling to balance it, she again drops to the floor. The book is too big to sit comfortably on her lap, so she places it on the floor in front of her. The book is bound in dark brown leather, with bold cream coloured writing that states below the title, "Herein lies the secrets of Titan, Orth, Bael and Ollin."

"Finally, a book about Titan," Kit exclaims. There is renewed excitement in her voice. Kit recognizes the names of Bael and Ollin from the stories Fury had told her. These are Titan's wicked children. The ones who imprisoned him in his icy chamber.

"Why is Orth named here?" This is the name of the world they live on. "What does that have to do with the *Travelers*?"

"Orth and Titan were the first Travelers to set foot on this world," offers the librarian. *"Together, they brought forth their two sons, Ollin and Bael."*

"Librarian! You're cheating! You cannot speak of the contents of a book before it is opened." Tyr stands over Kit, his face in a rage.

Seeing how upset Tyr is that Kit has this book, she quickly tries to open the cover, but it won't open. Using both hands she tries again, pulling with all her might to reveal the book's contents.

"I'd choose a different book if I were you. I don't think Titan would appreciate you reading his deepest, darkest secrets," Tyr says with a wink.

Kit sighs deeply and picks herself up from the floor. She returns to running her hands across the spines and almost immediately, she feels that same tingling sensation. When she looks to see which book it is, the title simply reads, *Tyr*. Kit looks back to see Tyr with a worried look on his face.

Kit's about to take the book from the shelf when she sees the books next to it are titled, *Mephitis, Tyche, Eris* and *Tiamat*.

Kit looks back at Tyr. He's got his hands stuffed into his pockets, and the worried look on his face has gotten worse. "I know who Mephitis and Eris are," she says with a thin-lipped grin, "but who are Tyche and Tiamat?"

"Tyr, Mephitis, Tyche, Eris and Tiamat are the five fates entrusted with the care of Titan and Orth," the librarian's voice says in reply.

"LIBRARIAN! ENOUGH!" Tyr is screaming at the top of his lungs.

"Sorry," the disembodied voice says in a not-so-sorry kind of way. *"It's been so long since I've had somebody ask me questions ..."*

"What secrets do you have?" Kit says in a sing-song kind of way. I wonder what secrets that hag *Eris* has hidden in here. Kit reaches for Eris' book, but her hand passes right through it, as if the book is merely an illusion. The sound of a woman's laughter can be heard.

"*Eris!*" hisses Tyr, "*Explain yourself!*" A shimmer of fireflies surrounds Kit, flying at her and giving her a stinging sensation each time one lands. Kit starts furiously swatting at the bugs, but with no effect. Eventually, she runs out of the aisle, waving her hands about her head as she does.

The fireflies coalesce into Eris' putrid human-like form. "She cannot be permitted to read about us, any of us. You push the boundaries of the rules every single day, *Trickster*, but today you've gone too far. Mephitis has ruled that she may not read any books about us in here. NONE!" Eris' eyes narrow and she gives Tyr an evil smile. "You remember what happened to Tiamat's friend, Amonar. You coaxed him into breaking the *rules* because you thought it would be fun. You forced Mephitis' hand in judgement."

"He did not deserve dissolution." Tyr's voice was somewhat repentant. "It was a joke, a gag, something to amuse me while we watched those fool Travelers play their stupid games." Tyr's eyes narrow, his voice threatening. "It was you, Eris. You were the one who called for Amonar to be destroyed, dissolved into nothingness. But still, Tiamat blamed me for what happened. He's never forgiven me for what *you* did."

"And yet they call *you* the *Trickster*," laughs Eris as she vanishes in a puff of fetid smoke. Tyr waves his hands in front of his face, trying to dispel the horrid aroma. "You're revolting, Eris."

Chapter 24

WHILE ERIS AND TYR were arguing with each other, Kit wanders down the aisles searching for her third and final book. When she reaches the end of the aisle, she finds a door. Unlike everything else in the Library, which is made of rich coloured wood, the door is made of stone, possibly marble. On the door is a black plaque with white lettering. It reads, "Librarian." Without hesitation, Kit pulls on the handle, and the door opens smoothly toward her.

Inside the room are beautifully carved wooden shelves, but each and every one of them is empty. In the middle of the room is a single small table, with a simple wooden chair. On the table, there is a very thick book, much thicker than any book Kit had seen in the Library.

As Kit steps into the room, the door closes behind her with an audible click. She continues over to the small desk to look at the book. When she sits on the chair, light shines down from above, illuminating the book. Letters on the cover flare to life revealing the books title, *The Font of Knowledge*.

Without regard for what might happen, Kit reaches out. As her fingers touch the surface of the book's cover, the room begins to spin. Everything turns into swirls of colour. At first, the colours are the browns and reds of the shelves in the room, but they quickly shift to bright blues and rich, vibrate greens. When the spinning stops, Kit struggles to keep her stomach from lurching.

When she gets control of herself, Kit comes to the realization that she is no longer in the Library or in the librarian's office. She is sitting on a large rock, in a glade by a small pool. The water is the deepest, most intense shade of blue that she's ever seen. When she pulls her eyes away from the water, Kit sees that she is on a small island floating in the vastness of space. Stars, by the billions, are twinkling all around her.

"Hello, Kit" says a voice, startling her back to reality, or whatever this is. Beside the pond, sitting cross-legged in the grass is an unremarkable man, holding an instrument made of a tree branch bent in a "U" shape, with spiderweb-thin strings. It reminds Kit of a lute, but it's somehow quite different. The man runs his fingers across the strings. A lovely melody fills the air, and Kit immediately relaxes.

I wonder if this is Tyche or Tiamat," Kit thinks to herself.

"I am not," he says while still playing, responding to the question that Kit had only *thought* about. "I am not a Fate, nor am I a Traveler."

"What are you then?" Kit asks before she can stop herself, speaking to him in the same cocky tone that she might use with Captain Harding.

"I am me. I was alone in this place before time existed. I existed in a great void. Perhaps I *was* the great void. It was very long ago, and I haven't thought about it in ages." He chuckles lightly to himself, seemingly lost in his own musings.

"Are you the Librarian?" Kit asks, her mind racing out of control, grasping at straws, and hoping to find something, anything that can ground her.

"Oh my, no. I am not she, but I would like to think I am her friend. I am, after all, her favorite book."

Kit blinks at the man, as he continues to play his peculiar instrument. "You're the book in her office, *The Font of Knowledge*?"

"I am not the book, but the book is me," he says in a playful sort of way. "Oh, little angel, it's difficult to explain in simple terms that you might understand."

"Try me!" Kit really hates being spoken down to, like she's a child incapable of understanding a concept.

"The universe, as you understand it, exists in a never-ending expanse, stretching beyond your sight and your comprehension. This is but one of many universes, each existing in another plain, and yet occupying the same space of every other universe. The book that you saw in the Librarian's office is but one of many instances, manifestations if you will, of my existence. So, even though the book is me, it's only one of the infinite possibilities that may occur or that will occur across time and space."

Kit's face goes slack. This man just unloaded an entire avalanche of information in just a few sentences. Even though she thought she was following, the snow quickly got deeper than she could manage, and her mind was quickly snowed under.

"Um, ya. Okay." Kit rubs her chin in a thoughtful manner. "I understand."

The man roars with laughter, practically falling over as he does. "I should have brought you here ages ago, little angel. Nobody has *ever* made me this happy before. You're very funny."

Kit chuckles along, watching the man's elaborate antics. She's suddenly reminded of Runt and Lump, watching them roll about in the grass, having the time of their lives.

When the man finally regains control of himself, he props himself back up and lays his instrument across his thighs. "So, little angel, what question do you wish answered?"

"What's your name?" Kit asks. "You clearly know me, but I don't know who you are."

"Is that the information you seek? You sit before the *font of knowledge* and all you want to know is *my name*?"

"It's not *all* I want to know," says Kit, "but it's a pretty common thing to ask somebody when you first make their acquaintance. Would you not agree?"

"I know many things, but I don't think I am well versed in the art of polite conversation. Afterall, I've spent eternity alone with my own thoughts. I have not ever had a conversation, not like this anyway, with anybody in all that time."

"Never?" Kit wonders. "You must be horribly lonely."

"Perhaps I am," he replies. "So that you'll know, I have no name, not really, but I have been called many names by those who have *felt* my existence. But the name I think I like the most is *Anu*."

"Pleased to meet you, Anu." Kit says with a slight bow.

"Pleased to meet you, too, Kit Standing Bear, Priest of Titan, Twice Touched, Wolf Friend." Anu picks up his instrument and begins to play again, a soft gentle tune, and something like a lullaby fills the air. "And what question have you decided to ask me?"

Kit peers up at the heavens, tapping her finger against her chin. "Up until now, I have not chosen what I wanted to learn. The Library was choosing it for me, telling me which books I should read."

"That is not entirely true," says Anu. "The Library was responding to what you need to know. When your hand touched a book that contained relevant information, it let you know."

"So, I need to learn of *Titan*, and the *Travelers* and the *Fates*? Those were the books that made my hands tingle when I touched them."

"Those books are important to you, and to the possibilities that lie before you."

"Possibilities?" Kit asks.

"Yes, possibilities. Even though there are predisposed outcomes, destinies if you will, none are written in stone, especially where you are concerned. The choices that will be put before you are yours to make, or ignore, whichever feels right to you in the moment. Sometimes a choice leads you in a specific direction. Sometimes it will offer you new choices. Sometimes, choices you've made in the past will affect the choices you will make in the future. A world of possibilities lays before you, Kit, a nearly limitless series of choices and outcomes."

"I know what I want to ask you, if it is allowed." Kit's hoping that Anu can, and will answer this question.

"I can only answer that question in part. What you want to know involves me predicting the future, and although I can speak to likely potential outcomes, I cannot say for certain how the future will unfold."

"Does that mean you cannot tell me who the three are? The three who will try to free Titan?" Kit is very disappointed that Anu could not or would not answer her question.

Anu smiles a sad smile. "I will speak of a likely possibility, but know this, it may not come to be." Kit's eyes suddenly get wide with excitement. Clearly, she wants Anu to spill it.

"The prophecy is real, and what it describes will come to pass. Who will be affected by the prophecy? That, my dear angel, cannot be told. There is one clear path that leads to any specific outcome." Anu watches Kit's crestfallen reaction. "I can say, however, that you are one of the three, as described in the prophecy."

"I am?" Kit suddenly gets nervous. She desperately does not want to be caught up in this prophecy, this destiny.

"You are."

"And the other two? Who are they?"

Anu closes his eyes for a moment as he considers the question. "The answer to that question is unclear, but I can say this with some certainty. One of the three has already crossed your path. The other is somebody that you have yet to meet."

"Is that as much as you can tell me?"

Anu smiles. "Ah, sweet Kit, you are a joy to me. Even though I cannot predict it for certain, I do believe that you will free Titan from his prison. The probability of that outcome is low, but you are wonderfully tenacious. You possess qualities that make your path wildly uncertain. Pondering your outcome brings me such joy."

"Because I'm a complicated girl and nobody understands me but my mother?" Kit laughs despite how frustrated she is with not getting her questions answered.

"Our time together draws to a close, but know this, little angel, unexpected bringer of joy in my life. You have much to teach Titan. If he is willing to listen, he will learn much from you."

"From me?"

"Don't be so surprised, there are many things you could teach to a number of those whom you believe to be gods." Anu stops speaking for a moment, looks up to the stars and nods his head. "You can speak with them, but you must hurry. Their mortal life is in peril."

Anu again turns his attention to Kit. "Thank you for sharing your limited time with me, Kit. You have made me truly happy for the first time in, well, forever. For the gift you have given me, I will give you one small, but highly significant piece of information."

"Yes? What is it?"

"You will be forced to make a leap of faith. Only in doing so will your true self be revealed. I have watched your life play out in countless scenarios. If you are to succeed in your quest, you must be willing to risk the lives of your friends. You will have no time to decide, just listen to your heart."

Listen to your heart. Those were the same words her mother had said to her on the night of her Rite of Way. Kit is just about to ask what this all means, but Anu vanishes. The floating island swells, and returns to normal, as though it had just sighed.

Chapter 25

AGAIN, EVERYTHING BEGINS to spin. The stars begin to swirl, their silver-gold colour changing to the same vibrant blues and greens they were when Kit was swept away from the Library. A moment later, everything comes to a stop. Kit finds herself kneeling by a pond, next to a rock on an island floating alone in the night sky.

This time, however, Kit's friends are with her. Lump is in his natural dog form, Danny is his usual charming self, and in his hand is Fury, back in his cane form.

Kit looks into the pond that she's kneeling in front of. Looking up at her from the depths is a man, a strikingly handsome man, dressed in shimmering blue and silver clothes. The man emerges from the water, standing before her, soaking wet.

Lump begins to bark furiously at him. His hackles raised, his teeth bared, he slowly begins moving forward.

"Silence your mutt, this is between *you* and *me*." The man's voice is low and threatening. There is a surging power behind his words.

"Who in Helja do you think you are, ordering me about like some child. I am a priest of Titan. This is Lump, my friend, my ally, my protector. Do yourself a favour and watch your tone, you pathetic sack of ..."

"Kit ..." Fury interrupts before she finishes her sentence. "I wouldn't ..."

"WHO. AM. I? You insignificant peace of flotsam, you random collection of useless essence. I am *Triton*. I am the god of water. I am the son of Gaia and Pele. I am the guardian of Haven, the guide of the departed, the tamer of the Makara!" He places his hands on his hips, puffing out his chest in a display of peacockery. He looks ridiculous. Exceedingly handsome, yet absolutely ridiculous.

"NEVER. HEARD. OF. YOU!" Kit screams back at him. Lump continues barking as if to put an extra exclamation point behind her words.

"Kit ..." Fury interrupts yet again. "He is who he says he is. He *is* the god of water."

"So what?" she screams at Fury. "So, what if he is, but why is he YELLING AT ME!"

"BECAUSE YOU'RE YELLING AT ME!" Triton screams back at her.

"Kit, just sit down," Fury says. "Sit down on the rock beside Danny." His gemstone eyes are practically glowing as he tries to maintain his own composure.

Kit starts to head toward the rock when she sees Danny. His face is as white as fresh-fallen snow. His eyes are vacant and unblinking. Kit takes a seat beside him, putting her hand on his knee to let him know everything will be okay. When Kit turns her attention back to the man, he's smiling at her. Kit suppresses the urge to stick out her tongue, and that snaps her out of whatever odd spell she's been under.

The man, Triton, moves closer to her until his face is directly in front of hers. "Why were you in the Library?"

Kit rolls her eyes at him. "Why does anybody go into a Library?" Kit replies with a sarcastic tone. "To read and to learn."

Triton chuckles. "And why are you here, right now, with me?" He waits, impatiently staring at Kit as she stares back at him. "It's not a trick question."

Kit groans to herself. "I don't know why I'm here. I'm assuming that you brought me here."

"And why do you think I brought you here, taking you from the Library. Why do you think I'm standing before you right now?"

"To ask me stupid questions?"

"I think he wants to tell you something," Danny interjects, his voice barely more than a faint whisper.

"At least one of you isn't brain-dead," Triton retorts.

"Forget you!" Kit yells at Triton. "You drag me out to here, wherever here is. I'm on an island in the middle of the stars, and you're upset because I can't guess what you're thinking." Kit hops off the stone she's sitting on and starts bearing down on Triton. "You say you are the son of Gaia, but right now, you're just being a giant, pompous jerk."

Triton takes one step away from the advancing Kit before his body grows to five times its previous size. "I have no time for impertinent little girls. I brought you here to share some information with you, important information that may save the lives of everybody in Aarall, but if you are too arrogant to listen to what I am going to tell you, then you can leave."

Titan raises his hand like he's about to send them all back to the Library when Kit raises her hands to stop him.

"I'm sorry, alright?" Kit takes a few steps back away from the giant-sized Triton. Not out of fear, but rather to allow herself to look up and see his face. "You've been aggressive with me ever since you popped up out of that pond over there."

Triton quickly reverts back to his previous size. "I have been aggressive because you have been aggressive towards me. It is in my nature to *reflect* whoever is before me."

"Like when I look into water, I see my reflection?"

"So, you're not just a pretty face," Triton says with a smile. "Mother told me you are highly intelligent, but I just couldn't see it – until now."

"I'm not that smart," Kit says without a hint of false modesty. "I'm better at swinging my hammer than I am at thinking my way out of a problem."

Kit's final comment makes the god laugh. "I'm not too surprised. If you'd take more time to think before you speak, maybe you wouldn't need to use your strength as often as you do."

"Try telling that to my mouth. It's not usually connected to my brain."

"Well then," Triton says with a smirk, "if you can try to keep your disconnected mouth shut for just a few minutes, I have information to share with you."

Kit is about to respond to Triton's comment, but she manages to catch herself before she does. She slams her mouth shut and gives Triton a tight-lipped smile.

"Better," he says. "I understand that you've met Tyr." Kit nods without saying a word. "The statue of Titan that overlooks your city, well, it was his idea to create it."

"That's ridiculous," Kit scoffs, trying to keep her anger in check. "Everyone knows that statue was made by Titan himself, as a reminder that he is watching over everyone."

"He's right," states Fury matter-of-factly, drawing a glare from Triton.

Triton puts his finger to his lips, shushing them all, like a teacher might do while trying to ask for quiet from her classroom. "It was his friend Tyche who made the statue," Triton explains. "He drained a great lake, and used his power to change the water. He made it into something else, something that could freeze or liquefy, but not evaporate. It changed all the living things inside the water as well. Do you understand what a terrible thing that is?"

Kit slowly shakes her head. She understands the words, mostly, but she doesn't really see the harm in what he did.

Triton takes a deep breath and slowly lets it out. He's acting like he's completely exasperated by her. "Water is a wonderous thing. It yields easily if you slowly pass your hand through it, but if you slap it, it can feel like it's as hard as stone. It can bring life to plants, when it is in the right amount, or it can bring death if there is too little or too much. When the sun heats it, it evaporates, turning it into a vapour, seemingly disappearing. But, when enough of that vapour gathers together, and it cools, it returns back to the land as rain. When it gets cold, it freezes. When it gets warm, it melts. There really is nothing else like it."

Kit can't help but yawn. Sitting through a lecture does that to her. She raises her hand slowly, hoping she's allowed to ask a question. Triton inclines his head to her and waits patiently for her to speak.

"Tyche, he's a Fate like Tyr and Eris?" Triton nods. "And Tyr asked him to make the big statue of Titan, the one that stares down at us at the Temple?" Triton nods again. "And he used water from a big lake, your lake, to make the ice for the statue?" Triton nods yet again, this time adding a small yawn like he's becoming bored with Kit's simplistic questions that are really nothing more than her repeating what he had just told her. When Kit sees the yawn, she scowls at the god. "Well, excuse me for boring you. You threw a lot of things at me, and I'm doing my best to keep up. I just want to make sure I've got it right so far."

"My apologies," Triton says, cocking an eyebrow at her. "Please proceed with your questions."

"Well," Kit says trying to get her thoughts straight in her head, "I have no idea why Tyr and Tyche would create the statue, but I don't see what harm it's caused. People come from all around to visit the statue and pray to Titan. It sounds like they did him a service."

"What's the harm? That's what I've been trying to tell you before you interrupted me with your questions." Kit flinches slightly at the comment, before she defiantly juts her chin out at him, causing the god to shake his head at her. "The water that Tyche took from my lake was full of life; fishes, crustaceans, insects, small water-borne animals, and creatures so tiny that you would never know they were

there. When he took that water and magicked it to make the ice statue, all those creatures were trapped within, neither dead nor alive, no
longer able to live their lives."

Kit blinks a few times at the implications of what Triton was saying. She was about to interrupt but managed to keep her lips pressed
together.

"The ice is melting and soon, very soon, the statue will lose its
structure and the magicked water will be released on the barony below. In it's magicked state, it will not behave like normal water. Instead, it will be like a great mudslide and it will utterly destroy everything in its path. The walls of Aarall will fall when it strikes them.
Everything within the city will be obliterated. The water will spread
out across the barony and eventually soak into the ground. When it
does, it will kill everything in the ground in the process. Nothing will
grow on that soil, ever again. The land will turn into a barren waste-
land.

Kit's jaw goes slack. "How do we stop it from melting?" she finally asks.

Triton's eyes are filled with sadness. "You cannot. The melting
is being brought on by Titan himself. His anger and frustration are
causing it. Ever since he was imprisoned, he's been seeking a way to
free himself; trying to recruit people, such as yourself, to aid in his
release. But something has changed recently. Titan has become infu-
riated, and that rage is spilling out across the north. It is directly af-
fecting this statue."

"How do we get the people out of Aarall then? We need to get
them out of the way of the water." Kit stands up, like she wants to
leave immediately and warn the people.

"There is no time for that anymore, Kitten." Triton motions for
her to sit down so that he can continue. "You will need to convince
Tyche to remove his magic from the water."

"Why don't you fix it yourself? If you're a *god,* it should be easy. Right?" Kit cocks an eyebrow at Triton.

"Tyche's magic is strong and not easily undone. Fate-magic is different from mine, from ours, and it cannot be undone by us." Triton's voice sounds like he is resigned to the fact that his water is gone.

"What happens if I can't get Tyche to remove the spell? What can we do to help minimize the damage?" Kit begins pacing about, wracking her brain, trying to think of an alternative, any alternative, that will save the people of Aarall.

"There is only one thing that I can think of," says Triton. He's shaking his head. He clearly doesn't like his idea. "If I wish to save the lives of Aarall, I will need to put other lives, possibly millions of lives at risk in the process." Triton continues shaking his head, looking sad.

"Millions?" the number doesn't mean anything to Kit. "There aren't that many people in all of Arnnor."

"The river Aar comes from deep inside the mountains. To save the people of Aarall, I would need to send the statue's magic water out to the sea. To do that, I must call the river Aar's water back to the mountains. The melting ice would then fill the dry riverbed. When I release the Aar's water, it will rush back, pushing the magicked water out to sea. The riverbanks will explode when the waters meet, destroying everything near its banks. Hundreds of your people will be killed."

"That sounds much better than everyone in Aarall dying." Kit says, hope springing up from her soul. "But you said that *millions* of people will die..."

"No, not millions of people, millions of lives. It would save many of your people, but my children, the creatures that live in the water, they will be utterly decimated." Kit can see in his eyes that he is pleading with her to not let this happen. "The world beneath the waves is complex and diverse, but it is also fragile; oh, so very fragile.

When the magicked water meets my water, the natural water, it will instantly kill every bit of life that it touches."

An idea pops into Kit's head. It's risky, but if it works, it will save lives, possibly millions of lives, if what Triton says, is accurate. "How long?" Kit asks. Triton raises an eyebrow, wondering what she's getting at. "How long until the statue melts enough that it will come crashing down on the city?"

Titan closes his eyes, casting his face to the stary heavens above. "Hours. No less than three, but no more than twelve. It's magicked, so it's hard to get an exact read on it."

"Send us back! I have a plan, and we have no time to waste." Kit turns to her three companions. "I'm going to need help from all of you, or my plan can't work."

A moment later, the heavens begin to spin, the stars once again swirling in a kaleidoscope of colours.

Chapter 26

KIT FINDS HERSELF SEATED at the Library's circular table with eight chairs, along with her party: Danny, Lump on a Log, Fury, back in his cane form, and of course, Tyr.

"Where have you been?" Tyr asks. He sounds both annoyed, and at the same time, relieved.

"I've been here, reading. Just like the rest of you." Kit looks at him like he's lost his mind. The memory of being someplace else tugs at her, but she can't get a grip on it. It's like water slipping through her fingers.

"No. That's not true." Tyr says with a skeptical tone. "You were here, and then you weren't." He motions his hand towards the rest of the party. "Same for you all. You were here, and then you weren't. And now you're all here again."

Kit's memories of her visit with Anu and Triton come crashing back. "The statue is melting. It's going to collapse and kill everyone if we don't do something to fix it!"

Tyr straightens up, a look of surprise crosses his face. "Yes. Yes, it is. But how do you know this?"

"It doesn't matter right now. We have no time to waste, no time for chatter. We need to move. Now!" Kit appears frantic as she looks to each of her companions. They're looking back at her, waiting for her to tell them the plan.

"Danny, can you change back into that firebird? Like when you saved me from the shadow demon?"

"You want me to kill myself so that I can turn into a phoenix?" Danny's eyes are wide, and a little bit wild at this point.

"You don't need to die, boy; you just need to call upon it. It's a part of you." Fury seems intrigued at this point, wondering where Kit is going with this. Tyr just looks annoyed.

"Okay," says Danny, perhaps just as curious as Fury. "If I can, what do I do next?"

"Fly, that's what. Fly back to the Fist. Don't ask permission, just ring the warning bells at the Temple. Everyone will follow the protocols. The villagers will leave their fields and head for the city. Those who live near the mountains will take shelter on higher ground. It's been ages since the bells have rung, but everyone will know what to do."

Danny smiles at Kit. "So, I'm the one to save the day, then? I'm already popular, but I'll be revered for this." He begins strutting around the Library, in a typical *Foxy* fashion.

"First, you're going to need to find it in you to transform." Tyr chides. "Now is not a good time to disappoint the lady." Tyr seems to be amused at this point. Not with Danny, but with Kit's take-charge attitude.

Lump woofs, waiting impatiently for his orders. Kit gives him a smile. "I need you to find the wolf-packs. Warn them of what's happening. Have them spread the word to the other animals. Have them scare everyone and everything away from the statue, if necessary. I don't know how animals communicate. Can you do this? Will it work?"

Lump woofs at her again. She's fairly certain he agreed, but now is not a time for uncertainty. "Do you understand, Lump?" Lump shifts from dog to human form, the transition is almost instantaneous. "Yes, I will follow commands. Tell wolves. Scare animals. Make friends safe." A moment later, he shifts back into his dog form.

"You, Fury, you're coming with me. We have a lot of work to do." Kit grimaces as she says this, her face become filled with worry. "A lot of work."

"And what of me, Kitten?" Tyr moves in beside her, much closer than she likes. Lump gives him a warning with a low, throaty growl.

"You, Mr. Fate, will seek out your friend, Tyche, and tell him to remove his magic from the ice." Kit pushes him away as she gives him his instructions.

Tyr crosses his arms in front of his chest. "Why would I do that, Kitten? I think I'd rather stand by and watch the mayhem."

Kit crosses her arms in front of her chest, mimicking Tyr's moves perfectly. "Because, dear Tyr. Because of the power of four."

The look of smug satisfaction disappears from his face. "What do you mean by that?"

"Eris was correct. I could hear you talking. I heard everything that was said and, if I got this right, and I think I have, you cannot interfere in the lives of the people of Orth. At least, not directly."

"So?" he replies, uncrossing his arms and putting his hands on his hips. "All the more reason for me to not speak with Tyche."

Kit follows suit, uncrossing her arms, putting her hands on her hips. "By action or by inaction, you cannot interfere in our lives. If you don't speak with him, you are directly contributing to the deaths of thousands of people. Tens upon tens of thousands." Kit shakes her head, like a teacher might when speaking with a student who doesn't want to learn a lesson. "If that happens, I'm guessing Mephitis will declare that you're in violation of your rules, and be subject to dissolution."

"How? What?" Tyr is completely taken aback. "I wouldn't. Tyche made the statue, not me. He'd be in violation. It's his fault and he'll be held accountable."

"No, sweet Tyr. That is not correct. You. It was you who charmed Tyche into making this statue. He made it for *you*. I'm guessing that the creation of the statue did not break any rules. You did not force anybody into doing something against their will. You merely placed an object before them. How the people chose to react to the statue, well, that was up to them."

The smug look again returns to Tyr's face. He's nodding in agreement. "I broke no rules. Mephitis even confirmed it after Eris complained. So? If it melts, it's not my fault."

"Not true," Kit says with the same smug look as on Tyr's face. "Your creation will be directly responsible for the death of people. If you do nothing to fix it, it's on you. It will all be on *you*."

"Fine. I'll speak with him, but it's not my fault if he won't undo the magic."

Kit could swear that Tyr was pouting at this point. She considers mimicking the pathetic look he's giving her, but she's got what she wanted from him. There's no need to risk it.

"Have him wait until I'm ready. If he does it too soon, it will collapse immediately and kill everyone in the area." Kit, once again, takes on a mantle of authority. Inwardly she feels like it suits her, like she was made to lead. "You'll know when it's time." She's about to address Fury when another thought strikes her. "If my plan fails and I am not ready before the magicked-ice falls apart, have him change it then. Magicked-water will cause far more damage than normal water."

Tyr looks at her with awe. "The Library has changed you, Kitten. Much more than I would have ever expected." Again, he sidles up to her. "I like it." He gives her a peck on the cheek and disappears from the room.

"Fury and Lump, you're with me. Danny, get changed and be on your way."

"I can't!" Danny moans. "I've been trying this whole time, but I can't. I don't know how to call it out."

"I'll help," Fury says with a playful note in his voice. A moment later, a gout of blue fire bursts from the mouth of the cane, enveloping a screaming Danny. Instantly, he transforms into his phoenix form.

"Did you kill him?" Kit yells at Fury. "What the Helja?"

"I didn't harm him, not really, anyway." The little draconic head is giggling and lolling about. "The fire wasn't hot, well, not that hot. He's practically immune to fire now anyway. He just didn't know it. He wasn't in pain. He was just surprised and maybe a wee bit frightened."

The phoenix swoops at Fury, knocking him to the floor. As the cane goes rattling across the room, Lump immediately gives chase, scooping him up in his mouth.

"You deserved that," scolds Kit. "Okay, enough of this nonsense. We're running out of time by the second."

Chapter 27

THE PHOENIX ERUPTS into flames and flies through the room, back toward the way they had come in; Kit and Lump, with Fury still in his jaws, following close behind. There is the sound of rushing water again. The floor of the Library shakes heavily. Lump continues without issue, but Kit's having trouble maintaining her footing. More than once she slams into the wall of the hallway when she loses her balance.

Ice and rocks are beginning to fall from the ceiling. The Library itself is collapsing behind them. Kit redoubles her efforts, trying to keep up with her cohorts who are now a good deal ahead of her. As the hallway bends, light can be seen from outside, and joy begins springing up in Kit's heart.

That joy turns sour when the entrance collapses. Ice and stone fall from the ceiling, completely blocking the exit. It seems that Titan's icy butt has slammed shut on her. If she wasn't gripped with terror, Kit might have even found the situation funny.

Kit continues to run toward the exit, pulling her battle hammer from its sheath as she does. Without slowing down, she runs full out into the wall, swinging her hammer at it with every ounce of her being. Both Kit and the hammer bounce off the wall, sending them careening back from whence they came.

Her hammer damaged the wall of ice, but only just barely. She picks up her hammer and starts swinging again and again. Chips of ice are flying off the wall with each swing, but at this rate, she'll be riding the statue down to the ground long before she breaks through.

Utterly exhausted, she drops to her knees in front of the wall. Rage is pouring out of her. Kit does not fear for her own life, but for the lives of the innocent people who will die if she fails. She wonders if this is the same rage Titan is feeling, as his children are left without him to look over them.

She leans back onto her heals and closes her eyes in prayer. "Titan, I *know* you can hear me. In my heart of hearts, I know that you are with me, now and always. If I am to save my people, my friends, your worshippers, I am going to need your help. I will need your *strength*."

Suddenly, Kit remembers her conversation with Hoarfrost. *"For Titan is with you; now and always. This mark will allow you to call upon him in times of dire need. You will be able to draw strength directly from him."* The meaning of what he had said now becomes crystal clear.

Kit places her hand on the now invisible mark on her neck. "Titan, hear me, I call for your strength, that I may do your will."

Kit's body is immediately wracked with a cold so intense that she feels like she's on fire. The pain is excruciating, but at the same time, it feels good. Oh, so very good. When she looks at her hands, she sees they are wreathed in an ice-blue aura. She quickly grabs up her hammer. It feels feather light in her grip.

Kit stands close to the wall and sets her feet. The power of Titan is still flowing through her, seeking a place to be unleashed. She switches to a two-handed grasp on the haft. With every ounce of her being, Kit unleashes all of her strength, her faith, and her soul into one single swing.

The wall simply explodes on contact. The force of the blow sends the stone and ice blasting outward. When the dust settles, she can once again see the light of day, along with her cohorts who are completely covered in snow and ice.

"Holy, Helja!" yells Danny from a snowbank fifteen feet from the path. "That was some explosive *gas* from Titan's butt! It blew out my flame!" He quickly tousles his now flame-red hair, dislodging the ice clinging to it.

Lump is bounding about, still holding onto Fury. It's pretty certain the dog thinks this is good fun, but judging from the look on Fury's face, he is not enjoying any part of it.

"Danny, can you switch back? You know, to a firebird?" If Kit has permanently blown out his flames, her plan would be ruined.

Danny spreads his arms out, closes his eyes and utters a single word. "Burn!" His body is immediately engulfed in bright red flames just before transforming into phoenix form. He quickly does a couple of loops, perhaps in celebration, before speeding towards Aarall.

As Kit watches in wonder as Danny flies away, she's brought back to reality when a torrent of muddy water takes her feet out from underneath her, sending her careening down the mountainside. In seconds she's caught up with Lump who is running down the muddy path for all he's worth. She quickly grabs a hold of him, using her enhanced strength to pull him on top of her. The poor dog's eyes are wild with terror, his legs flailing about in all directions.

"Shift to human form," she yells at Lump. "Shift back and hold onto me."

He immediately does as he's told. Kit now has the shaggy-haired young man clinging to her like a child might cling to his mother. His face is buried into her neck. Kit can hear him whining, even over the din of rushing water and roaring mud falls.

"Don't worry, my friend, I've got you. You're safe with me."

After several more seconds of free-fall descent, they finally come to a stop. Kit is caked with mud and debris. It looks like she's slid about halfway down from where they were a few moments ago. A quick check of herself and Lump reveals that there are no severe injuries. Lump sits on the ground and begins licking his wrist.

Kit sits next to him, taking his hand in hers. There are some abrasions, but nothing too serious. "You'll be okay, Lump. Those cuts will heal quickly." She gently kisses the wound, like a mother might do for a child. "I need you back in dog form now. We don't have much time."

Just as she finishes speaking, the high-pitched peal of the Temple's alarm bells rings out across the landscape. "Ah, Danny, well done," she exclaims. "Well done, my friend."

Lump quickly kisses Kit on the mouth. "Love you, Kit," he says just as his body switches back into a dog. He gives himself a violent shake, throwing bits of mud and ice in all directions. He smiles his best doggie-smile and bolts off down the path.

"You have many admirers, young Kit." Fury is floating in front of her. His jewelled eyes are dancing with mischief. "If I may be so bold, you can count me among them."

Kit blushes hard at his words. "Let's get going before another torrent of water knocks me off the side of this mountain."

Outside of hitting some slick patches where she nearly loses her footing, the remainder of the hike down the path goes smoothly. Kit races past the large altar at the foot of the statue and continues on, bounding down the staircase three steps at time.

She can hear Fury as he floats along beside her. "Fly, Kitten, fly!"

When she is about halfway between Aarall and Titan's ice statue, Kit finally comes to a stop. She looks back at the statue. The facial features and other fine details in the carving look like they're starting to sag.

"How long?" Kit asks, barely able to catch her breath. "How long since we left the Library?"

"Three hours, twenty-seven minutes and seventeen seconds," Fury replies. "The collapse might happen any minute now."

Kit begins running about, looking at the ground as she does.

"What are you doing there?" There is a hint of amusement in Fury's voice. "Did you lose something?"

"I'm looking for holes in the ground. Any type of sign that there might be firebugs here."

"Ooh, I love firebugs. I used to eat them by the hundreds, back when I was myself, and not this *walking stick*."

"How did you find them before you were a dog's play-toy?" Hopefully, she hadn't insulted him with her comment, but she's worried that Fury isn't taking the situation seriously.

"Simple!" Fury states as a matter of fact. "I just put my ear to the ground and listened for them. They make quite a racket under there, don't you know."

"Can you do it now?" Kit could swear he was just stalling, trying to make her sweat.

"Nope," he replies with a spoiled-child sort of retort. "Play-toys have no ears, or can't you see that."

"You're not a play-toy. You're a magical cane hosting the essence of a once powerful sky dragon." She gives him a look of complete frustration and impatience. "Better? Can you help me now?"

"Sorry, Kitten, but I can't help you. I wasn't kidding when I said I have no ears."

"But you can hear me. So, you can hear the bugs." Kit's practically screaming at this point.

"And you have ears to hear me say I can't do it." His beady little gemstone eyes blink at her as he sticks his forked tongue out at her.

"Oh." It suddenly dawns on Kit what he's been trying to say. She quickly drops down to her knees and presses her ear to the ground. She waits for several minutes, straining to hear what she can. "I hear nothing but the rumbling of the ice statue." Kit's face contorts in horror as she thinks the situation through. "It's about to let go!"

"Well, that's interesting," Fury says in a sing-song kind of way. "This is something I have to see." He floats away from Kit, staring intently at the giant statue.

As predicted, the statue begins to slump badly. It looks like the god's face is sagging, dragging the rest of the head down with it. Titan's hands drop off from the ends of his arms, careening downward.

Then, the statue begins to shimmer. For barely a moment, the statue becomes translucent, a wonderous shade of blue-green, before it completely loses its form and comes crashing down in a torrent of water.

"Fantastical!" screams Fury, his voice barely carrying over the sound of the water rushing towards them. "I estimate you have about thirty seconds before that wave of water hits you."

Kit takes her hammer in her hands. She still has Titan's strength coursing through her. She can only hope and pray that it will help.

Trying to calm her mind, Kit bends down on one knee, holding her hammer into the air above her. She presses the palm of her other hand on the ground.

"Titan! Hear me!" She screams with all her might. She looks up at the wall of water racing toward her. "In your icy prison, I call upon you. For the sake of your Temple, for the sake of your people, I call upon you. Rend open the earth. Unleash your fury." The head of Kit's battle hammer crackles with energy. As when she unleashed this spell against Pental, small bolts of lightning begin to lick the head of her weapon. The lightning cascades down the handle, and into her arm, the power growing inside her. She uses the strength of Titan to hold onto the power, to let it continue to build inside her. Kit smiles a deadly smile, watching, as the water bares down on her.

She quickly grabs hold of her hammer with both hands; bolts of lightning streaming from it in all directions. With all her might, she brings the hammer down on the ground in front of her.

A thunderous crack unleashes as her hammer falls. The shock wave throws her backwards several dozen feet. Where her hammer struck the ground, a gaping hole appears. Cracks in the ground begin to radiate outward in multiple directions, taking serpentine paths. The cracks continue to open wider just as the wall of water reaches them.

The torrents of water pound into the gaping cracks, opening them wider still. Kit watches, her heart racing out of control, as the ground swallows it all up. In all directions, the cracks continue to spread, taking the water that was once the statue of Titan, along with them.

When the event finally comes to an end, there is a large lake in front of her, with many finger-like tributaries running out from the center.

"An interesting solution to a difficult problem," a voice, but not Fury's, says in a matter-of-fact sort of tone. "My mother was right. You are intelligent."

Kit looks beside her to see Triton. He's dressed in azure-blue from head to toe, and he's carrying a silver-blue trident, encrusted with barnacles and seashells.

"Hardly a single life was lost. Most impressive, indeed."

"Everyone lived?" Kit asks, joy springing from her heart.

"No, not everyone. The people of Aarall were all saved, but the wildlife nearby suffered. Lump was not able to complete his task."

"Oh, Helja no, is Lump okay?" Tears come pouring down her face. She couldn't have sent Lump to his death!

"Oh, my sweet angel, don't cry. He is a child of Fenrir, and she would not allow him to be taken from this world, not yet, anyway."

Kit swipes the tears away from her cheeks. "He's okay? He didn't die?"

Triton helps dry her tears. "He is in good health and in Fenrir's care. He reached the wolves and together they spread the word as fast as they could. Many of the animals listened, but many more scattered in fear. They tried to herd them up the mountain, even when the waters were coming, they tried."

Kit sees that Triton is also crying at this point, his words catching in his throat. "Fenrir's children saved many of the creatures, but many wolves perished as they tried. Lump, too, was caught in the flood, but for your sake, I'm guessing, Fenrir pulled him from the water to safety."

Kit suddenly feels a warmth crossing over her. A moment later Danny is at her side, crushing her in a warm embrace.

"You're amazing, Kitten. You saved the city."

Kit bursts into tears, sobbing uncontrollably. She presses her face into Danny's shoulder and begins to bawl her eyes out. "*We* saved the city. All of us, together."

There is a small popping sound, spraying Kit with water. She looks around to see that Triton has vanished. A moment later, the air begins to shimmer and sparkle, and a number of people appear from within the glistening teleportation sphere.

"That's my girl!" booms the voice of Captain Harding. "I thought Danny had lost his mind when he started clanging that damned warning bell. He was raving about a flood and how you were going to stop it."

Runt is next to greet Kit, bowling her over, covering her in wolf-slobber.

"Thank Titan, you're alive!" exclaims Indie as he pulls Kit up off the ground, smothering her with his own embrace. She immediately presses her lips to his, letting all her love flow into him. His shock passes quickly, and he returns the kiss for all he's worth.

"Okay, this has been a harrowing experience, but let's not lose our self control." Kit pulls away from Indie's embrace to see a stern-faced Father Hoarfrost, causing Kit to blush so hard that she thinks her face is about to catch fire. "Never, in all my many years of treading upon Orth, have I witnessed anybody quite like you, sister Kit Standing Bear. You truly are the Hand of Titan!"

Runt begins to bark in a high-pitched, excited way. Kit turns to see him barrelling into Lump, the two of them rolling about in a joyful reunion. Beside the fray is a Berrat huntress, perhaps a little older than Kit. She doesn't recognize her face, but she knows her eyes.

Deep brown, the wisest, kindest eyes she's ever seen. Kit rushes to the girl, wrapping her arms around her.

"Thank you! Thank you for saving Lump! I can never repay you for your kindness." As soon as Kit finishes hugging her, she drops to a knee and kisses her hand.

She can hear Indie behind her saying, "That's Fenrir." There are a chorus of gasps. When Kit turns around, the entire group is on bended knee. All except for Runt and Lump who are continuing their own personal greetings.

"Your job is not done, sweet Kit." Fenrir takes Kit's chin in her hand, pulling her gaze back. "This was but the first of the challenges Titan will set before you. Look for me on the night of the Feast of Titan's Bounty. After the ceremony is complete, I will tell you more."

Fenrir then walks over to Father Hoarfrost. "Titan's peace unto you," she says in the traditional greeting. "May Tyr find mercy in his heart, so that you will no longer have to endure the curse that he has set upon you."

"You know? Of my curse?" Hoarfrost's hands are shaking badly as the deity addresses him.

"I do. Your suffering has not gone unnoticed." And with that, Fenrir stretches out her arms over the small group. "My blessings upon you, children of Orth."

There is a bright flash of light, followed by a warm breeze that smells of earth and wildflowers.

Chapter 28

THREE DAYS HAD PASSED since the statue collapsed. There was considerable damage to the landscape, but the peoples of Arnnor banded together to perform the necessary repairs. Some people were talking about creating a new village on the shores of the newly formed lake.

Kit and her friends were given the freedom to take some time for themselves, which they all happily accepted. They found themselves a quiet spot on the Temple grounds where they'd meet, spending some quality time together.

Today Kit presses her back against an ancient oak tree's massive trunk, twirling the stem of a daisy between her fingers. "Does it hurt?" she asks Danny as he lays in the tall grass, looking up at the clear blue skies.

"Does what hurt?" he asks, rolling over onto his stomach.

"When you change, into that firebird thing."

"Oh, that," he tousles his now bright red hair. "Not at all; it feels awesome. It's both comforting and exhilarating at the same time. But flying! Sweet Titan, there is nothing like it."

"It sounds like I missed an awful lot." There was a tinge of jealousy in Indie's voice. He reaches down, picks up a handful of dirt and flings it into the air. "Don't get me wrong, my vampire combat training was interesting, but ..."

"I wish you were with us, too," Kit says. "The Library was incredible. And now it's gone."

"Which books did you read, Kit?" Danny moves closer to where Kit is sitting by the tree.

"I don't remember exactly what I read," Kit says, as she tries to recall the text. "I read a book about languages; I think I did, anyway."

"Languages? Seriously?" Danny plops down on the ground beside Kit, prompting Indie to do the same, but on her other side. "The first book I read was about the creatures of Orth. It was about ..."

"About what?" Indie asks. Apparently, he held a keen interest in the subject matter.

"I'm not sure. It's like I remember everything, but when I try to talk about it, it becomes murky in my mind."

"Me, too," says Kit as she continues to twirl the daisy between her fingers. "I think that's the way it works. What we read was meant for us, and us alone. We can't share what we learned."

"Maybe that's why that Berrabbithi guy, Anan, was writing stuff down in his journals. Maybe he figured out that it allowed him to speak of what he had learned once he left the Library." Danny seems pretty pleased with himself for coming up with his explanation. He didn't know why, but it felt right to him.

"Okay, can we change the subject?" Indie's voice is strained, on the verge of yelling. "I get it. You guys did a bunch of amazing things, played with gods, saved the city. I get it."

"It was pretty cool," Danny remarks, almost like he is trying to rub it in.

Indie spins around, glaring at him with what almost looks like hatred.

"But I'd have traded places with you in a heartbeat. I still would," adds Danny.

"What? Why?" Indie is utterly taken aback by the comment.

"Because you got a kiss from Kitten, here." Danny elbows Kit in the ribs and waggles his eyebrows at her. "Do you have any idea how hard I've tried to get her to kiss me?" Danny starts puckering his lips, making wet kissy noises in Kit's ear.

"New subject!" Kit yells out, as she knocks Danny over with a hard elbow into his ribs.

Danny promptly falls onto his side, feigning a life-threatening injury. "Oh, that's very cute," he says, now grinning from ear to ear. "You two even blush together now."

Moments later, much to Kit's relief, the conversation is interrupted by Lump and Runt racing towards them. As soon as they arrive, Lump switches from dog to human form.

"Titan's snowballs," Indie yells out. "You're human?"

"No, friend Indie. I am Lump." Lump gives Indie his very best smile. "But now I am also human like you."

Looking like Indie's head might explode, Kit interrupts the conversation. "What's up Lump? You and Runt look like you were in a big hurry when you got here."

"Hello, friend Kit. Father Hoarfrost wants to see you before tonight's Festival." Lump's eyes suddenly look up into the tree, searching for whatever it was that had caught his attention.

"Whatcha looking at there, Lump? Spot a squirrel?" Danny can't help but laugh at his own joke.

"Maybe," Lump says, his eyes still searching through the tree's branches.

"Lump!" Kit yells, a bit louder than intended. "What does Hoarfrost want?"

"You. Now." Lump's gaze never leaves the treetop.

"Alright," Kit says, brushing loose grass and dirt from her backside. "I'll see you guys tonight, I guess?"

"We'll be there," Indie says. Again, there's a hint of jealousy in his voice.

"I'll be sitting with Captain Harding, while you two will be sitting up at Father Hoarfrost's table."

Kit takes Indie's hand in hers and gives him a small kiss on the cheek. "Once the ceremony's over, I'll be joining you at your table. I don't want to be up there any longer than I need to be." Indie shrugs his shoulders slightly at Kit's display of affection.

"I'd trade places with you in a heartbeat, Indie. In a heartbeat." There is no joking in Danny's tone. Like Kit, he brushes the loose debris off his backside and starts walking back towards the Temple. Lump switches back into his dog form and takes off to join Danny, with Runt on his heals.

"C'mon, Kit says tugging on Indie's hand. I don't want to keep Hoarfrost waiting today. The Festival is going to be starting in a few hours, and I'm going to need to do some serious work to get my hair under control.

Indie pulls Kit around, so that they're facing each other. He gently lifts her chin so that he can look directly into her eyes. "You're beautiful already. No need to change anything with your hair." Kit's face immediately blushes, but she manages to hold his gaze. "Well, that's new." Indie tilts his head to the side, while maintaining eye contact.

"What's new?" Kit says, a playful tone coming through in her voice.

"The gold in your eyes. That wasn't there before."

"The what? My eyes aren't gold, they're brown, just like they've always been."

"Not anymore," Indie replies, still staring into Kit's eyes. "You're eyes now have a very thin ring of gold in them. It's really beautiful."

"It's got to be a reflection or something. C'mon, let's go."

When they make it to the foot of the staircase leading up to the Temple, Indie takes Kit's hand in his and lightly kisses it. "I'm going to see Harding. I'll see you at the Festival."

Kit gives Indie a quick wink before bounding up the stairs. By the time she gets to the top, she's barely breathing hard. When she looks back down, Indie is still standing there, staring up at her. He gives her a quick wave before heading off to see the Captain.

Kit makes her way through the oddly empty Temple. It seems that everybody is preparing for the Festival. Those who do not attend the festivities inside the Temple's hall often have their celebration at the ice statue, which is now a large lake just outside the city walls. It leaves Kit wondering where everyone will go for the celebration.

When Kit gets to the hallway leading to the High Priest's office, it, too, is strangely empty. There are always a few acolytes milling about outside his door.

Just as Kit is about to knock, the door opens revealing the old brother, Snowbank, inside. "Hello, Kit," he says with his cracked rheumy voice. "You're just in time."

"Just in time for what?" Kit asks, taking a few steps away from the entrance.

"Please, Kit," Father Hoarfrost calls out from his office. "Just get in here."

Kit reluctantly enters the High Priest's office, keeping her distance from brother Snowbank. "Still in costume, I see," she says as she walks past him.

"No need to startle the locals," Tyr says with a grin. "The Frost Forest brothers are always welcome at the Fist." Kit waves her hand dismissively at him as he gives his weak explanation.

"You wanted to see me, Father?"

"Well, he called for you, but I'm the one who wanted to speak to you."

"What do you have to say to me? You could have sought me out without dragging Father Hoarfrost into this." Kit is not trying to hide her distain for Tyr.

Tyr feigns that her words cut him deeply. "After everything I did for you, Kitten? I saved the city and all the villages in Aarall."

"You saved your own skin." Kit retorts. "Had the magicked water killed people, you'd have been vaporised or nullified, or whatever it is that happens to your type when you break the rules."

"Call it a win, win then," Tyr says with a wide grin. "But you got the credit for it. You're the hero being honoured tonight."

"You're an idiot!" Kit yells at Tyr. "Do you really think I did any of that for glory?"

Tyr seats himself on Hoarfrost's desk, looking at Kit with pride in his eyes. "No, I know you didn't. You don't do anything for yourself, at least nothing important. You, Kitten, are an enigma. A wonderfully complex puzzle, encased in the most beautiful wrapping I've ever seen."

"Why am I here, Tyr? I don't want to be a part of your *games*." Kit steals a look over at Father Hoarfrost, who is being unnaturally quiet. He's sitting in a chair in the corner, staring down at his feet.

"We're not playing *games* any more, Kit. Armageddon, Ragnarök, End of Days, whatever you want to call it, is on the horizon. The prophecy will come to pass and the world as you know it will be forever changed." Tyr's voice is serious, almost remorseful. "But that's not why you're here. You're here to decide Hoarfrost's fate."

"I'm what?"

Kit's eyes dart to Father Hoarfrost, wondering what Tyr is talking about. Without looking up from the ground. "I must select who will die, who will pay for my curse."

"What curse?" Kit practically runs to Hoarfrost's side, waiting for him to look her in the eyes, but he continues to stare down at his feet.

"What curse?" Kit yells, now directing the question to Tyr.

"The curse I placed on his family when Hoarfrost's ancestor killed brother Edur. My friend. My only friend who wasn't of my own kind." Rage is boiling just under Tyr's seemingly calm exterior. That rage gives a hateful edge to his words. "All Edur wanted was to learn from me. He was a brilliant man, insightful, capable of accepting facts even when they flew in the face of everything he'd ever been told."

Tyr takes a moment to gather himself. He is on the edge of losing control, something he's not willing to do.

"I showed Edur the Library and all it's wonders. He read the texts. He read of the Travellers, and their *games*. He learned the *truth*."

"And what was this *truth*?" the anger in Kit's voice is gone. Her experience in the Library was profound. She learned things that she could have never imagined, not in her wildest fantasies.

"The truth of the Travelers, the Fates, the games. He couldn't keep this information to himself. He had to share it with Father Chilblain, Hoarfrost's direct ancestor."

Father Hoarfrost groans, pressing his face into the palms of his hands.

"And what did Chilblain do when Edur told him of what he'd found? He executed him! Right here, in this very office, all those many years ago." The calm in Tyr's voice was now completely gone. All that remained was loathing.

"He executed him? Why? Why would the High Priest execute somebody because he had information? That's not possible."

"It is possible," Hoarfrost groans out. "What Tyr is sharing is the truth. My ancestor killed a man to save himself, this Temple, and his seat of power. Edur's tale would have changed everything. The people wouldn't have praised Titan, they'd have spurned him."

"What truth?" Kit feels the room beginning to spin. Looking like she's about to pass out, Tyr pulls out a chair, carefully sitting her in it.

"The truth that Titan is a monster." Father Hoarfrost finally looks up. His eyes are bloodshot, like he'd been crying for hours. "Was a monster," he corrects himself, now staring at Tyr, challenging him to disagree with his words.

"Chilblain was a monster," Tyr continues. "Edur didn't need to die for what he had learned. The Temple could have changed its teachings; moulded the narrative so that the people could have learned the truth, without destroying the Temple in the process."

"What does any of this have to do with a curse?"

"Tyr made Chilblain pay for his sin. He made him pay by forcing Chilblain to kill his best, and only friend. He made him repeat that every cycle, at the Feast of Titan's Bounty. When Chilblain died, the duty fell onto the next person in Chilblain's bloodline."

"And you call Chilblain a monster?" Kit throws her chair at Tyr, hitting him squarely in the chest with it. The chair simply disintegrates on contact. "You are a sick, twisted ... whatever you are."

Where the chair did nothing, Kit's words seemed to have cut Tyr deeply, for a moment at least. "Did you know that you are Hoarfrost's only friend? The only person in all this world that he truly cares about?"

Kit looks over at Hoarfrost, his face, once again, planted firmly into the palms of his hands.

"So, I am the one to die, then? If that is my fate, then I accept it. But release Father Hoarfrost from this ridiculous curse. It serves no purpose except to nurse your hatred and remind you of a past that should have been forgotten by now."

"I will not choose her," Hoarfrost grinds out between clenched teeth. "I will not let you kill her. I am the last of my line. Take my life and end this. NOW!"

"NO!" Kit screams, "I accept my death, but please, let him be free of this torture."

"Again, you would offer your life to save a friend, young Kit?" a melodic voice fills the room, the same voice Kit heard when she offered up her life in place of Indie's. "You're quite right about her, Tyr, she is a remarkable creature."

"Your presence is not required Tiamat. Leave. Now." Tyr was looking about the room, presumably waiting for Tiamat to show herself.

"You cannot take her life, Tyr, even though I know you wouldn't anyway. Her life belongs to me now. Nor can you take Father Hoarfrost's life. Your curse only allows you to take his friends away from him. You cannot kill him." Tiamat's voice was hypnotic, almost soothing. "You have no choice but to release him from the curse. The cycle has been broken."

"Fine!" Tyr says with total resignation in his voice. "I release you and your descendants, whoever they may be, of the curse."

No sooner had the words been spoken, than Hoarfrost collapses to the ground, weeping uncontrollably. "Thank you," he calls out. "Thank you for not taking her."

"Tiamat was right," Tyr says, directing his comment towards Kit. "I couldn't have killed you, even if Hoarfrost had selected you." With a wave of his hand, Tyr simply vanishes.

"Tiamat?" Kit calls out, in a quiet, tentative voice. "Are you still here?" When there is no response, Kit runs over to help Father Hoarfrost from the ground. He somehow looks younger, like a great weight has been taken from him.

"I'm sorry, Kit, I'm sorry." The old man picks himself up off the ground, Kit helping him while he does. "I tried my best to insulate myself, to stay away from people, to form no friendships."

"Except I'm irresistible!" Kit says with a shrug and a smile. Father Hoarfrost returns the smile, in spite of the situation.

"You need to get ready for the Festival, Kit. I'll be okay." The old priest pats her hand, giving her another reassuring, thin-lipped smile. "It's a big day for you, *sister*."

"You do know that none of that is important to me, right, Father?"

"I know, but your brethren, and the people need this. These celebrations give the people a much-deserved break from the mundane. You, little sister, will bring them hope that their god will once again be among them.

"Father," a concerned look once again fills Kit's eyes. "About that."

"Not now, Kit. Let it go. When it's time, we can speak of this at length, but for now, you need to get yourself ready."

"Okay, Father," she says giving the back of his hand a gentle kiss. "Titan's peace be upon you."

"And with you, too," he replies with a warm smile.

Chapter 29

KIT RACES DOWN THE halls to her dormitory room in the acolyte's section of the building. After the ceremony, she'll be moved to the priests' quarters. From what she's heard, they're not much different from her existing quarters, but they're ever so slightly larger, with an actual window instead of a slit.

Everything in her room had been cleared out, except for her priestly robes and a small satchel containing her toiletries. There is a small bottle of winterberry oil sitting on top, most likely a gift from sister Miyuki. She often dabs a bit of the oil on her wrists. A scent that Kit just adores.

Kit quickly bathes, cleaning what felt like a year's worth of grit from her body. Afterwards, she slips on a simple cloth dressing gown that covers her from neck to toe, and runs back to her room. When she gets there, she stands in front of her tiny mirror, trying to remove the tangles from her hair.

"Can I help?"

Kit turns to see Lin standing in the doorway, wearing a beautiful sky-blue dress, with bright green trimming.

"Sweet Titan, you look beautiful!" Kit's eyes are wide.

"Oh, thank you for saying that. My grandmother sent this to me today." Taking Kit's complement as an invitation to enter her room, Lin walks in and holds out her hand for the comb.

Kit gives her a sheepish smile as she hands it over. "It's a complete rat's nest. I don't think there is any option, short of cutting it all off."

"That's just nonsense," Lin retorts as she takes the small bottle of winterberry oil from Kit's bed. She pours a small amount of it onto the comb and rubs it in with her fingers. When she puts the comb to Kit's hair, it glides through it like a knife through warm butter. The tangles simply disappear.

"How'd you do that?" Kit asks. There is a touch of awe in her voice, causing Lin to blush slightly.

"I put a small enchantment on your comb," she says, like it was nothing at all. "Winterberry oil is an amazing reagent."

"What's a reagent?"

"It's just a fancy name for ingredient. It's a pretty simple enchantment, but it's really effective." As if to punctuate her statement, Lin quickly runs the comb through Kit's hair multiple times, leaving it smooth and shiny; the winterberry fragrance filling the room. In seconds, Kit's hair is perfect.

"Now, let's get you into your robes and down to the dining hall. I think we acolytes have outdone ourselves this year. Everybody was really motivated to make it, well, perfect." Kit couldn't help but smile, thinking back to previous years when she was on *Festival Duty*. A time when acolytes were forced to make sure every detail was just right, so when the guests arrived, it was a magical experience. Kit hated those duties.

"I'm pretty sure I can dress myself," Kit says, raising her eyebrows at the offer.

"Oh, I know," Lin responds, without missing a beat, "but this is a big day for you. Don't you want to look your best? I'm pretty good at it."

Kit quickly checks her hair in her tiny mirror. She could say with all honesty that she had no memory of her hair looking so beautiful. She takes the strip of bright red strands in her fingertips, letting them trace their way down to the tips. Suddenly Kit remembers what Indie had said about her eyes. She looks at them in the mirror, seeing a slight, but definite golden ring around her once pure-brown eyes.

"Okay," Kit laughs, "do your thing."

Lin bolts over to the bedroom door, slamming it shut. When she turns around, she sees Kit dropping her dressing gown to the floor, revealing her petite yet utterly perfect shape. She also notices the two thin vertical white lines between Kit's shoulder blades. They're practically imperceptible but they're there, nonetheless. Feeling somewhat ashamed for staring, Lin quickly turns away while Kit slips on her small clothes.

"Okay, let's get my priest robes on," Kit laughs, raising her arms over her head, like a child waiting for a parent to dress them.

"Whoa," Lin gasps as she pulls the robes over Kit's body. "Your robe is amazing."

"What?" Kit says, staring down at herself. Priest robes are typically simple, functional garments, meant to be worn anywhere. What she was wearing was anything but *simple*. They were made of the same basic material of normal robes, but there was also intricate ice-blue stitching throughout the garment. It created an almost ethereal look to them.

Suddenly, a shadow in the corner of the room catches Kit's eye. It's that of a hare. Kit quickly looks about, but there is no hare in the room, just a shadow on the wall. The shadow-hare bows its head to Kit. The memories of her Rite of Way come flooding back to her, and she recalls the hare that gave its life for the stoat's hungry children. Kit suddenly realizes that she's holding something. When she looks down, she finds a small, smooth stone in her hand. The same stone her mother had given to her on the night of the Rite. Kit inclines her head to the hare and slips the stone into one of the many pockets hidden within the folds of her robe.

"Kit?" There's a tinge of concern in Lin's voice. "Are you okay?"

Kit looks back down at her gown. When she raises her head to look at Lin, she has a look of pure joy. "I'm great," she says in reply. "Are we ready to go?"

Lin holds out Kit's holy symbol necklace, waiting for Kit to let her slip it over her head. "As soon as you put this on, we'll be ready to go." She slips the necklace over Kit's head and steps back to look at her. "I thought I was going to do more, you know, to dress you up for the ceremony, but those robes are perfect just the way they are. Let's get going!"

Chapter 30

LIN IS PRACTICALLY bouncing as she and Kit walk to the Temple's main dining hall. Things had been moved around to allow the hall to accommodate as many people as possible. A din is coming from the room, audible long before they get to the doors.

"Wait here!" Lin says to Kit, practically screaming to be heard over the voices in the hall. She stands in front of the open, double doors blocking Kit's view of the room. Lin waves her arms furiously, hoping to be noticed. A moment later, the room suddenly goes quiet.

Lin turns toward Kit, motioning her to come, but Kit's feet are frozen to the ground; not from cold, but from abject terror. It suddenly becomes clear that these people are waiting for *her* to make an entrance. Lin scowls at her, trying to coax her forward.

"C'mon, you big chicken. Let's get going!" Lin's eyes dance with mischief. "C'mon! If you don't come on your own, I'm going to drag you in. How do you think that's going to look?"

Kit quickly begins running her hands over her robes, trying to press out wrinkles that aren't there; a habit she had apparently picked up from her mother. Not wanting to let her fear get the better of her, she puts on her game face and starts stepping forward.

"Smile, Kit! Smile! You can't go in there looking like you're going to take off somebody's head."

Lin's comment makes Kit laugh, genuinely laugh. She still has that happy look on her face as she enters the dining hall. As soon as the crowd catches sight of her, it goes crazy with cheers, applause and more than a few cat calls. Lin is quite possibly the biggest cheerleader of them all.

The hall was decorated to the point of looking horrendously gaudy. There were more streamers and glittering lanterns than Kit could take in. Between that and the hundreds of people that were jammed into the room, Kit hardly even noticed Father Hoarfrost at the end of the room's center aisle, coaxing her forward.

Lin gives her a gentle nudge to get her feet moving. Kit wants to scowl at her, but the sheer delight on Lin's face makes her laugh. Once Kit's feet get moving, she practically runs down the aisle, while the throng continues clapping and cheering. Many are calling out her name, sounding an awful lot like a chant that might be heard at a sporting event.

When Kit finally arrives at the front of the hall, she looks up at Father Hoarfrost who is standing a few steps higher than she is, on a raised dais. He holds up his arms, motioning for the room to quiet down. Instead, it has the exact opposite effect, causing everyone to cheer all the louder.

Kit slowly turns to face the people, tentatively raising one of her hands to them, while thanking them for their support. It seems that's what they had been waiting for because they finally start to quiet down. Just when it seems everyone has calmed down, somebody yells from the back of the hall. "Kit Standing Bear, champion of Titan!" The entire crowd once again erupts in clapping and cheering.

Father Hoarfrost comes down from his dais and leads Kit up the stairs to a place beside him. He once again holds out his hands, asking for quiet. A few moments later, there is silence.

Father Hoarfrost clears his throat, hoping it will help project his voice so that everyone can hear him. "Thank you!" he calls out, almost like he was testing how loudly he could speak. "Thank you, everyone, for joining me for the Feast of Titan's Bounty!" He is forced to pause for a moment as a few individuals start cheering again, but it dies out very quickly.

"As you all know, we celebrate this day to commemorate all that Titan has provided for us, bestowed upon us, if you will. Our winters are often harsh, forcing many families to remain indoors while the worst of the winter's storms hit the region. We mourn those who do not survive the winter, as they join the Great Cycle, but we also look forward to the warmer seasons and the harvests that they bring."

The old priest pauses for a moment to look out over the multitude of people gathered in the great hall; people from all across Arnnor, Berrathia and even Lycos, the kingdom on the far side of the Gaelinora Sea.

"On this day, we welcome the children who have joined the ranks of our novitiate, as they begin their journey to acolyte, and then on to priest, if they can pass the challenges set out before them." The crowd begins to murmur slightly, some of the people looking to the entrance of the dining hall. "So, I would like you all to welcome the newest, youngest members to the Temple." The High Priest claps three times in quick succession, and a small group of children enter the hall, being led by sister Nevara. The crowd once again begins cheering, but with more control so as not to frighten the children. They seem to range in age between five and eight cycles, with the older children taking up the rear of the procession. When they reach the front of the hall, they all bow their heads to Father Hoarfrost. The cheering dies off almost immediately, allowing the High Priest to continue.

"Titan's blessings upon you, young novices. May your time in the Temple be filled with prayer, hard work and personal growth," the High Priest says in a gentle, fatherly tone.

"Titan's blessings upon you, Father Hoarfrost," they reply in perfect unison, in a somewhat sing-song kind of way. One child starts clapping, spinning on the spot. The display ends abruptly when he sees the look sister Nevara is giving him. She quickly claps her hands three times in succession, and the children turn to face the crowd, some of them a bit slower than the others. Once again, the crowd cheers for the children, but just long enough to be respectful. As though on queue, the clapping dies off and the children bow their heads to the people in perfect unison. Following sister Navara's lead, they exit the hall in single file.

Father Hoarfrost smiles warmly. It seems the procession of the novices is a part of the ceremony he truly enjoys.

"Now," he says with a somewhat solemn tone, "I will announce that one of our own will be leaving the Temple." The crowd immediately begins talking, likely trying to guess who it is that is leaving the ranks. It happens, on rare occasions, but those who join the Temple rarely choose to exit of their own accord. Father Hoarfrost holds up his hands again, and the crowd immediately goes quiet.

"I'd like to invite acolyte, Danny Fox-Dancing to come join me here on the dais." Danny steps away from his front row table to join Father Hoarfrost and Kit up on the dais. Kit's jaw is agape, thinking, no hoping, that she misunderstood the High Priest.

As Danny climbs the stairs of the dais, he gives Kit a quick wink. It's only then that Kit realizes that he's dressed in traditional Berrat garb, exposing freshly tattooed tribal markings on his wrists and upper arms. Father Hoarfrost puts his hand on his shoulder while Danny smiles and waves politely to the crowd. The hall is utterly silent.

"As I'm sure you all know, Danny played an instrumental part during the Great Melt. As a direct result of his actions, and his bravery, many hundreds of lives were saved." No sooner do the words leave the High Priest's mouth than the crowd goes crazy, clapping and cheering in much the same way as they did for Kit during her entrance. Father Hoarfrost once again holds up his hands, calling for quiet.

"Even though Danny had never chosen to take the Rite of Abandonment trial, in light of his unprecedented heroism, I offered him the title of Priest." Again, the High Priest pauses until the crowd settles down. "But he chose not to accept my offer. Instead, he informed me that he would be returning to his village in northern Berrathia."

"Why?" Kit asks Danny, a bit louder than she intended, drawing a scowl from Father Hoarfrost.

"Danny's reasons for deciding to return home are his own, and not for us to question." The last part of his statement is seemingly directed at Kit. "But know this, on this night, the last night he will spend at the Temple, we will honour Danny Fox-Dancing, in thanks for what he brought to the Temple and in hopes that he will someday return to us.

The crowd begins clapping, with some random cheering interspersed with it. Somebody from the back of the crowd yells, "I love you, Danny!" which spurs on many laughs and a *lot* more cheers. Afterall, everybody loves Danny.

Kit's eyes are glassy when Father Hoarfrost turns his attention to her.

"In the many days I've lived, I've seen some truly amazing things, but I'm not sure if any of them compare to the stories Kit has shared with me about another hero who played a huge roll in protecting the lives of Arnnor." The crowd seems somewhat taken aback by these comments. Outside of Kit and Danny, nobody else was ever mentioned as a part of the team.

Kit, on the other hand, knew exactly who the High Priest was talking about. Her glassy eyes immediately start overflowing, tears of joy and pride pushing the sadness away. Right beside where Danny was sitting is her favorite *actual* golden retriever, Lump-on-a-Log, his tail frantically sweeping the floor behind him. Kit quickly pats her thighs, calling Lump to come join her on the dais. There are a few groans and many more laughs as Lump races up the stairs to take his place beside Kit.

"Well, I guess I'll just finish my introduction then," says Father Hoarfrost, once again staring down at Kit. "I give you the Temple's mascot and a true hero in his own right, Lump!"

The crowd goes nuts. They yell and scream until a blood-curdling howl brings the celebration to a terrifying halt. All eyes turn to Runt, who is sitting at his place, next to where Lump had been. He punctuates his personal cheers with a few quick barks, bringing about a wave of laughter across the hall.

Suddenly the room begins to fill with the most heavenly aromas of breads, spiced vegetables and charred meats. Necks are starting to crane as the crowd searches for the source of the culinary delights that are about to appear.

Father Hoarfrost can't help but smile. He's been trying to give Kit her just rewards and announce her formal acceptance to the priesthood, but the food is making it very difficult.

"Call in the food," Kit says, understanding that her accolades could wait. In fact, she'd be okay if they never happened at all.

"No way, little sister, you're not getting out of this that easily," the old priest couldn't hide his pride-filled smile if he tried.

"Please, friends, please!" Once again, Father Hoarfrost has to rein in the attention of the crowd. "I can smell sister Miyuki's banquet as well as you can, so let me bring my long-winded speech to its conclusion."

There was a good deal of laughter before quiet took hold.

"In closing, I have the honour, no, the privilege, of announcing the newest member to the priesthood, the savior of Aarall, Sister Kit Standing Bear!"

Once again, the crowd erupts in an overwhelming display of joy. Hooting and whistling, many were banging their hands on their tables while many more were stamping their feet. Kit might have even been embarrassed the way the crowd was carrying on, except that her attention is completely overtaken by hugs and well wishes from her friends.

The crowd is even louder a moment later when sister Miyuki leads a parade of servers into the room, each carrying huge trays of food.

Indie gives Kit a crushing hug. "When the music starts, make sure you save the first dance for me." Kit was about to reply when Danny pushes himself between them.

"Sorry, friend, but I've known Kit much longer than you have. The first dance is for me." Indie looks like he's about to fly into a jealous rage when Danny pats him on the chest. "Not to worry, my friend, she'll save the much more important and meaningful last dance for *you*." He gives Kit a quick wink. "Won't you, Kitten."

Indie stands blank faced, stupefied, by Danny's suggestive comment. Danny quickly grabs him by the scruff of the neck, at least as best as he can, since Indie is nearly two feet taller than he is. "C'mon, let's not waste any more time, that food smells so good! Let's eat!"

Indie quickly turns to Kit, giving her a small shrug as he allows Danny to lead him to their table at the front of the hall. A wistful look crosses Kit's face as she sees her friends all gathered together to share a feast.

"Go ahead," Father Hoarfrost says. "It was long ago, but I was once a young man. Go celebrate with your friends."

Kit quickly embraces the old priest, hugging him for all she's worth. "Thank you. I love you, Father!" And with that, she races down the stairs to join her friends in the feast that has just arrived at their table.

Chapter 31

THE PARTY WENT ON FOR many hours and by the time Kit and her friends left the dining hall, she was stuffed to the point of exploding.

"The night's not over, Kitten," Danny said with a suggestive laugh. "We need to take you to your new priest quarters."

"Sweet Titan, can't we just call it a night and get some sleep?" Kit was practically pleading with them to not keep the festivities going.

"Do you really think we don't know what day it is now? It's well past the midnight hour, which means it's tomorrow." Silverleaf is giving Kit a not-so-gentle poke in the ribs with his elbow. Kit can only groan in response. "Happy Birthday Kit!"

The entire group begins singing happy birthday, much to Kit's chagrin. "Can't we celebrate after we get some sleep? I'm exhausted."

"You heard the lady; she wants to go to bed!" Indie starts trying to corral her friends, to push them out of Kit's way.

"Time for the last *dance*?" Danny says as Indie pushes him off to the side. In perfect unison, both Kit and Indie glare at Danny.

Amara grabs Danny by the scruff of his cloak and picks him up off the ground. "And what exactly do you mean by that?" Amara is a good three feet taller than Danny, creating a somewhat comical appearance as she shakes him, waiting for an answer.

"Amara! Put Danny down. All of you, I'm going to my room – alone – and I'm going to get some sleep. I suggest you all do the same." Kit manages to project an air of authority, but she struggles to not laugh as she watches Danny feet kick helplessly in the air.

Silverleaf gives Kit a quick peck on the cheek. "Happy Birthday, Kit. Sleep well."

Everybody follows suit, except for Indie, who gives Kit a substantially deeper kiss. When he pulls away from his embrace, Kit's face is flushed, and her knees appear to be wobbly. "I'm going to get some air," she says, trying to not look affected by Indie's amorous embrace.

"Would you like me to join you?" Indie asks, clearly hoping that she'll agree.

Kit stands, staring at Indie, not knowing how to reply, without hurting his feelings. As if on cue, both Runt and Lump move in beside her. Neither of them shows any sort of overt aggression, but their body language is telling Indie that he's not welcome. Kit gives her furry bodyguards a scratch on the head as she gives Indie an awkward grin. "Not tonight," she starts, her face immediately beginning to heat. "I'm just going to enjoy the night air for a while, and then I'm going to get some sleep."

It was hard to tell from Indie's reaction if he's angry, or just disappointed, but whatever it was, his reaction disappears as Amara uses her free hand to grab him by the upper arm and drag him away. "C'mon lover boy, you heard the lady. The morning's light will be the start of a new day, and then we can all give Kit her birthday presents."

"Thanks, Amara," Kit says with a wink. "Tomorrow's another day."

The shortest route to the Temple grounds would have been to follow the group back to the dormitory, but Kit chooses to go in the opposite direction, so as to put some distance between her and her friends. It's not that she wouldn't have enjoyed their company, but something was nagging at her and she wanted some alone time.

Kit took the first stairwell she could find and headed up towards the Temple's main floor. As she enters the Temple's main hall, she sees that there are still a few revellers hanging around, all of whom clearly had too much honey-wine to drink. When her eyes fall on the large statue of Titan in the middle of the hall, her heart begins to ache for the giant ice statue that she'll never get a chance to look upon again.

"Don't despair," says a voice from behind Kit. "The true statue of Titan, the one he built himself, is still standing. The pilgrimage will be somewhat farther though if you choose to see it."

Kit turns to see Lump and Runt lying at the feet of a young Berrat warrior. They are, as always, in complete rapture of their god Fenrir.

"The *true* statue of Titan?" Kit asks, as she bows her head to the wolf god.

Fenrir gives Kit a knowing smile. "When I was your age, I travelled to Iceford, on the Northern Isle. My friends and I were drawn to the location. In the dead of winter, we crossed the North Sea on foot. A path had frozen over, allowing us to make the otherwise, impossible journey. None of us knew why were following the path, but we each new that we must. When we arrived, we witnessed Titan's first and true temple. A statue of him, had been carved into the cliff of a great, barren mountain. His face looked to have been tormented, his hands bound by manacles with chains that were attached to the ground beneath him."

As Fenrir told her story, Kit remembers the visions she had while she was undergoing the Rite of Acknowledgement. In her mind's eye, the statue was just as Fenrir described.

"At the base of the statue," Fenrir continues, "was the entrance to the Temple within. My friends were not permitted to enter, but I was." Kit's mouth is agape. Her mind racing at the prospect that she had seen this temple in her visions. "That was the day I was offered immortality, Kit. The day that Titan bestowed his blessings upon me."

"Is that what you wanted to speak to me about?" Kit asks. "When I saw you after Titan's statue melted, you said you would seek me out after the festival."

Fenrir laughs, a sweet melodic laugh that echoes off the walls of the Temple. "No, that was merely the ramblings of an old woman's memories." Fenrir sits at the foot of Titan's statue and invites Kit to sit beside her. Runt and Lump both quickly move to take up a spot near their god, but they manage to leave enough room for Kit. "What I wanted to speak with you about is Pental."

"Pental?" Kit's voice shakes as she says his name. It had been a while since she even thought of him.

"After your encounter with him, he travelled to Silverhawk, the city north of Aarall. I could not find out who he met with their, but he left shortly after arriving. Last we saw of him, he was heading towards Berrathia. We lost sight of him after he crossed the boarder."

"Why is that important?" Kit asks. Her curiosity pushing aside her fear of Pental.

"I'm not sure," Fenrir answers with a shrug. "I had expected him to head for Faol, to report back to his master."

"His master?"

"All vampires are controlled by whoever sired them, the vampire that turned them. I believe that Pental was sired by Faol himself, which is why he's as powerful as he is."

"Do you think he's connected to the poachers?" Kit's mind is racing as she tries to put the pieces together. "I've been thinking hard about them lately. I couldn't figure out why somebody would want to turn the wolves against the people, but I think I had it backwards. I think this was all about turning the people against the wolves. I think the poachers were meant to be seen as saviors, rescuing the people from the wolf plague."

"To what end?" Fenrir asks, pushing Kit to continue on her train of thought.

"Well," Kit starts, "if the poachers are seen as heroes, then it's possible that ..." Kit starts shaking her head. "No, they can't be with Pental. Pental is trying to cause division across the lands. He wants the Berrat to turn on the humans. The poachers were all humans, and if they're seen as saviours, that will make the humans more popular. It might not make a difference in Berrathia, since the poachers weren't working out of that kingdom, but it might make the Berrat living in Arnnor like us more."

Runt gives a quick bark, followed by a number of whines. "Did you understand what he just said?" Fenrir asks Kit.

Kit's eyes go wide. "I did, but how?" Not a moment passes before Kit answers her own question. "The Library! The book I read about languages."

"Maybe," Fenrir replies with a wide grin, "but I don't think so. You've always had a connection with the wolves of Orth, but it's only recently that you've become aware of it."

"And that's why I could understand Runt saying that they're killing off the wolves to hurt you?" Kit looks into Runt's yellow-green eyes. "Is that what you think?"

Lump shifts into human form. "The wolves are Fenrir's eyes and ears across the land. If they are killed off, the information chain is broken."

"Why didn't you just protect the wolves yourself?" Kit asks Fenrir.

"I am not allowed to directly interfere, I can only influence others. Like the other deities, I am bound by the rules of the *game*, as decreed by the Fates."

"I don't understand. What do you mean the game?"

"I cannot say more about it," Fenrir replies. There is fear and sadness in her eyes. "I risk dissolution if I speak further."

Lump switches back to his dog form. He rests his head on Fenrir's lap and whines softly. "It's okay boy," Fenrir says to him as she gently caresses the fur on his head. I was not meant to live forever." Fenrir gives Kit a wistful smile. "One last thing before I leave you, beware of those within the Temple, not all are your friends."

Kit suddenly remembers brother Rime and his reaction to seeing Runt as a wolf. Only enemies can see him in his true form, unless allowed by Kit. When she turns to ask Fenrir, she's gone. Kit pulls her two furry friends in close to her. "I guess she doesn't like long good-byes."